Writing
Is
Easy

Open
A
Vein
.com

The Rogues Gallery

Writers Present

OpenAVein.com

Writing is Easy: Open a Vein.com
Copyright © 2010 by Michael Ray King, Rebekah Hunter Scott, Jeff Swesky, Tracy McDurmon
Cover Art by Tracy McDurmon. All rights reserved by ClearVeiw Press Inc.
Copy Editor Nancy Quatrano

King, Michael Ray
Scott, Rebekah Hunter
Swesky, Jeff
McDurmon, Tracy
   Writing is Easy: Open a Vein.com
   260p. ill. cm.
   ISBN 978-0-9799623-7-0 (sc) 978-0-9799623-9-4 (ebook) 978-0-9799623-8-7
   1. Self Help – Writing – Fiction – Short Stories. I. Title.
AC1-999
818
Library of Congress Control Number: 2010930992

ClearView Press, Inc.
PO Box 353431
Palm Coast, FL 32135-3431
www.clearviewpressinc.com

Printed in the United States of America

Acknowledgements:

The Rogues Gallery Writers would like to thank the following people and groups for their love, support, guidance, and encouragement over the years:

Donna & Walter Swesky, Tracie Arnold, Caroline Wiest, Professor Danny Lawless, the Table 609 critique group, the Florida Writers Association's Ancient City Chapter, Professional Writers Group, Rik Feeney, Stephen Woodin, Pat Matheny, Bobbie King, Saunda Thomas, Jenny Chambers, Alicia Hunter, Amy Dutta, Matt Hunter, Carrie Hunter, Evan Hunter and Jeff, Rollie and Elsa Scott.

Additional thanks to the following "readers" who unselfishly gave their time to critique *Writing Is Easy*: Rob Davis, Helen King, Roberta Hubbard and Diane Legg.

Extra special thanks to Nancy Quatrano for her excellent and detailed final edit of *Writing Is Easy* and Vintage Photos of St. Augustine for the AWESOME back cover pic!

Table of Contents

Writing is Easy

The Rogue's Gallery Writers

If you are a writer and you are not published, it is your own fault.

Harsh? No, these words speak the truth. As writers in the early twenty-first century, we are capable of getting our work published in a myriad of venues. The only thing stopping us is ourselves. This may not have been true for our writing predecessors, but the ability to get published today is our reality.

Oh, but you won't necessarily make much money, is that your particular cop-out? I rested on that one awhile myself. Think about it, though. When have writers ever really made much money? Yeah, I know. There are the J. K. Rowlings and Steven Kings of this world, but for every one of them, I know there are literally millions of struggling writers.

Here is our story. We are a published writers group. Contained in this tome is a collection of some of our work. Hopefully you'll read and laugh, cry and mourn. But more than that, if you aspire to write, we hope that when you walk away from this book you will say, "I can do that!"

Some of our stories may not resonate with you. Some of them may thrill you. We believe that is what every writer wants above all else. Yes, money and fame are cool ideas, but isn't it the excitement and satisfaction of knowing your writing touched someone, that drives you to the next word?

Here is our story, how we came together and how we came to be published. This is something you can do. Our hope is that we inspire other writers to engage and actively pursue publication in one of the most fertile environments writing has ever known.

How the Rogue's Gallery Writers Came to Be – Michael Ray King

I am a charter member of an incredible writer's group called The Professional Writers of St. Augustine. The group formed in October, 2003 and in the course of the next four years, I learned more about writing and publishing than I had in my previous forty-five years of life. Three years into this group, my brain was about to explode. I needed desperately to share what I had learned with other writers.

I asked a dear writer friend, Susannah Castle, if she would be willing to join a group of writers if I formed the group. Susannah is a reluctant writer, but one of the most talented humor writers I've ever met. She hemmed and hawed about the idea for a year.

In the meantime, I kept looking around, trying to find someone as serious about getting published as I was. In early 2007, I re-met Jeff Swesky. We had both attended the Professional Writers of St. Augustine, but he had moved away for a couple years. We immediately hit it off, and I knew I had found the first piece to my writers group puzzle.

Right about this time, Susannah had a change of heart and let me know she was interested. She had a friend named Tracy, a wonderful poet who wanted to join, as well. Tracy was added to the group bringing us a softer, more poetic persona. Susannah's husband Al joined as a "non-writer". Al turned out to be an incredibly talented writer who could bring his life experiences to us one moment, and write about "pet" alligators that made us laugh, the next.

Somewhere within the first few meetings we jelled as a group. Everyone felt it. A cohesiveness borne of diversity. One day, I met a young woman named Rebekah Scott at another writers group. She immediately struck me as a perfect fit for our group. Susannah and I had discussed group size and we agreed four to six would be the perfect size.

Since the five of us, Jeff, Tracy, Al, Susannah and I had bonded so well, we were hesitant to mess with our chemistry. I knew though, that Rebekah would offer us an overdrive, an intangible push to another level and I convinced the group to give her a try. The Legare Gang was born.

At the same time the group was forming, I was bringing ClearView Press Inc. into existence. Through a great friend and mentor, Rik Feeney, I had come to understand the publishing world a little better. He walked me through setting up an S-Corp and I was off and running.

With my own publishing company and a book in the final stages of completion, I was on my way to the writers dream. I released my first book in March, 2008. I found, however, that my brain was still overloaded and I needed to share what I knew with my fellow Gangers.

I proposed to the group that we put together a collection of our short works and publish it through ClearView Press. In no time, we had a thick manuscript ready for the editing process. Somewhere in the excitement of putting together the book, we came up with the idea we would market to writers groups. Our feeling is that if we could do this, so can other writers.

After nearly two years, Susannah and Al decided to drop out of the group. Their hearts were not into the book project. We sadly parted with our special friends knowing we would miss them.

The four of us decided we needed to forge a new name for the group, one that would mimic the gusto of Legare Gang and give us an identity as well. It took months to come up with the name, but a chance remark by Rik Feeney at a luncheon dropped our wonderful name right in our laps – The Rogue's Gallery Writers.

Here in your hand is a collection of stories, humor, poetry, and art that is intended not only to entertain, but to inspire. Over the years, I have met many writers much more talented than I. In fact, I imagine there are a good number of you reading this that are going to say, "I can write better than that." I say to you – prove it. Not that I don't believe you can't, but simply because I know that the best writers NEVER get published.

The reason many writers don't get published is that it takes a desire and a work ethic to get there. But I also stand by the earlier statement that if you aren't published, it's your own fault. The Rogue's Gallery Writers is proof positive of this fact.

Are we good? Absolutely. Are we the greatest writers ever? We don't claim to be. But what we are is published. You can be too.

Go to our website, www.roguesgallerywriters.com and see how we put The Rogue's Gallery Writers together. There are also many links and tips that will help you along your way. We want to help. We want to share. We want you to know what we have found.

Thank you for picking up this book. We sincerely hope that at the very least, you will be entertained. More than that, though, we hope you will be inspired. Get your work out there to the world and see where it takes you.

Somewhere down the line, we hope to meet you and share stories. It will truly make our day, by the way, if we hear that we inspired you to step forward with your writing career.

What the Rogue's Gallery Writers Mean To Me - Rebekah

When Mike King asked me to join the Le Gare writers group, I wasn't sure what to think. I didn't know any of the other members, and wondered if they'd accept me or be writing snobs, or hacks or whatever. But I went because I was curious, and because, deep down, I did want to improve my writing, and I wasn't sure if I could do it on my own. I had penned a few manuscripts, bought *Writer's Market* a few times, and collected a humbling helping of rejection letters. I figured I needed a support network or I was doomed to stagnate as a writer.

Then when Mike asked me if I offended easily, I wondered what the hell I was getting myself into.

My first meeting with the group was invigorating. Sure, when I read my first free-write to the rest of the group I was sweating through my clothes and my voice took on this odd, wavering timbre that I didn't recognize. But sitting around the kitchen table, looking out at the other writers, listening to words they unleashed from their own wells, I felt something click into place. This was going to work. This was going to be great.

The raw, unadulterated talent that sits around the table with me every other week often takes my breath away. What's great about this group is, despite coming from such diverse backgrounds, we all feed off each other like some six-headed parasite, gaining strength with each meeting, growing, changing. The last meeting I attended, I was actually worried that *I* would offend the other members with my free-write—I had officially come out of my writing shell.

Since joining the group almost two years ago, I have been published in several literary magazines, won an award for one of my short stories, completed my third novel and am starting a non-fiction book, attended three writers conferences, met face-to-face with agents, and have had several proposal packages requested. Of course, I'm still amassing a sizable stack of rejection slips, but I am sending out more queries with greater confidence and am certain that because of the encouragement and support from the Le Gare Gang, I will see my name in print many more times in the years to come. Now that we've morphed into The Rogue's Gallery Writers, I'm even more convinced of this future.

Most importantly, I have these friends whose opinions I deeply respect, and whose work I thoroughly enjoy. I look forward to every meeting, and leave each time feeling challenged, inspired, and invigorated.

But never offended.

What the Rogues Gallery Writers Mean to Me – Jeff

We all want to be accepted. We all need to fit in.

For us writers, these statements couldn't be truer.

I wrote my first original short story based on an assignment for a 10th grade Home Economics class. We had to write our interpretations of how a female student would handle being picked on and bullied by fellow students, while being put upon by certain teachers. I wanted my version to be edgy, so I wrote a dark satire about a graphic school shooting during a time when "school shooting" was not a common term yet.

Not only would my teacher not let me read the story aloud like the rest of the class had done, she ripped it up, threw it away, and failed me on the assignment. She even announced my grade to the class.

I didn't write another short story for nearly eight years.

But once I returned to writing, I couldn't stop. I had a few of my friends read some of my horror stories. The comments varied only in the language used, "Swesky, there's something wrong with you." "You're a psychopath." "Dude, you're fucked up."

After that, I became guarded about reading or sharing my work. At readings I would pick my tamer, candy-coated stories—or stop reading just before things got twisted or vulgar.

When the organizer of the Rogues Gallery Writers (originally the Legare Gang,) Mike King, approached me to join the group, I was skeptical when he told me they were not easily offended. I thought, "yeah, right—wait 'til they get a load of me." But not only were they *not* offended or repulsed, they actually enjoyed my work. Even my most depraved pieces. In fact, they were actually disappointed if I held back.

As I said, every writer wants to be accepted. Every writer needs to fit in. But it may take time for you to find the proper group. For me, it's most definitely the Rogues Gallery Writers. Not only because they accept me, but because they also inspire me. They push me to do better. The talent level in this group is incredible and each writer is diverse and special, and proof of this is packed into this collection. There's always something to be learned from their works. Their feedback during critiques is vital and has helped me to solve many difficulties in my own works. They've made me a much better writer.

More than just a terrific critique group, they're like a family. People I rely on to help me forget about my problems even if for only a couple hours. People whose opinions I highly value. It's the one place where I can laugh my fucking ass off on a regular basis; laugh so hard I nearly piss myself.

Now that we're devoting our meetings to transforming our passions into professions, I feel like the "dream" is finally within reach.

What I like About the Rogue's Gallery Writers - Mike

Writing this is much more complicated and involved than I had imagined. This writer's group connects on so many different levels at once that my mind is overwhelmed. The adjectives I dream up pale in relation to the reality of sharing stories with these exceptional writers.

We laugh. Oh my god do we laugh.

We cry. We cry together. Not typically a "manly" thing to say, but I've always believed it takes a strong man to cry.

We revel in stories and humor and life – given freely with that special artist's naïveté that allows vulnerabilities to show – in the interest of putting forth a work in progress. The diversity of writing in this group is amazing. Tracy's poetic touches, Rebekah's ability to paint incredible visuals from mere words and Jeff's dark, gut-wrenching stories detailing pain and loss, all overwhelm the senses.

I am a Rogue junkie. We support each other. We cheer each other on. When one of us gets published, the entire group is energized. Heck, we are all pumped up when one of us tells of a mere submission made – because we all know the angst of putting your work out into the world.

Dumas may have written "all for one and one for all" for his musketeers, but we carry that mantra forward, and I have to tell you, it feels really good. Yeah, I used one of those nasty adverbs on purpose. There is no apt description of what it feels like to be in this group that doesn't end up being a pathetic understatement. Every writer should experience the Rogues Gallery Writers, but I am jealous and will defend our little group's nucleus to the bitter end.

Tracy, Rebekah, and Jeff are a writing force to be reckoned with. I am beyond privileged to write with these incredible people. Whether we are the most talented writers in the world is not of any relevance to us. Whether we persevere and support each other in our quest to be the best writers we can be, is of ultimate value to this group. There is no price I could ever attach to the ongoing friendship and creativity we share.

The Rogue's Gallery Writers absolutely rock. Thank you all for coming together in such a profound and intimate way. I love you guys!

Write long and proper.

What I like about The Rogue's Gallery Writers – Tracy

"To be or not to be."

That's my answer to the question, "What do I like about the Rogue's Gallery Writers?" and being a part of their madness. What a great group of simply diverse, wonderful people, each with an open heart and an open mind. I have learned through them, the magic of writing, cried with them on richly emotional pieces, laughed with them to the point of tears and sore cheeks. I have journeyed with them through their eyes and visions of complete insanity and magnificent illusions and realities.

To be a part of this group has been a fantastic adventure itself, in not just their writings, but also in the awesome people behind the words. I truly have been blessed. Even with our individual struggles and differences, we come together as one, and grow and share our love and passions for writing. Not to be part of this group would truly be a story of sorrow and tragedy in itself. With Mike, Jeff and Bekah, you can express your mind and your heart, the core of any good writer. Writers need such a support system and much more. This group does that.

Thanks guys for your love, encouragement and inspiration. I hope our story continues in yet another time and place …

Peace.

Rebekah

Incubation

LeeAnn unbuckled her belt and pulled down her fly, glancing around to make triple-sure no one was watching. It was always a gamble, peeing outside, but it was a risk she often took. She felt much safer doing her business by the grove of live oaks at the edge of the playground than at home behind the bathroom door with the broken lock. Momma's boyfriend Morris had already walked in on her twice, claiming he'd knocked first, even though LeeAnn could swear she'd never heard a sound. Morris must be the world's quietest knocker.

The air was heavy, flat and sickly yellow, amplifying the maraca of cicada wings to their crescendo. Every so often a hot breeze rolled by, but instead of bringing relief, all it brought was the stench of the stagnant marsh on the outskirts of the trailer park. LeeAnn would rather be sweating than breathing in the scent of salty rotten eggs.

Just as she pulled up her shorts, she spotted a bird lying at the base of one of the ancient trees. Its body was smashed and ruined, a sneaker print visible in the surrounding dirt. LeeAnn knew the owner of the shoe print was Jimmy Doyle. Jimmy lived two trailers down and had once thrown a stray kitten into the marsh to see if it could swim, even though alligators were known to lurk just below the algae-covered surface.

"You poor thing," LeeAnn whispered, but didn't touch it. Bitsy had warned her plenty about touching anything dead—she could get worms that way.

She gazed up into the tree. Spanish moss hung from the branches, lifeless as animal furs. Resting in the fork of one branch was a ragged bird's nest. She looked down at the dead bird, wondering if it had left any babies behind, or if Jimmy Doyle had already found a snake to feed them to. Wrapping her fingers around the lowest branch, LeeAnn pulled herself up, grasping and panting until she was eye-level with the nest. Inside were two eggs no bigger than a couple of olives. LeeAnn thought about leaving them there, hoping that another bird— the father perhaps—would come and take over until they hatched. But she knew better.

Taking a leftover wad of toilet paper from her pocket, LeeAnn lifted the eggs from the nest and wrapped them inside. Then she carefully descended the tree, one hand gripping the branches, the other clutching the eggs. She hurried home, hope blossoming in her heart.

Once she was safely inside the room she and Bitsy shared, LeeAnn set the eggs on her dresser. Now that she had them, she was unsure of what to do with them. She knew from her science class that eggs needed to stay warm, and that the mother bird would turn the eggs every so often. She touched one of the eggs; the shell was hard and smooth as a gumball. It still felt warm, but she worried that it wasn't warm enough. She switched on the plastic lamp beside her jewelry box and angled the dingy shade toward the eggs, but decided the light was too hot. The last thing she wanted was to hard-boil the poor things.

Instead she opened the top drawer of her dresser where she kept a few mismatched socks, some underwear and several undershirts, mostly hand-me-downs from Bitsy. LeeAnn wasn't jealous that Bitsy had moved on to training bras though—Bitsy had become the main target of Morris's harassment, especially when Momma was working late at the diner.

Morris would snap her bra strap and pinch her budding boobs and once in a while even try to kiss her. Bitsy would holler about calling the cops, but would end up simply leaving the trailer and staying gone until Morris went on home. LeeAnn figured that her own lack of development put her somewhere below Morris's radar for now.

She balled up a pair of underwear the faded pink of chewing gum, shoved it in the back corner of her drawer, and arranged a few socks around it. Then she settled the eggs inside the underwear nest. There, she thought. It would be nice and dark and warm for her little eggs. She would be sure to turn them every day, and in a few weeks she'd have two baby birds to take care of.

LeeAnn switched off her lamp, washing the room in the same sour yellow as the outside world, and lay down on her rumpled bed. She stared out her window into the marbled square of sky and imagined taking care of the babies once they hatched. She pictured their fluffy little bodies and big black eyes as they cheeped at her, convinced she was their momma. She would keep them safe inside her dresser drawer, and sometimes take them outside and show them the world, pointing out insects and lizards and other birds, explaining to them that someday they would learn to fly. They would perch on her shoulder as she walked to school, and give playful tugs at her hair and earlobes, and when she eventually did teach them to fly, they would test their wings and give it a whirl. But they'd always come back to her. She was their momma, after all. They would love her and never want to leave.

***

As soon as Bitsy got home, LeeAnn showed her the eggs.

"Where'd you get these?" Bitsy asked, sounding skeptical.

"That big ol' oak tree by the playground," LeeAnn explained. "Jimmy Doyle killed their momma."

"That asshole." Bitsy looked down at the eggs. "You just gonna leave 'em in your drawer?"

"Till they hatch, yeah."

"They ain't gonna hatch, you dummy."

LeeAnn frowned. "How come?"

"They just ain't. They need their momma sitting on 'em. Or one of them incubating machines. They ain't gonna hatch sitting in there with your undies."

LeeAnn knew her sister was wrong, but didn't say so. Arguing with Bitsy when she was in a mood was pointless.

Instead, LeeAnn said, "We should tell on Jimmy."

"Tell who? And what's the point, anyway—the momma bird's dead." Bitsy reached into her shirt and adjusted her bra strap. "Ain't nothing no one can do 'bout it now."

"I know, but maybe he'll get in trouble."

Bitsy snorted and moved to her side of the room, where she flopped down on the bed. "Nothing will ever happen to Jimmy. He'll go on being his asshole self. That's how it works, Lee Lee."

LeeAnn watched her sister stare at the water-stained ceiling and suddenly felt like crying.

Still, she kept vigil over the eggs. Every day she turned them, checked to make sure they still felt warm, and even talked to them a little. She remembered how her old neighbor Mrs. Holiday used to talk to her plants, convinced that they would grow bigger and more quickly that way. Bitsy always said Mrs. Holiday was crazier than a shithouse rat, but LeeAnn tried it anyway. And when no one else was around, she pulled open the drawer and sang songs to the eggs—songs from the radio, show tunes, Christmas carols, anything she could think of.

One afternoon LeeAnn was belting out Jingle Bells, when she looked up to see Morris standing in her doorway.

"Oh," she bolted up from her bed. "I didn't know anyone was home."

Morris stood there in his grease-stained shirt and dirty blue jeans and regarded her with a lopsided smile.

"We got a regular Loretta Lynn here," he said.

LeeAnn glanced at her open drawer. She felt like she was standing in front of a stray dog—if she didn't make a move, he would simply take a few sniffs and move on.

"Where's your momma at?" he asked.

"Work."

"What about Bitsy?"

LeeAnn shrugged. Bitsy used to hang out by the pool, but this summer the pool was filled with slimy green water and no one had been swimming in weeks. LeeAnn wasn't sure where Bitsy hid these days.

Morris nodded and leaned against her doorway, his smile now more of a smirk. LeeAnn stiffened and looked at her drawer again. She longed to shut it. She didn't know what Morris would do if he saw the two little eggs tucked away inside her faded underwear, but the bad taste in her mouth told her it wouldn't be good.

"You're gettin' taller, girl," Morris said.

LeeAnn felt a sickening lurch in her stomach like she sometimes got on the swings. And even though she was wearing a t-shirt and shorts, she felt naked.

"How old're you?" he asked.

"Nine," she said.

Morris nodded again and straightened back up. "Almost there."

"Almost where?"

But Morris simply winked and hooked his stubby thumbs through his belt loops. "I'ma go up to the diner and visit your momma. I'll see ya'll later."

It wasn't until he'd left her and she heard the front door shut that LeeAnn realized she'd been holding her breath. She exhaled in a whoosh and went to her dresser. The eggs were still snuggled safely inside. She reached in and gave their hard shells a few strokes.

"That was Morris," she said. She thought about explaining further, but decided that was all she wanted to say about him.

***

One week passed, then two. LeeAnn turned the eggs, talked to them and sang softly, and still nothing happened. She began to wonder if Bitsy had been right, that she was foolish for thinking that she could hatch two baby birds in her underwear drawer. She thought about asking Bitsy if she should just give up, but her sister stayed away from the house for longer and longer stretches. When she did come home, she hid behind books, buried her face in magazines, or simply crawled beneath her covers and slept the day away.

Still LeeAnn was determined not to give up.

Until one day she came home, headed straight for her drawer to turn the eggs, and discovered they were gone. She pulled the drawer out as far as it would go on its splintery track, but she didn't see the eggs anywhere. Gone was the cubby of cotton and elastic. Her drawer was in complete disarray, like a piñata of panties had exploded inside.

She didn't understand. No one ever went into her drawers. Whenever Momma actually remembered to go to the laundromat, she tossed the girls' clothing, wrinkled and still damp, onto Bitsy's bed and left it up to the girls to sort it out and put it away. And Bitsy wouldn't have rifled through LeeAnn's drawer—last thing she would want was a bunch of her old underwear and socks when she got brand new ones from WalMart at the beginning of every school year.

Which meant only one other person could have gone into LeeAnn's room, into her dresser drawer.

Fighting back the angry tears that burned like pepper in her nose, LeeAnn rushed through the narrow hallway and into the cramped kitchen at the back of the trailer. She found Morris helping himself to leftover macaroni and cheese the girls had shared for dinner the night before. He sat at the rickety table and hunched over his bowl like a hungry wolf over a fresh kill. LeeAnn stopped at the kitchen doorway and was suddenly afraid to take another step, afraid to open her mouth and turn loose the accusations that were crammed inside. She wanted to disappear.

But it was too late. Morris had already noticed her. Despite the poor light filtering through the grimy curtains, his black eyes glittered as he sat back in his chair.

"Well, well, it's the mother hen." He shoveled up more macaroni, chewing with his mouth open as he looked her up and down.

"Where are my eggs?" LeeAnn whispered.

Morris swallowed and chased his mouthful with a swig of beer. "I ate 'em," he told her.

LeeAnn gaped at him, her knees as rubbery as the noodles Morris slurped through his cracked lips. She felt her chin tremble, but she told herself she could not cry in front of this man.

"You're a liar," she said, trying to keep the whistling panic from her voice. "They was bird eggs, not chicken eggs. You can't eat bird eggs."

Morris laughed. "I can eat anything I damn well please, little LeeAnn. I cooked me up a bird-egg omelet, and it was dee-licious. I would'a saved you some if I'da known you was hungry."

LeeAnn just stood there, silent rage simmering in her heart and shooting through her veins.

"Don't believe me?" Morris asked.

LeeAnn shook her head.

"Ask Bitsy. She begged for some. Loved every bit of it, too."

LeeAnn glanced over her shoulder and saw a thread of light beneath the bathroom door. She looked back at Morris, who was leaned back in his chair, rubbing his stomach with one hand. He winked at her, and then she smelled it—the scent of cooked eggs, thick and rotten, a hundred times worse than the marsh. She saw a flash of her baby birds, feathers wet with goo, their eyes fused shut, their beaks emitting weak little chirps as Morris doused them with salt and pepper and scrambled them alive in her mother's cast-iron skillet.

She turned, fled down the hall, and stopped in front of the bathroom.

"Bitsy?" she said.

Her sister didn't respond.

"Bits?" LeeAnn knocked softly, her knuckles hollow on the thin door.

Still nothing.

With a sweaty hand, LeeAnn turned the knob, wobbly in its socket, and pushed open the door, blinking against the harsh light from the naked bulb over the sink.

Bitsy was huddled on the bathroom floor, her knees pulled to her chest, her forehead against the open toilet. Her face was pale, her eyes vacant. On the floor in front of her was one of her training bras, folded in half. Resting on top were LeeAnn's eggs.

LeeAnn shut the door behind her and settled onto the floor beside her sister. Neither one spoke for a few minutes. LeeAnn could smell sour puke on her sister's breath, could feel the occasional shudder that went through her sister's body, rattling her own each time.

Finally Bitsy let out a long sigh. "I went into our room and found him in your underwear drawer. He was holding a pair up to his face. Sniffing it, I guess, the sick sonofabitch. I yelled at him, asked him what the hell he thought he was doing. He came after me then." She shuddered again, and rose up on her knees toward the toilet, where she gagged and spit.

"Are you okay?" LeeAnn asked, afraid to hear any more.

Bitsy sat back down, wiping her mouth with a shaky hand.

The two girls sat, leaning against each other, looking down at the tiny eggs.

"They ain't gonna hatch, are they?" LeeAnn asked after a few minutes.

Bitsy sighed again.

"Don't know, Lee Lee. Don't know."

Story's Inspiration:

This story is based loosely on true events from my childhood. I'd always wanted to write about my attempt to hatch a bird egg in my underwear drawer, and the setting and characters who showed up to tell the story seemed to fit just right. I wanted the reader to form his own conclusions as to what exactly happened, but also wanted to leave a faint light for the two female characters to possibly find in their dark world.

Q&A:

1. Why leave the ending so open?

   I wanted the reader to draw his or her own conclusions as to what happens to the girls after this scene. Depending on the reader, the girls would either be destroyed by their circumstances or figure out a way to overcome them. I would like to think that Bitsy's character is strong enough to do the latter, and that she cares enough about her sister to lift her up, too. But not every reader is an optimist.

2. There's a pretty obvious metaphor in this story. Was that the intention from the outset?

    Because the story is looscly based on real life, it really wasn't the intention at all. When the characters and setting started to take shape, however, the metaphor of the bird eggs and the sisters just sort of happened. It made for a much more interesting story than some dorky kid in suburban New Jersey trying to hatch a robin's egg in her bedroom.

3. What was the inspiration behind Morris's character?

    I've met all kinds of people in my life. Mostly good people, but I have known a few who are pretty evil, plain and simple. Morris was sort of the embodiment of the evil I have known.

Jeff

Mr. 22 Caliber

We decide to stop at Brad Witten's house after school. We are a little worried about him. Yesterday, he beat Shawn Bradley to a pulp between classes. Shawn had made the terrible mistake of making fun of Brad's father who had died a few years back. There were rumors that it had been suicide.

Of course, Brad's a little sensitive to this subject and doesn't take jokes about it lightly. Shawn ended up with two black eyes, three broken teeth, and a busted nose before teachers grabbed hold of Brad. And now he's suspended from school for ten days.

There's no answer at his front door. We hear a loud popping noise behind the house, so we go around to his backyard. Brad is spread out on a lounge chair with a bottle of Jack Daniels in one hand and a pistol in the other.

"Brad, what the fuck?" I ask.

"He-ey guys."

"What the hell are you doing with a gun?" Donnie asks. Pete and Scott are with us too, but they keep silent and distant.

"What, this?" Brad snorts and holds it up to his face. "It's just a twenty-two."

"So, it's still a gun."

"Yeah, are you crazy?" I ask.

Brad straightens his arm and the blast from the pistol startles me, startles all of us. Brad laughs out loud. "Goddamn squirrel, I'll get you yet." He takes a long swig from the bottle and laughs even harder.

"Brad, are you crazy?" I ask again. "You can't go shooting off a gun in your backyard."

"Oh, knock it off, *Mom*. It's just a twenty-two. It's like a pellet gun. Good for shootin' squirrels and cans and not much else." He shoots again.

"Would you stop shooting?"

He grins at me, points the gun towards us, and pretends to squeeze the trigger. He makes a gunshot sound from his mouth and takes another drink from the bottle.

"Not funny, man. Not funny at all." I realize I'm the only one talking now; even Donnie has taken a step back. Stupidly, I take a couple steps forward and lower my voice.

"Come on, man, put the gun down. You don't need to be drinking and shooting around like this, that's how accidents happen."

He looks at me and points the gun to his head. He holds it there staring at me with a dead serious look that frightens me. Then he winks and grins and moves the gun from his head. He takes aim in the yard again and blasts his mother's bird feeder. Feed sprays out in all directions.

"Oh-h! *That* was a good shot," he insists. He takes a long drink from his Jack Daniels, and without looking over, says, "Why don't you guys leave me be. You're a real drag, right now. Can't let a guy have a bit of fun."

* * *

In school the next day, we're not too surprised to hear reports that Brad has died. Yet another rumor of possible suicide in his family. Since we're known to be his friends, school authorities, teachers, and police question us again and again asking if he was showing signs of depression or acting unusual in anyway whatsoever.

"No," we keep telling them. No, not at all, none whatsoever. Hell, we don't want to be involved in this mess.

Story's Inspiration:

Back in high school, a couple of us went to a friend's house after school. He was out back drinking and shooting a .22 Caliber pistol. That image, among others from my high school days, stayed with me and I always wanted to use it for a story or novel. Although nothing destructive happened in real life, I decided to explore the possibility of the situation getting out-of-control.

Q&A:

1. Why did the teenager have access to a .22 caliber gun? And booze?

    Access to the gun is a reminder of how careless gun owners can be with their weapons. How many times do we hear about a young child accidentally killing themselves? Gun owners need to keep the firearms secured and locked up. Alcohol is easy for teenagers to acquire—drugs too for that matter. If it's not at their house, someone always knows someone who can get it for them.

2. Did his mother, friends, and teachers not see that this boy was troubled and needed counseling?

    This is another reminder, or warning, that I've placed in this story. How many times after a school shooting do people come forward and say things like: "He was dark and disturbed." "He was a loner; an outcast." "He often talked about doing things like this." The problem is, the warning signs are often ignored, and this needs to change.

3. Why did his friends plead ignorance to Brad's aggressive, out-of-control behavior?

    Could be any number of reasons. Maybe some of them didn't want to be considered uncool if they spoke up like the narrator. They could've been afraid that Brad might snap if pushed. Maybe they had their own problems and didn't want to take on another one. It takes a strong person to ignore these factors and do what's right.

Mike

Guardian Angel

When the time comes, pull the cord.
Freefall exhilarates. Frightens. Freefall delivers beauty and danger. Jake licked his lips. Skydiving dominated his heart like a medieval lord jealous for his lover. Jake strangled the parachute cord in his right hand.

A roaring sea-rush of air surrounded him. He plummeted, a vertical freight train, headed for mother Terra in an unplanned and certainly unorthodox flight. A city dotted with rooftops and church steeples approached at an alarming pace. *Wouldn't it be a hoot to be impaled by one of those suckers?* he thought as he admired the heaven-pointed church-fingers.

Lights popped on like kernels of corn at critical mass as dusk handed off its remaining diffuse light to the night. Faint smells wafted up from a thousand houses – apple pies, wood fires and lover's scents mingled as one. He flattened out, the resistance of air acting as invisible hands on his shoulders, abdomen, legs and feet, lifting him from the earth. He glided and soared, his nose dividing air to his cheeks so that it flowed past his ears and roared its approval. The knowledge that eagles feared him wrenched a maniacal laugh from his soul.

He ripped at the cord and the chute yanked him heavenward. The world slowed down to a single moment in time – his descent, the movement of the early evening moon and his mind. *Nothing to do now but float back into oblivion and obscurity.* Unless he could maneuver over the lake and drown . . .

Everyone called Jake a junkie, but he had a secret that none of them could imagine – he could fly.

***

Terry hooked down the back alley off Main Street. These days, downtown produced very little business, but she needed rent money. She frowned, lips downturned tight and white at the way the grubby old bums fawned over her, asked for free samples and tried to cop a feel.

Goes with the territory, she thought as she smoothed her silk dress, hands parallel and in sync from her breasts to her hips. Normal people made life look so easy. They go about their lives like nothing mattered other than the next new television program or the latest song. A place to live surpassed her dread of the next man she allowed to violate her self esteem.

A man in an Armani suit spun around the corner. His quick steps carried purpose and he gave an impatient tug at a thick black mustache. Terry sized him up and raised her rates with every step. Expensive suit wearing his body in tight, clean lines – ca-ching. Creases were sharp and shoes that shone in the evening light like a silver window on the skyscraper at the corner of Main Street and Elm Avenue – ca-ching. This man wanted the transaction to happen immediately – ca-ching.

His ebony hair mimicked the black that makes you think of deep caves and Tom Sawyer. Maybe she could play Becky Thatcher for him and make a little more money. Negotiations she enjoyed. Men often squirmed and waffled in and out of confidence when paying for her services. Beware the man who knew what he wanted and how much he would pay. Whenever the man took control right from the start, bad things tended to happen.

He stopped about four feet away, assessing every curve of her body with his dark gaze. His eyes brushed over her feet, then took a slow, deliberate path up to her eyes. She knew she looked good. She always looked good. Men whistled at her all the time and the bums stayed away for the most part because her beauty intimidated them.

A light autumn breeze twirled up inside her skirt and the pleats lifted slightly. That raised the price another ten dollars. She took a curly lock of blonde hair, wrapped it slowly around her right index finger and made certain the cute dimple of her cheek would catch his attention. He silently continued his inspection.

Finally he said, "you'll do", and motioned her to follow him.

"Hey, I don't work for free, mister".

The dark man turned, reached out and clamped her throat with an iron grip. "I said, you'll do. That means, come with me. I am not here to dally and dicker with you. You are here to give me what I want, when I want it and be happy with what you receive."

The cool breeze rose again and traveled up her skirt to her brain. She had known fear before, but now fear knew her.

***

Jake missed the lake again. He woke sprawled face down in a dumpster, no longer cushioned by air but by trash bags. Nostrils blew out the stench of urine intermixed with garbage. His dry mouth and growling stomach protested their neglect. He struggled to get to his feet. When he finally did get upright, he swooned and almost fell back.

Jake leaned on the green metal wall and collected his thoughts. He also waited for his vision to return and his breathing to stabilize. He checked his fingers, the ones that poked through cutoff holes in his leather gloves. They were clean enough so he wiped the crud from his eyes. He always suffered a short nap after a flight.

His dumpster sat in an alley about ten yards from a streetlight. The fact he never could remember how he landed vexed him. Sometimes he landed in the county jail house. Now that would be a trick to remember, floating down through those cell bars with nary a scratch on him.

The methodical click of high heels on pavement pricked his ears and he steadied himself. Even purported junkies had their pride. He hated waking up in a dumpster. People always got the wrong impression. He rubbed his eyes again.

A woman strutted toward the light, slow and deliberate. A silken white dress stopped well short of her knees and wore her like a lonely man's fever dream. Even in this light, her legs dredged passion from his most latent desires. Her breasts were cradled in the most magnificent V that he'd ever seen on a woman. It moved, she moved. She moved, it moved. They were in concert with each other, the dress and this blonde goddess.

Her golden hair followed a manic course from the top of her head halfway down her back. As she strolled by, the back sway of the dress caught Jake's eye, a pendulum swing full of rhythm and promise.

A man, straight out of a mafia hit-man assembly line, approached and rudely looked her over. Of course, the intrusion of any man at this point was sucked, especially a rude man. The light breeze flowing through her back carried their initial conversation with it. Her dress tantalizingly lifted and Jake's heart slithered to his loins.

The intruder turned away, then whirled and clamped her throat with his right hand. Rage flew through Jake like the junk folks accused him of using. The intruder just identified himself as evil. Jake needed to soar, to fly high enough to dive down and annihilate this ruffian. He focused and tried to make the magic come, but nothing happened. Despite his best effort, he was nothing more than a junkie fresh from a filthy dumpster.

***

Terry thought to scream, but the man's grip closed too tight around her throat. She lifted to the balls of her feet. Her dress rode up higher than she liked. She nodded and hoped the man would let go before she choked. He released his grip and tilted his head toward the street corner as he walked away. Terry followed. *Run you fool,* her mind screamed, but the heels strapped on her ankles robbed her of that option. Where could she run to anyway? This man obviously noted her immobility. She struggled to keep up, but he did not slow down.

A limousine screeched to the street corner and the driver hopped out. The dark man turned on his heel. His scowl guided her through the door opened by the nimble driver. She slid in facing forward. As she glided across the black leather seat, two men leaned forward. One grabbed her right knee as she attempted to finish her slide.

The door closed behind her. The dark man's footsteps faded into the night. The other man facing her latched onto her left knee. Both lurched forward onto the limo floor maintaining their grips on her knees. The large man on the left pinned her head to the seat by her throat while a short, grinning man ripped her new blouse. Her scream only made the small man's grin explode into a dull yellow collection of poor dentistry.

***

When the blond bent over to get in the limo, Jake knew he had to stop this. Before the door closed, he noted a pair of hands reaching for her from within the limo. The ruffian slammed the door and walked down the street. This couldn't be good.

Once, Jake had witnessed a rape in the alley. The woman wasn't nearly as pretty as this lady in white, but the whole episode disgusted him anyway. He intervened and promptly got the shit kicked out of him. Fortunately, the woman got away while he paid the price.

This woman would not see another day. The evil man's nonchalance screamed that these men didn't care what happened to the woman. The men in the limo would toss her out the door when they were done, most likely off the nearest bridge.

All he had to do was focus. Dream. Imagine himself up there with the birds and jets. He sat behind the dumpster rocking back and forth mumbling his little chants. He could never be sure if these chants helped, but they certainly didn't hurt. Airliner lights overhead gave him bearings as he sought to enter the realm between space and earth.

The earth fell away from his feet; the dizzying ascent nearly blacked him out. He hovered just under the jet, knowing it should be screaming fuel combustion bombs in his ears, but only the silence of death met his mind. This time there would be no parachute. This time he needed wings.

***

Virtually no air trickled down her throat. The big man's grip kept her with only enough oxygen to stay conscious. They ripped off her panties and the small man's face dove between her legs. She willed herself not to feel his fingers probing, taking turns with his tongue. The big man's other hand was alternately squeezing her right breast to the point of extreme pain or slapping it with violent strokes. Then he stopped.

She couldn't breathe. She prayed. She begged the universe. The rip of his zipper jerked her limited attention. The big man pushed the smaller one aside with his legs. He sat back and lifted her by her neck until her head hit the ceiling. Reaching up with his other hand, he brought her down to her knees with her face buried in his crotch.

Another zipper ripped as the big man clasped two fistfuls of hair, shoving her head up and down, laughing as she gagged. Now she really couldn't breathe as he held her head down with both hands. She felt the short little grinning man saddle up behind and enter her. Just as she thought she would pass out, the big man lifted her head and spoke for the first time.

"You like that little cunt?" He slapped her hard. "You like my cock?"

Her face rocketed forward again. Pain in her throat mushroomed from the raw breaths she grabbed when he slapped her.

She tried to pass out. The big man kept bringing her up before she could. She knew she was going to die.

***

Without a rip cord and a parachute, Jake felt naked. Air trickled into his dream and he knew he would be freefalling any moment. *How do you imagine wings into being?* He had parachuted in the Marines. He knew what that felt like, but wings?

Jake could dream up a hang glider, but he needed more control. He needed to be able to accelerate rapidly. The explosion of air on his face tumbled him into an ugly flopping blob until he straightened out and pressed his chest against the onrushing wind. He closed his eyes and imagined roots growing out of his back.

A sickening feeling of unnatural growth between his shoulder blades gave him hope. He imagined the roots to be wings in a tremendous twelve foot wingspan. He imagined them strong, full of muscle and well practiced in flight. They caught the wind and he cut a path downward, diving to the edge of the city where the limo headed just moments ago.

He tucked his new wings and lengthened his body to increase speed. He would see the limo soon. Jake stared at the interstate heading out of town and made sure no vehicle passed that resembled a limo. He barreled over the road and decided to imagine more than ever before.

***

The big man ripped at the remnants of her dress and the little man continued to rape her. The sunroof opened, shooting napkins and pieces of clothing up and out.

"Great idea!" The big man yanked her up and off the little one, bringing on a flurry of what had to be curses. He had her by the neck again, this time with her feet on the floor. As the big man unfolded himself to his full height, she felt her toes leave the floor. This had to be the end.

***

Jake caught the glint of white reflected off the limo as it passed under a series of lights on a bridge. He imagined the sunroof open. The woman's head popped out with a pair of hands at her throat. He circled the limo to get a good look at the woman's plight. Jake peeled back the roof metal behind the tall man with his mind as the goon choked her. He left an icicle shaped chard directly behind the asshole.

Jake made the brake pedal depress suddenly, throwing the man against the woman. Then Jake mentally stomped the gas pedal and impaled the big man while the woman flew up in the air. Jake settled underneath her so she landed between his wings. In his mind, he took the little man by the throat and launched him a thousand feet into the air. Then Jake turned him over to gravity.

The big man struggled to pull himself off the metal spike. Jake imagined it curling back into the man, stapling him to the limo. Jake veered off, flipped the back bumper of the limo up in the air and gloried in its crunching tumble.

The woman on his back whimpered. Because of him or them he couldn't figure, but more important worries sprung to mind. He'd never learned how to land without passing out.

***

The last few minutes became a blur. In one moment the big man choked the life out of her, the next he gets impaled and she is thrown skyward. Something flew underneath her and she settled on its back. She must be in that place between death and life.

The limo startled her when it ejected the small man like a firework on its way to please her. The limo flipped into a devastating tumble with metal and blood flying everywhere. She closed her eyes and thought she heard a voice.

***

Jake glanced over his shoulder and tried to console the woman. "I've never really landed before. I just wake up someplace, so I hope whatever happens doesn't hurt you worse."

What a stupid way to make someone feel better he thought as he glided toward the lake. Maybe this time he wouldn't miss it. Of course, if the water didn't wake him up, he would drown, which would be alright with him too. He'd always thought that if he could just land in the water, he might wake on impact. That way he could sort things out better. After all, he hadn't had any dope for weeks.

He headed for the shoreline and the familiar fatigue overtook him. More intense this time though. He hoped the wings would carry him to the water after he faded out.

***

Terry's eyes opened while every muscle in her body remained guardedly relaxed. Her swollen face and sore throat throbbed like mosh pits. Her naked breasts straddled the back of some man's head – not unusual for her. Night sounds of crickets and a small stream tugged at her ears. Was the limo a dream? Had she died?

Terry slid off a grubby, bearded man and checked him out. Definitely not her type. The bums back in town would welcome this guy as a soul brother. They all looked the same. They lay beneath a willow with a small stream tripping along behind them. Early morning crept through the canopy of faded leaves and branches with a hint of sunrise peeking through. She searched for her clothes but found nothing but soft grass. At least the bum was still clothed. Maybe she hadn't fucked him.

She stood and explored the perimeter of the willow's waterfall branches. The bum remained motionless. *Maybe he's dead* she thought, breasts cupped protectively in her hands. She ran fingers across his left wrist. A heartbeat pumped life through the dormant man. Her back hurt where she'd dreamed the big man had slammed her against the sunroof. The soreness between her legs told the familiar story that someone fucked her. Had it really been the little man?

The more she thought about it, the more confused she became. She needed answers and the only source appeared to be passed out beside her. She crawled under the low-hanging branches to the brook, cupped her hands in the cold water and dropped it directly on the man's left eye. A groan rose up, but no movement.

She repeated the water torture eight times before the man grunted, "Enough already."

"Hey, I didn't know if you were dead or what," she said as he rolled to his right side.

"Shit, I missed the damn water again, didn't I?"

"What the hell are you talking about? Who are you and why am I naked?"

The man rose up to one elbow and looked at her for the first time. "Holy shit."

"What's the matter, haven't seen a naked woman before?"

"No. No." The man looked away. "It's your face. It's all bruised up. They musta beat you the whole time they had you."

"It was just the big guy. Wait a minute. That limo shit really happened?"

"Yeah, I was in the alley when that first guy choked you. I knew it wasn't going to go well for you."

"Did the limo wreck? How did I get out without dying, or am I dead already?"

"That's a long story, and yes the limo wrecked. I made sure of it."

"You? How'd you do that? Do you really expect me to believe all this?

"Lady, you can believe what you want. I don't know what to believe these days myself. Here, take my jacket. It should just about cover you up."

"Thanks. Hey, what are these holes in the back?"

"Oh, that musta been where the wings poked through."

"Wings? You've got to be shittin' me. What is going on here?"

Jake searched her bewildered eyes and sighed. "A few weeks ago, I found I could fly with the jets if I just imagined myself there. Real hard. Then I would imagine a parachute and I'd float back down. I never could actually land, though. I would wake up in dumpsters or jail or in trees. I thought about not using a parachute just to see if I'd die, but if I did, I wouldn't be around to know it, would I?"

Terry's eyes narrowed as she raised her voice, "So you *are* one of those bums around town always getting' high or drunk. I might've known."

"Look, I just didn't want someone as beautiful as you getting hurt. Obviously I didn't do the greatest job, but at least you're alive. Those men were going to kill you."

"Yeah, they were, weren't they?" Terry glanced his way. She lowered her eyes as she continued, "I'm sorry. I suppose I should thank you."

Jake rose up and leaned against the tree. "I just wish I could've gotten there sooner. It's just not right what they did to you."

"That first man who shoved me in the car. Did you see where he went?"

"Yeah, he walked down the street about two blocks and went in the hotel."

"He's gonna come looking for me you know. Can you do to him what you did to those other assholes?"

Jake stared at the crud caked on his shoes. "I don't know. I didn't even know I could bend metal and flip a car until I did it. I've never been able to fly when anyone's watching, either. I tried to show some of the guys once, and they all laughed at me."

"It's still dark. Maybe you could like, do him in real quick like?"

"You want me to just go and kill this guy?"

"He was the one that set me up to die, wasn't he?"

"Well, yeah...."

"And he will back to find out what happened."

Jake rolled into a fetal position. "I don't know. This is different," he whispered to the grass in his face.

"Please, the man will find me and kill me and you know it."

"But to just kill him in cold blood?"

"So what they were doing to me was warm-hearted? The least you could do is try."

"The least I could do?" Jake jerked up straight and glared ice-daggers at her. "I saved your ass lady, remember? I don't just get up and go kill people though. It just isn't right."

An awkward silence floated down through the willow branches. Terry shifted weight from one foot to the other. "I'm sorry. I shouldn't have asked. I wouldn't be here if you hadn't . . ."

"Look, I don't even know your name."

"Terry."

"Nice to meet you Terry. I'm Jake. Jake Holiday. Why don't I try to get us back to where we can work through this stuff better. Where do you live?"

"The Confederate Point apartments on Spruce Street."

"I know the place. I know I'm grubby and all, but I think I'll need to hold you to get you up there with me."

"What? What do you mean, hold me?"

"Whenever I fly, I kinda like rock back and forth with my eyes closed and imagine I'm up in a plane overhead. I never end up in the plane, just under it. Then, all of the sudden, whatever got me up there lets go and I imagine a parachute, or wings, and I float back down. That's all I know. But if I'm not holding onto you, I may go up to the plane by myself and leave you behind. I still might, even if I'm holding you. But it's the only thing I can think to try. Understand?"

"Not really. Maybe. Hell, I don't know. No funny stuff?" Jake frowned.

"Ok. Sorry. Let's do it."

Terry settled in his lap, pulling the front of his jacket tighter as he put his arms around her waist. "Just don't panic when we're up there. I seem to be protected for a few minutes once I'm up, so I feel pretty sure I can hold you. But if you start kicking and screaming, I don't know what will happen."

"Do I need to close my eyes and rock like you?"

"It wouldn't hurt. I haven't a clue if it will help though."

"Let's do this before I chicken out."

"Ok. Hear that jet overhead?" She nodded. "Just close your eyes and concentrate on being on that jet."

"Ok."

"Lean your head back on my shoulder and relax. Remember, I have you. Don't panic." Jake closed his eyes and began a slow, gentle rock.

"Gotcha." Terry relaxed into his arms and focused on the distant sound of the jet. She felt Jake's arms wrap her tight, but not too tight. These arms had held a woman before, she could tell. She began to realize there might be more to this man than his quirkiness.

She opened her eyes. The willow fell away below her feet. Air caught in her throat as they sped upward, two human missiles headed for an unseen jet. She didn't feel any wind or sense of movement other than the visual. She clenched her eyes shut again. Far better to tuck her head down on his shoulder and forget about what was going on.

***

Jake opened his eyes as he positioned himself underneath the plane. He'd never spoken while he was so close to the jet, so he decided to try it out. "I'm going to imagine a parachute for each of us. Have you ever used one?"

"You have got to be kidding, right? You get me all the way up here before you ask about whether I've used a parachute?"

"Well?"

"No. And you'd better not let go of me."

"Ok. Ok. I'll do the wings thing again. It just seemed to take more out of me than I'm accustomed to." Jake closed his eyes and focused on the process of growing wings again. "Where exactly do you live?"

"Why?"

"I'm gonna try and land in your apartment if that's ok."

"Go for it. I need to get into some clothes that don't stink."

"So, where do you live?" Air and Terry's scream pelted his ears - freefall. "Hold on and don't panic," he yelled over his shoulder as dagger nails dug into his neck. He flattened the descent out gradually so his rider didn't get jolted off his back.

Her hot breath behind his right ear whispered, "219A."

Jake focused on the apartment number and headed in the general direction of the apartments. Once he regained his bearings, he accelerated his glide toward the apartment building. Her nails clawed and imbedded in his skin, and he liked it. Once they got there, if they got there, he wondered if she would lighten up on him. As they neared the building, he continued to focus on 219A.

***

Terry woke up in the corner of her apartment, rolled up on her shoulders, ass over elbows. She ached as though she'd been in this position for some time. Jake lay on the back of a toppled over couch. "You sure got the better end of that deal," she muttered as she unfolded herself to her feet.

She staggered to him, knees weak and a schoolgirl's concern for this man who saved her life. *The stench of those goons needs to go away.* Terry trained her ear on movement from the living room as she showered, but all was silent. Once out and dried off she changed into jeans and a long-sleeved blouse and made two cups of coffee.

A groan startled her as she thought about everything that had happened. "Did I actually make it? Is this your apartment?"

"Yeah, you made it alright. I ended up on my head in the corner over there."

Jake glanced in the direction of her finger. "I'm sorry. I don't know how to land well. Hell, I don't know anything after I pass out."

"There's coffee on the kitchen counter and the shower's down the hall to the left. You can use my razor, but make sure you clean up after yourself." Terry sipped her coffee and glanced Jake's way as he righted the couch.

"I can take a hint. Wouldn't mind a good hot one about now anyway."

Terry buttoned the next-to-last button closest to her neck. She'd left it open on purpose while Jake was in the room. Metal scratching metal at her front door turned her feet to lead blocks. The knob on the door lock turned. She managed a shaking hand on the lock to attempt to stop it from turning. Jake's shower roared in her mind like Niagra Falls. Outside the door someone pounded with what sounded like iron fists.

She whirled around, coffee flying in a hurricane arc, and ran to the bathroom as the door exploded open. She heard the dark man's gruff voice shout, "You!" as she reached for the doorknob. Without looking back, she shoved and fell through the door and glanced off the side of the toilet. She scrambled to the door and fumbled with the lock. She knew once again, she was going to die.

***

The water had just got hot when Jake when Terry blasted through the door. "What the fuck?" He turned off the water, opened the shower door and looked around for a towel. Terry sprung to her feet in a wink, slammed the door shut and shrieked, "He's here."

The doorknob exploded. Terry whimpered and fell back into the corner of the bathroom.

The door creaked open in a slow-motion arc despite the knob's sudden demise. The chrome barrel of a pistol peeked around the doorjamb followed by the sinister, dark man from the alley. His brows furrowed and he pointed the gun at Jake's chest.

"Who the fuck are you and what are you doing with the bitch? She's supposed to be a corpse."

Jake felt the dark man's finger squeeze the trigger. He closed his eyes. He focused on the gun and imagined it frozen – absolute zero frozen. Tongue-stuck-on-the-flagpole frozen. The dark man's hand frostbite-frozen. Ice age-frozen.

The man screamed as he twirled about trying to release the gun, all the while his hand turned white, then blue. Jake focused and the blue traveled up the man's arm, disappeared under his shirtsleeve and reappeared at his neck.

The right side of the dark man's face turned sky blue, the color creeping up under his hairline until a final scream belched forth in a white-frost fog from the man's mouth. He crumpled to the floor. His right arm shattered with glass chards of steaming crystal flying everywhere. Dizziness stuck Jake like the cold blast of a violent northeaster. As he blacked out, Terry's arms thrust out beneath him.

***

Terry scrambled over to Jake and caught his head before it played a nasty game of chicken with the toilet. She cradled her arms around his neck and rocked back and forth.

"Oh shit, oh shit, oh shit. C'mon Jake, wake up." She glanced over at the frosty corpse beside her. "Jake, I don't know what this is, and I don't know who you are, but I need you. I don't know what to do and I don't have anyone to call. Please, please, oh God, please wake up."

A few minutes later, Jake moaned and she caught herself by the rim of the toilet mid-rock. "Jake, come on, Jake. We gotta get this guy out of here. Wake up."

Jake shook his head. "Holy shit. I actually froze the bastard."

"Hey, I'm sorry about how I treated you back under the tree. I mean the bum thing and all. You saved my life twice now." She stopped herself from running her fingers through his wet hair. "How are we going to explain this?"

"We drop him off the roof."

"What?"

"I imagined him at near absolute zero just before I passed out. See the steam coming off him? He is so frozen, we drop him off the roof, and I'll imagine he'll shatter into a million pieces. Grab that throw rug in the living room while I get dressed."

She shifted her eyes into the hallway, then slowly back to meet his. "Jake, I think you must be my guardian angel. Where the hell you've been the last five years is beyond me, but I think I need to change my life. Once we dump this guy, are you going to stick around?"

"Let's get rid of this goon before he thaws. We don't want to touch him with our bare hands or we could get hurt." He paused as he rose to his feet. "I've been a drunk. I lost my family. I'd have never thought I could deserve a fine woman like you again."

"Jake, I'm a hooker, I'm no fine woman."

"You are to me."

Terry smiled. "I suppose that's all that matters." She jumped up and came back with the carpet. Ten minutes later, a body dove off the roof of the twenty story apartment building like a Mexican cliff diver without the grace. The sound of a thousand crystal glasses crashing to the pavement brought a smile to their faces as Jake slid his arm around her waist.

He looked to the sky and pointed at a jet flying silent overhead in the night sky. She followed his gaze.

"Whatd'ya say we fly out of here? Find a place to start our lives over," he asked.

Her kiss held all the answer he needed.

Story's Inspiration:

I trained myself to write short, tight stories over the years, consisting of less than two thousand words. For this story, I was determined to run it past five thousand to prove to myself I could write length into my stories. While I have no aspirations of jumping from perfectly operating aircraft, the line "when the time comes, pull the cord" popped into my head. I figured this was a great jumping off point …

Q&A:

1. In writing a longer short story, what challenges struck you as the most daunting?

Wrapping up. There actually is a lot more tension I would like to go back in insert into this story. Back-story on Jake and Terry. What the villains were up to – that sort of thing. There also are many opportunities I missed to ratchet up the tension within the word count I presently have.

2. Jake fills the role of an anti-hero here, not your clean-cut kind of guy and he actually gets there late. Was this planned or did your 'characters run the show'?

I planned it that way. Terry is not exactly your model citizen. Basically they're two down-and-outers with good hearts. I wanted them to drive the story and I wanted the villains to be without any moral stature – kind of a not-so-good vs evil scenario. The point with Jake and Terry is that good can step up to the plate.

3. This story runs a sci-fi plot. Is this your preferred writing genre?

The truth is sci-fi is my passion. I love to read it, I love well-written sci-fi movies but I struggle to write sci-fi material. This piece is an experimental foray into sci-fi. My typical writing deals with muted sci-fi themes that rely heavily on character driven plots. I sometimes think the sci-fi in my stories gets lost in the characters themselves which ultimately does not bother me much.

Tracy

Touches On a Rainy Day

White, just pure, rolling white stretched out far beyond my reach.
Frangipani filled the air. Whispers of tranquility touched everywhere.
Unbeatable softness enveloped us, the untouchable rain rang out
melodies.
These touches on a rainy day bring peace, in a cleansing way.
Untouched by the cares of the world.

Pinks.
Passionate pinks, lined the outer whites creating shade .
Touched by the essence of giggles and kisses.
Soft caresses and gentle purrs.
Untouched by the cares of the world.

Blues, blues, bountiful blues, circled in around the rolling whites.
Blowing stroking, the gentle sighs.
Airs of innocence tingeing their smiles.
Warmth of the touches filling them deep inside.
Sharing a moment, finding their path.
Untouched by separation, fears, or lies.

Purples.
Purples of violet.
Morning glories and amethyst lighted the corners, and blended with
smiles and laughter amongst their stares.
Touched by the Perfect Passion snuggled together, binding their cares.
Untouched by the sadness which always seemed to linger.

Guldens glistening, golden glare.
Power in the light that leads them there.
Eyes close and dreams return.
The silence is hushed with heartbeats and
Oneness occurs.
Sleep persists , Happiness confines the pair.
Touched by the source, that rules the beyond sky.
Untouched by darkness that at times does arise.
To be touched on a rainy.
Awesome touches on a rainy day …

Rebekah

Five Easy Minutes

I was horny and suicidal.

Don't ask me why—the two don't exactly go together like biscuits and gravy. Besides, Tommy says I'm never horny. I am, as he puts it, a cold fish. But Tommy likes to say things like that just to piss me off. He's a regular Prince Charming.

The suicidal part came first.

There I was, cleaning out Peeps' cage, when that damn bird nipped the back of my hand. Hard, too. I squealed, pulled my hand back and saw a little pinch of blood.

"Ow, you little shit," I said and sucked on the bite.

Peeps twittered like an old lady and rocked back and forth, his head feathers up like he was daring me to come at him.

I sighed and looked around. Tommy was on Saturday shift at the plant, and the only sounds in the house were Peeps muttering and the clothes dryer ka-thunking around in the laundry closet. I took it all in, the matted carpet and paneled walls and dingy TV screen and water rings on the coffee table, and Peeps' tilted birdcage in the corner, and suddenly I wanted to kill myself. I thought about rummaging through Tommy's nightstand, beneath the dead batteries and old Penthouses, for his gun. I saw myself loading the gun, bringing it to my temple, and pulling the trigger. I shivered—it would be so easy. I'd never realized that if I really wanted to kill myself, I could do it in five minutes. Five easy minutes.

I hadn't even thought I was suicidal. Maybe I wasn't. Picturing yourself robbing a bank doesn't make you a thief. I guess I was just amazed that more people didn't kill themselves. We're surrounded by hundreds of ways to do it—just find a tall bridge or some heavy traffic or a bottle of pills and there you go. I guess it's all our damn responsibilities that stop us. Responsibilities to our boring jobs, our asshole boyfriends, our pet birds.

As I stood at the front window, picturing our bedroom wall painted with my brains, I saw a truck with a trailer hitched to it pull up across the street. The driver's door opened and a man got out, his head wrapped in a bandana and his chest stained with tattoos. He swaggered to the trailer and opened it, pulled down a metal ramp, then disappeared inside. An engine roared to life. The man came out riding a lawnmower.

He backed into the street and shifted gears. The lawnmower lurched forward, took the man over the curb and into the grass of the crazy old lady across the way. I watched him ride in lazy circles around her yard. He sure was tan. And sweaty. It was a hot one today. Hot and humid, with a sun so bright there was no place for shadows to hide.

He weaved between the trees, circling them like a buzzard, and somewhere inside me, a heat began to spread. It was a weird feeling, like remembering that you hadn't eaten all day and suddenly your stomach is pissed and your hands are shaking and you're out of your body with hunger. That's when I knew I was horny—I wanted this man in my room, in my bed, between my pilled sheets, between my stubbly legs.

Once the lawnmower man had finished the front yard and headed toward the back, I ran to the kitchen and grabbed a plastic cup. It was Tommy's—the white and orange one he'd gotten from Hooters. Each time he takes it back he gets a free refill of sweet tea. I cracked ice from the tray into the cup, filled it with water from the tap, then brought it to the window and waited.

Finally the muffled hum of the engine grew loud again, and out from behind the crazy lady's house rode the lawnmower man. Before I could chicken out, before I could see Tommy's ears grow red and his cracked palm make a beeline for my face, I fluffed my hair, stepped into my flip-flops and flung open my front door.

The lawnmower man was riding toward his trailer when I waved to him and held up Tommy's Hooters cup. He cut the engine and the world went dumb.

"That for me?" the man asked, wiping his brow with the back of his forearm. I about died with that move right there.

"Thought you'd be thirsty in this heat." I said as I crossed the street.

"Forgot my cooler this morning." He reached out and took the cup; the tips of our fingers kissed.

He couldn't have been more than twenty-five, but his face and the sun appeared to be close friends. When he smiled his skin folded like an accordion, but his teeth were white and straight as piano keys. Behind those mirrored shades were eyes I'm sure had seen a lot.

I watched as he gulped down my water. His Adam's apple was a sharp stone in his neck. He surfaced and belched, not to be rude, but to show his appreciation. At least that's how I took it.

"Thanks," he said. His upper lip was wet, sweat mixed with water. I bet it tasted salty.

"No problem." I didn't say anything more for a minute—I was suddenly shy and didn't know what the hell I was doing. I stared at his tattoos flecked with blades of grass and dirt. Across his stomach were the words "I'm Broken" in fancy letters. Above that was an angel, her wings clipped like Peeps', her eyes large and sad. I wondered if she was the one who broke him.

He took a few more swigs from the cup, then licked his lip. "Well, guess I better get back to it. I'm running behind. Hungover as a dog, too."

"You—you're backed up?" I twirled my hair with one finger like a goddamn schoolgirl. "Because I was wondering if you could…you know…cut my lawn….If you have time."

The man looked up at the sky as if telling the time by the sun. I knew it was only ten-thirty. Ten-thirty and hot as a mother.

"Tell you what," he said, "I've got some more jobs off Route Ten. If we don't get no rain this afternoon, I'll come back 'round three and take care of your grass. Sound good?"

"Sounds great."

He angled his mirrored shades at me and I smiled. I wondered if we were both thinking the same thing, if we both knew we weren't just talking about 'taking care of my grass.'

Just to be sure, I put a hand on his arm, gritty and greasy and hard. "I'll see you at three." I saw my reflection wink in his shades. I couldn't believe it—I wasn't even a winker.

It was the wink that seemed to send him the message. His skin folded again as he smiled, his white teeth gleaming once more.

"See you then," he said.

***

At two-thirty the clouds stumbled in, bulging with ugly bruises. I stood at the sink, stared out the window that overlooked my weedy back yard and watched them settle across the sky. It figured.

Well, I told myself, it's probably better this way. I was crazy to think I could pull off an affair, even though Tommy has run around plenty. For some reason I never really minded—it took some of the pressure off me. I am a cold fish, after all. If he needs to get his rocks off with some tramp he meets after work, that means he'll come home a happy man—maybe even offer to clean up after dinner or pick up his dirty clothes.

If *I* ran around? Forget it. I'd be tossed into the street so fast I wouldn't even have time to grab any of my stuff. Most of the stuff in the house is Tommy's anyway. I'd want to at least grab my picture of Daddy—it's the only one I have left. And maybe a cardboard box to sleep in, since I wouldn't have anywhere else to go.

The sky cracked open at five minutes to three—first a few pings and then the sound of rocks pouring onto the roof. Peeps chirped nervously and paced his perch, shaking his whole cage. I watched gray bullets of rain shoot sideways, washing weeks of pollen from the plastic lawn chairs out back. At least I'd remembered to cover Tommy's smoker this morning. He doesn't take care of much, but that smoker is his baby. One spot of rust and he'd shit a brick.

Thunder and lightning arrived, rowdy and loud as a couple of drunks. The lights flickered but didn't cut out completely. I closed the blinds and thought of Tommy's gun again. Five easy minutes. I could even do a murder-suicide and take Peeps with me.

I'd stretched out on the scratchy couch and was reaching for my Enquirer when the front door burst open and Tommy stood there, vacuum-sealed in wet clothes.

"Tommy!" I bolted up and felt my face go hot, like he'd just caught me swiping bills from his wallet.

"Goddamn, it's a shit storm out there," he turned and waved to J.J., who was backing his pickup out of our driveway.

I stared at him, there in his blue uniform, his name patch dark with water, his workboots leaving damp prints behind him as he shut the door and headed toward his easy chair.

"Why aren't you still at work?" I asked.

"Power went out," he said. "Generators didn't kick on like they're supposed to. Heads're gonna roll tomorrow, but instead of sitting around with our thumbs up our asses, bossman told us union guys to go on home."

He grunted as he leaned forward to untie his boots. Somewhere above us, thunder snarled, prowling closer. The light outside had faded to a greenish-purple and the confused streetlights had stuttered to life.

"Get me a beer, will ya babe?"

"Sure." I went to the kitchen, threw open the fridge and grabbed a beer from the sticky shelf. My hands were shaking. I'd really dodged a bullet. I couldn't even imagine what Tommy would have done if he'd come home and found some tan, sweaty guy in his bed, boning his girlfriend. I'd be cleaning blood off the walls for a week—the lawnmower man's and mine.

I was hunting around the cupboard for Tommy's favorite Koozie—the one with the foam boobies on it that he'd gotten at South of the Border—when the doorbell rang.

Shit.

I froze, beer in one hand, booby Koozie in the other.

"Babe, can you get that?" Tommy called. "I just sat my ass down."

"Sure," I hurried from the kitchen and across the living room, my heart roosting in my throat like a big, overfed hen.

Through the peephole I saw the lawnmower man, shirtless and slick with rain.

"Who is it?" Tommy called over the noise of the TV he'd just turned on.

"Don't know," I said. I shoved the beer into its Koozie and opened the door.

The lawnmower man smiled when he saw me. His sunglasses were gone. His eyes were brown with heavy lids—the kind that make me melt like chocolate on a dashboard. I almost forgot that I had a hotheaded boyfriend ten steps away and damn near invited the lawnmower man inside.

"Nice," he said, "I like a woman who meets me at the door with a beer."

"Oh." Without thinking I hid the beer behind my back like a little kid caught with a pop he's not allowed to have. "I'm sorry…." I stopped, every other word going right out of my head.

He hunched forward. "I hate to be rude here, but can I come on in? It's raining something fierce."

"We don't want any," Tommy called from the depths of the house. I glanced over my shoulder and saw the back of his head. He had turned on ESPN and likely wouldn't budge for hours.

The man looked past me. "You got company."

"Listen," I said quietly. "I'm really sorry, but you need to leave. I thought you wouldn't come because of the rain so…." God that sounded bad. *Sorry, but I couldn't wait ten minutes for you so I went ahead and called someone else to take care of my grass.*

The man nodded, then handed me Tommy's Hooters cup, now smudged with dirt and dotted with grass clippings.

"I forgot to get this to you earlier," he said.

I took it without a word.

"Well then, guess I'll see ya 'round."

He tipped his head like a cowboy and ducked back out in the rain, kicking up sprays of water as he went.

I shut the door and leaned against it, my heart racing like those cars in the Daytona 500. I stayed there a few minutes, trying to get it together, then walked back into the living room.

"Who the hell was that?" Tommy asked without peeling his eyes from the TV screen.

"Oh, just some guy wondering if we needed mowing."

"Mowing? What the hell kind of jackass mows in this rain?"

"Don't know," I said. Then added before I could stop myself, "The yard must look like hell."

Tommy looked up at me, though his eyes hadn't turned dangerous yet.

"You're lucky I had a nice, easy day—" He stopped.

"What?" I asked.

"What're you doing with that cup?"

I looked down at my hand. That damn Hooters cup.

"Oh," I said. "Nothing. Just putting it away."

"Why's it got all that shit on it?"

"It's just dirty is all." I wiped it on my shirt.

"What the hell're you walking around with a dirty cup for?"

"I don't know, Tommy, because the damn doorbell rang while I was holding it."

Tommy eyed me another minute. I swear I about threw up right there, certain he could see through my skull and read the thoughts printed on my brain.

"All right then," Tommy said. "Just as long as you weren't fixing to pour my beer into a dirty-ass cup."

"Don't be silly, Hon," I said, my voice about to smash into a million pieces.

I crossed the room and handed Tommy his beer, safe and cold in his booby Koozie. As I turned back toward the kitchen he slapped my ass.

"Tell you what," he said. "How 'bout you fix us a nice dinner and I'll clean up after? Promise I won't drop one dish."

"Sounds great."

In the kitchen I threw the dirty cup in the sink and leaned forward with my head in my hands. As I listened to the TV drone on and Peeps chirp away and the rain nail our roof and Tommy let out a long, low belch, I thought again of the gun buried in his nightstand.

Five easy minutes.

Story's Inspiration:

I wrote this piece one day in June after watching two men mow my neighbor's lawn. They were hot and sweaty, and I wondered what they would do if I came out and offered them some water—would they think I was just being nice or that I had ulterior motives? I tried to capture the dialect of Southern Georgia/Northern Florida and read it to my writers group with a Southern accent.

Q&A:

1. The narrator is a young woman who is somewhat intelligent— why is she with such a cretin?

    In real life, women stay with cretins for all sorts of reasons. When the narrator imagines getting kicked out of her house, she believes she wouldn't have anywhere to go. Her only mention of family is a solitary picture of her father, so it's safe to assume she either has no other family or can't rely on it. Sometimes a few years of self-imposed isolation and psychological abuse can convince a person he or she can't do any better.

2. Again, you leave the ending fairly wide-open. What was your intent this time?

    I think the narrator is simply marveling at the ease with which one can commit suicide if one wanted to. Committing suicide sometimes seems the easier choice out of certain situations, but that doesn't mean she is in fact suicidal. Because it was just as easy for her to arrange a possible affair, yet she didn't follow through with that, either. This narrator is a person who lets life happen to her, and life can be as shifty as the weather.

3. She only didn't follow through with the affair because her husband came home early. If that hadn't been the case, would she have followed through?

    Probably. At least to get a discount on her lawn care.

Jeff

Keepsakes

At the funeral home, my aunt told me that you never get over losing your mother. It's the nurturing you miss. That special bond between a mother and daughter that can't be replaced, but you learn to get by. During bad days you envision good memories to push those tear-stained cheeks into a smile.

For me, it's been the routine things. I can't tell you how many times I've picked up the phone to call her since she passed.

I'm at Mom's house now—going through the possessions in her bedroom. Dad didn't want to be bothered. Actually, he's hardly talked since her death. He just parks himself in front of the living room television and watches black and white movies. Only, he seems to stare at them more than watch.

In the bottom drawer of her nightstand, I find oodles of fabric with partly crocheted designs. One has a teddy bear with only one arm and no legs. One says, "Home Sweet Ho."

The top drawer is filled with hundreds of greeting cards for all occasions. They're dated back years and years. What had she planned to do with all of these? Buried under the cards I find her Bible; a black leather King James Version with crease marks along the spine. The binding is coming undone; the pages will soon begin to fall out.

I flip through the Bible, and am shocked. Mother was so organized and kept the house immaculate, yet her Bible has scribbles, crumbs from pencil erasing, and little scraps of paper throughout. Near the back of the Bible, in Revelation, an old black and white photo slides free. Actually, it's more like brown and yellow. It's a portrait of an older man posing and smirking at the camera. His light, thinning hair brushed back and teased by the wind. The wire-rimmed glasses seem too small for his face, maybe because his eyes are squinting from sunlight. He stands in front of a large tree wearing a white long-sleeved dress shirt pressed to perfection against his thin frame. A diagonally striped tie is knotted at his neck, but the thin bottom part hangs down lower than the wider portion suggesting he left the house in a hurry and did not notice the uneven tie job. It looks like a nice picture taken after Sunday morning mass.

I study this mystery of a man, and he means nothing to me. Yet his picture somehow reminds me of a conversation I had with Mom in her hospital room shortly before her passing. Her bedside table was cluttered with flowers and get-well cards. She was sitting up so I could massage her back to stimulate blood flow to prevent bedsores. A steady hum enveloped the room and occasional blips sounded from a machine on the other side of the partition. The woman over there seemed in much worse condition than my mother. My nose stung from the scent of alcohol-rubbed metal and over-bleached linoleum. A color television mounted from the ceiling and wall spat out worthless daytime programming.

My mother looked over her shoulder at me and smiled. "I'm worried about you," she said in a raspy, yet comforting voice.

"Don't be ridiculous, Mom. I'm not the one who's sick."

"You know what I mean."

I didn't have a response.

"He's making you miserable. You know this. You tell me time and time again. He doesn't respect you. He's verbally and physically abusive. That's no kind of husband to have . . . and what kind of father would he make if you two decide to have children?"

I felt an ache in my womb. I already knew the answer to that question. It was one thing I never quite told my mother the truth about.

"Mom—stop."

"There's a good man out there for you; one who will treat you right. You need to leave Thad—he's no good for you."

"Oh, how would you know?" I snapped. "How would you know that I would be better off without him?"

"Honey—life's too short . . . don't make the same mistake I made. The right man is out there for you. And when he comes along, believe me, you'll know it. Don't live out your life in regret."

"What are you talking about? What mistake did you make? What are you regretting?" I asked.

She turned her head from me and wept. Her reaction was so unexpected that my hands left her back as if I had been touching a stranger. I tried to soothe her, to find out what mistake she had referred to. She refused to answer.

Fearing the worst, I no longer wanted to know.

I continued to massage Mom's back while my eyes locked onto the prone shadow against the partition beside us. The occasional machine-assisted, deep breath from that side of the room kept me company.

This recollection makes me sick to my stomach, because looking at this man's picture closer, I see a resemblance. The large smooth forehead, the slightly sunken eyes, the prominent nose, and retracted jaw. It's the similarities I had always looked for in my father, but could never find. Even the way this stranger's head is slightly tilted to the right resembles me . . . it's exactly how all of my pictures turn out.

No, this *doesn't* make sense. This *can't* be what it seems.

Sure my father has been stubborn his entire life and never said so much as a kind word to my mother, just: "Get me this and get me that." "Stop lollygagging and get cleaning." "Get back inside the kitchen and make my dinner."

But still, would she cheat on him? She was such a pious woman. She attended church every Sunday no matter the weather or her health. Well, at least until those last few months. Father, on the other hand, never attended church.

Yet, I'm an only child and Mother was in her fifties when she gave birth to me. It always seemed strange that they conceived so late in life. Maybe Father wasn't fertile—although he would have blamed her regardless. But Mom, in her later years, met the love of her . . . ?

No, I don't want to think about this. It's making me nauseous. My head is reeling.

I look at the back of the photo. The time worn writing is barely legible. The ink has been worn to a light gray, but I can decipher some portions. One part says, "Life's choices are never easy, and I know that yours was the most difficult." The middle is too faded to interpret, but I do see words like "love" and "miss". The last sentence reads, "I respect your decision and agree to not interfere."

It's signed, "Your Beloved." There's no name, but the date jolts me. It was written almost 33 years ago. Only a few months before . . . I was born.

Story's Inspiration:

This idea came out of an assignment from a creative writing class. The professor brought in a bunch of old photos and spread them face down on a table. We each had to blindly pick a photo and develop a story around it while describing the photo in detail at the same time.

Q&A:

1. Does the daughter feel less love or closeness to her mother after she discovers the assumed affair?

    I think she would feel hurt that her mother never told her the truth and angry that she'd never met her real father. Yet I believe she would still love her mother the same and maybe, over time, even begin to understand why she'd decided to keep this secret.

2. What made you decide the daughter to have an abusive husband?
    These are two women who have kept big secrets—the mother's affair, the daughter's miscarriage—and probably tend to keep a lot of their feelings inside. I felt there needed to be strong motivations for the mother to even bring up the subject. The first was that she was dying and didn't have much time to warn her daughter, and the second was that her daughter wasn't just in an unhappy marriage—she was married to an abusive man.

3. Did you pull the information described in the hospital room, i.e.: sounds of machines and the smell of alcohol, from real life experiences?

    Yes, I still remember trips to the hospital to visit my grandfather. He seemed to always be there for one thing or another, but he survived heart disease and cancer to live into his mid-eighties before dying of natural causes. I was a young boy when visiting him and all the chemical cleanliness and machinery in an environment that housed sick and dying people always made me feel uncomfortable.

Mike

The Road Home

Smooth jazz plays on the radio as I wind around the rural mountain roads of West Virginia. I'm thinking of Momma's favorite painting as I lean my head against the driver's side window frame. Cool evening air washes my face of the day's stress. An October breeze kicks up fallen leaves into lazy cyclones that whoosh past my van. I focus on the steady rhythm of the paver lines on the road while music snuggles into my thoughts.

An airbag explodes into my chest and face. The unmistakable, sickening crash of metal on metal rips at my ears. My manicured hands fly off the steering wheel to protect my face. Glass clinks in crystal clarity on the pavement, yet my mind sees only an empty road.   The van is headed over the side of the mountain. Darkness overtakes my mind, my heart and the world around me . . . .

A sharp, stabbing pain digs at my ribcage and I remember a car crash and confusion and a valley. My chest is sore from the impact of an airbag, but I look down at the steering wheel and everything appears intact.

In fact, I'm back on the road – intrigued by the vivid hues of the foliage. I slow down and turn left onto a cobblestone road that hints of familiarity. Dazzling gold and red and deep maroon leaves transfix my eyes. I peer up the bumpy road hoping for a sign or something to trigger a memory as to why I am here.

I pull the van off the road, open my door and get out. The dirt under my feet is dry; the browning grasses and weeds reek of of autumn. I smooth my denim skirt, stand tall and inhale slow and long through my nostrils, catching every scent, every whiff of the day; the musky scent of leaves fallen under recent light rains, the hint of winter's forthcoming bite, my old, sixth-grade wool sweater. My pain is gone. In fact, that last breath I took was so good, I exhale slowly in anticipation of another.

My van idles next to me, all white and gleaming and the prevailing breezes push the exhaust fumes away from me. I don't want to get back in that ridiculous vehicle.

Wood smoke tickles its feathery finger under my nose. Tears nestle in the corner of my eyes as I think of home and how it would be to walk through Mom's front door one more time; soft like a butterfly-nestled-in-a-summer-rose, sweet like her special hot chocolate on a snowy night, warm like a fireplace quilt pulled over me as I nap on the couch.

I gaze at the sharp curve in the road and see a wooden plaque nailed to a tree. I look back at my van. I'm not sure which way to go. Deep inside I know I belong in the van, but the scent of Momma's peach cobbler dances under my nostrils and coaxes me home.

"I can always come back as long as I don't kill the engine. I'll just leave it running."

I run up to the plaque and trace the letters I burned there when I was eight; M – i – k – e – y. I named this curve after my older brother. He was riding his bike when a car killed him. He was ten. I was a devastated little sister.

I follow the old trail to Momma's house. I hear voices. Not just any voices, but the ones of years gone by: my uncle laughing in his beer-voice after a long day in the fields, my mother as she clanks dishes around in the kitchen, and most unmistakably, my brother's staccato war whoops as he battles invisible foes in the backyard.

I cry just outside the door as I strain to hear what Uncle Bill and Mom are talking about. I realize that no matter how much I strain, my ears will not be allowed to eavesdrop on the exact content of the conversation. There is nothing stopping me from walking through that door and right into Momma's arms – except the van parked at Mikey's curve.

I sob so loud the voices stop. I realize I am sitting, leaning against the front door. I jump to my feet and feel my face blanch as the door swings open. Momma looks at me with a bewildered expression on her face.

"Tammy, sweetheart, you're early. You shouldn't be here yet," she says. "You've left important things undone." She opens the screen door and engulfs me in her most special hug.

"Momma, I just wanna come home, that's all. If I go back, it's gonna hurt."

"I know. I know, darling, but you have to wait until the time is right."

"Why can't now be right? Why can't I choose? I just wanna come home." I wipe my nose on my sweater and realize how young I'm acting – like I did when I got rapped across the knuckles as a kid.

"Sweet, sweet Tammy. You never were one for following the rules. I suppose I shouldn't be surprised to see you here but, that doesn't change the fact that you have a life to live and you must see it through. Trust and believe I'll be the first one to welcome you home – when the time is right. Do you know how much I love you, sweetheart?"

"I know how much I love you."

"And I love you so much that I am sending you back to where you're supposed to be. I know you'll have a fine life just as I know one day you'll be back here with me. So go, child, and make your momma proud. I know you will, I've always known. I love you."

I'm dizzy. I hear the van idling behind me. I glance at the plaque and whisper a soft goodbye to Mikey. The breeze climbs up the mountain and I gag on exhaust fumes. My eyes sting. I stagger to the van door and climb in.

Except – I'm not in the driver's seat, or any other seat. In fact, I'm on the ceiling, on my shoulders with my feet up in the air – on one of the backseats. My ribs ache. My head feels light, dreamy.

But I remember Momma. I remember her favorite painting and the smell of wood smoke and peach cobbler and big hugs but most of all, I taste, hear, smell, see and feel the love I thought I'd lost when she died.

I smile through the pain because I know I will do great things in my life. Momma told me so.

Story's Inspiration:

The Road Home is a story written off of a *24 Hour Short Story Contest* prompt. The word count limit was 1100. I used my memory of a car wreck and some memories of living family members. My mother is not deceased, but I imagined what life might have been like without her. Also, like Lavender Hour, I experimented with writing from a female perspective.

Q&A:

1. You state you used memories of "living family members". Did you change their names?

   Yes. I had recently been involved in a nasty car wreck and I wanted to incorporate that experience into a story. I rely heavily on characters for my stories, so I figured I'd let family model for me. None of the characters actually match up with any reality within my family. All my sisters and mother are still alive. It was fun using some of their personality traits though.

2. What about the names? You used your own name for the dead brother. How did you pick the others?

   Interesting question. I kind of liked looking at myself as the fondly remembered 'dead' brother (sometimes I wonder about myself…). I used Uncle Bill because of the old tv show "Family Affair". The other names I wanted to be common. Nothing that would take away or add too much to the characters. Tammy is a nice, safe name and Momma, while we don't use this name for our mother in our family, lent kind of a down-home country charm to the character.

3. Working with an 1100 word limit can be tough. Do you have any methods that help you make your word count?

   Yes, it's called rewriting. I do quite a bit of it. Usually on a piece of this length my first draft will weigh in around 1600 to 1800 words. Then I begin to hack away at unnecessary sentences, then unnecessary words and a couple times I've had to use contractions to make it in just under the word count wire.

Tracy

Let Her Cry

Just let her cry, she has so many tears.

Just let her be alone, just let her go.

Her passion is her weakness and her strength

Each tear washes away her pain drop by drop.

She's cried so much all her tears will bring hope one day

Hope for no more tears. Let her cry

Her heart needs peace, peace from all the pain, peace from

All the confusion, she knows she needs to cry.

She knows she needs to let someone back inside.

Her pain has given her an unspoken, unknown beauty,

 she hides it well. To her it means everything,

That pain inside, that pain she tries to hide.

There's a smile somewhere inside, let her smile, make her smile.

Her words are different now because of the pain and the forced

Smiles. There are so many things left unsaid, she tries, let her try.

Just let her try, just let her cry …

Rebekah

Variations on Mr. Cornflake

In the spring of 1983, my sister turned me into a fairy.

She claimed to know the formula, the magic potion to turn an ordinary tomboy with dirt under her nails and stained hand-me-downs into a beautiful fairy, complete with gossamer wings and delicate little feet. I sat in the bathtub, hardly noticing the water going cold and the bubbles popping into oblivion, as I watched her work. She carefully measured a capful of strawberry shampoo, squeezed in drops of bathwater from her waterlogged Barbie doll's hair, and swirled the mixture. Her brow furrowed in concentration, she lifted the potion over my head and poured. I closed my eyes and imagined the transformation that was likely taking place before her. My hair was probably turning from mousy and straight to curly and blonde, perhaps with a tiny, glittering crown. My skinned knees were healing, my freckles were giving way to smooth, creamy skin. I felt her rubbing the potion into my hair and heard her muttering a few nonsense words—the magic spell.

Then she said, "Ta-dah!"

I hopped from the tub and hurried to the sink, my hair dripping and slick with congealed soap, my flesh coated in goosebumps. The mirror reflected the same girl I'd been before. Still the tomboy with brown hair and crooked teeth. Still short and pudgy. No tiara, no wings.

"Nothing happened," I said.

"I can tell you're a fairy," she told me. "You're probably just too dumb to see it."

She wrote and illustrated volumes of stories, *Mr. Cheerio, A Horse Named Bob,* plays starring our Cabbage Patch Kids and My Little Ponies for us to perform. I made a few attempts at my own manuscripts, but Mr. Cornflake just didn't have the same charisma, the same flair, as Mr. Cheerio.

One of her books was entitled *Stupid Bekah.* I was the main character. It chronicled the antics of an annoying, unintelligent little sister who constantly said the wrong thing, missed punch lines, took things without asking, and basically irritated everyone and ruined everything in her path. The illustrations of me were even less flattering than the descriptions. I found the book while snooping through her dresser. I ripped it up and threw it out the window of the bedroom we shared.

"What happened to the book I wrote?" she asked me later.

"What book?" I asked, wide-eyed.

"You know what book, Bekah. Where is it?"

"I don't know."

She stood across the room, hands on her hips, glaring at me from behind her glasses. "Liar," she said. "You really are stupid, Bekah."

I was crushed.

When she started middle school, things really got brutal. Anything I said was eligible for ridicule, nothing I wore was right. But despite her taunts, I was still determined to impress her.

"What do you think?" I asked, modeling a meticulously color-coordinated outfit—turquoise and pink—right down to the socks and shoelaces.

"It's okay," she told me, "if you're starting an ugly club."

Or I'd seek out her advice when I was experiencing drama typical of any fifth grade girl.

"I think my friend is mad at me," I'd say, on the verge of tears.

"You probably deserve it," she'd reply.

Then we were in high school. She dyed her hair, then shaved it. She wore combat boots with fishnet stockings and safety pins on her flannel shirts. I was never brave enough to venture beyond the realm of torn jeans and dark lipstick, which I always wiped off before I came home. She smoked pot and dropped acid. I felt rebellious drinking Peach Schnapps and NyQuil. She once threw an entire ice cream sundae at a girl who made fun of her jacket. I talked about people behind their backs and smiled to their faces. She was the real thing. I was just an imposter. A Mr. Cornflake.

But somehow that didn't matter anymore. We became confidants. Co-conspirators. She taught me how to smoke a cigarette. We sat together on her dresser and blew sloppy smoke rings out her window, coughing and giggling. She taught me how to sneak out of the house. We practiced shimmying down the huge evergreen that stood in front of her second floor window. Soon we were nimble as cats, able to make it from window to ground in twenty seconds flat. During family gatherings we swiped alcohol, smuggled it off into empty bedrooms and dared each other to drink it. Our throats ached from laughing so hard as we stumbled and slurred.   Between these moments, inside the hysterical laughter, the commiserating about crappy relationships and disloyal friends and strict but absent parents, we were equals. We were best friends.

We went to college on opposite coasts. Still I envied her life and spent my time trying to catch-up. The places she traveled, the things she tried, even the seedy apartments and shady friends— everything was about her was so alive.

Which was why I was blind-sided when I found out she'd tried to kill herself.

She told me about it when I was visiting her at art school one spring. We sat on the rooftop of her apartment, sharing a bottle of wine and smoking cigarettes.

"So don't get mad," she began, "but I tried to commit suicide last year."

"*What?*" I stared at her. "When?"

"Right before Christmas." She flicked her cigarette; ashes fluttered onto the tar paper below.

"But…*why?*"

She shrugged. "I wasn't happy. Stressed out. Work, school, breaking it off with what's-his-name." She was so calm about it, like she was telling me she'd tried a new recipe that didn't quite work out.

I, on the other hand, was livid.

"You were thinking about killing yourself and you didn't even *call* me?"

"What were you gonna do? You live like, a thousand miles away."

"Still, you could have at least *talked* to me about it."

She laughed and held up her wrist, where I finally noticed fragile red lines running across it. "What's there to say? I didn't go through with it."

"How could you even *think* about killing yourself!?" I was raging. It blew my mind that the person whose life I had always admired could decide it was something so disposable.

"I wasn't really thinking about anything, I guess," she said. "I was depressed and drinking, I saw a knife and I went for it."

"Jesus Christ!" I took a swig of wine, my lips making a hollow *thup* on the bottle.

"I didn't want to bother you," she said. "You're so busy with school and stuff. Plus you're so far away."

"I think you being suicidal would have taken precedence over anything else I had going on."

I felt betrayed, like she hadn't trusted me to handle her at her worst, her most vulnerable. I'd always believed we were as close as two people could possibly be. Yet when she should have been running to me first, she'd shut me out.

"Why didn't you call me, really?" I asked, crushing my cigarette out.

She shrugged again; a ghost arm of smoke escaped her lips. "I didn't think you could relate. You've always had it so together and your life is so easy. You wouldn't have understood."

"*I*'ve had it so together?" I laughed out loud. "All I've ever done is try to copy you. Don't you know that?"

She just looked at me.

"Hello? *Mr. Cornflake*? Remember?"

"Oh, yeah…."

"I've always tried to emulate you. Everything in my life has pretty much been a variation on Mr. Cornflake."

"Great," she said, laughing. "Well, congratulations. You're better at my life than I am."

"But don't you think that's kind of pathetic? Not ever doing anything original?"

"It's not pathetic," she said. "You didn't copy everything. Just the parts you liked. You'd be a complete moron to copy my mistakes. That's where you made your own life."

"I guess."

We sat there, looking out over rooftops, air-conditioning units and satellite dishes, above the medley of car horns and laughter and barking dogs.

"I always kinda liked Mr. Cornflake," she said after a minute. "He wasn't a jerk like Mr. Cheerio was."

"Yeah, Mr. Cheerio was kind of a jerk."

"I mean, he had his reasons…he had a hole in the middle of his body. That's gotta be tough."

"Yeah, but he was interesting," I said. "Mr. Cornflake was flat and lame. Who wants to hang out with a loser like that?"

She blew another smoke ring, looked at me and smiled.

"I do," she said.

Story's Inspiration:

I wrote this story for the Florida Writers Association's collection of stories about family relationships. Almost every story I write has a character who is much like my older sister, so I chose to write a short story to illustrate our relationship from childhood up to now.

Q&A:

1. You say this was all based on real life—your relationship with your older sister. Did you ever feel like you were living in her shadow?

    Not at all. The thing about my sister is that she is so completely different from me that we were never in competition for anything. Our taste in clothes, guys, music—nothing was similar. I never felt like she cast a shadow over anything because her shadow was way the hell on the opposite end of the universe. Thank God. I can't imagine actually competing with her for a guy. She'd probably fight dirty.

2. What do you think was the turning point in your relationship? You go from always trying to get her approval to you two being equals. How did that happen?

    When she started middle school we didn't hang out quite as often, and then one summer we babysat together and were sort of thrown back together, only now she found me less obnoxious, and I found her less cruel. We became allies and allowed each other back into our respective lives.

3. What is your relationship like with her now?
    She's my best friend. All my sisters are, but her especially because we are the closest in age and went through a lot of the same things together. She lives in LA so I don't see her very often, but we are always in touch and up in each other's business all the time.

Jeff

The Pleasant Sting of a Rose Thorn

George Viner gazed out the bay window towards the hidden sun as its light filtered through the autumn leaves of his oak trees. It was a season of change, a change that George could relate to. He released the curtain and took a deep, raspy breath.

"Betty," he hollered towards the kitchen. "I'm going for a walk."

"Give me a minute and I'll get my walking shoes on," she hollered back.

George moseyed to the entrance of the kitchen where Betty was cutting up vegetables in preparation for tonight's dinner. He smiled. 54 years of marriage and all throughout, she always began preparing at half past three and served promptly at five o'clock.

"That's okay, dear. Why don't you stay here?"

"Don't be silly, George, it'll only take me a minute." Betty put the knife down and dried off her hands.

"No, don't concern yourself. Really."

"But we always walk together—I look forward to our afternoon strolls."

"I want to walk by myself today."

"Why George? I want to go."

"Damnit Betty, can't you take a hint? I don't want your company today!" George turned before he could see the hurt set into her eyes. He couldn't take that image; it would tear him up. Yes, they always took their afternoon walks together, but George took his morning strolls alone. It gave him a chance to think and reflect on things. But he'd missed this morning's outing due to a doctor's appointment.

Outside, it took George a couple blocks to get his legs warmed up, especially his right hip, which he usually complained about . . . but not today. Instead he thought about the cause of the injury. His senior year in high school, state championships, he took a helmet to his hip bone as he dove into the end zone for the game-winning touchdown. The greatest and most painful play of his shortened football career.

For a brief moment, he could hear the roar of the crowd once again. He remembered how the adrenaline masked the pain of his career-ending injury. And how, after his teammates finished mobbing him, he looked straight to the sidelines to find that beautiful cheerleader named Betty Sue looking right at him with admiration.

A teenager roaring down the street in a Mustang brought him back to the present. On Crescent, the road parallel to and directly behind his house, George crept into Miss Kramer's backyard. The senile old lady had been a florist during her prime years, but dementia had set in early, so her children sold her business and hired a nurse to help care for her. But she never lost her touch and maintained beautiful rosebushes on both sides of her house. Oh how Miss Kramer's rosebushes saved his marriage on more than one occasion.

George took out his pocketknife and cut off several red roses, and while gathering them together, he gashed his thumb on a thorn. It stung like the devil. But he didn't mind, he actually relished the stinging sensation. A small bubble of blood formed and George sucked on the wound.

He continued his stroll, occasionally sucking on his thumb until the blood began to clot. He walked a mile or so down Crescent taking in all of the nature and beauty around him, not taking anything for granted, until he reached the public park. He approached the lake, admired the flocks of ducks and the songbirds that whistled from the tree branches above. George sat on his favorite bench and rested the bundle of roses beside him while enjoying the cool breeze from the lake. He felt his mind clear; during the walk he had tried not to think about that morning's appointment or the stomach pains he'd been experiencing for months, but hiding from his wife.

Just then a squirrel bounced up to George holding a meal between its claws. It dropped an acorn at George's feet and ran off. He stared at the acorn in wonderment and then crumbled into himself, sobbing, shaking, wondering how he was going to tell that beautiful cheerleader, his high school sweetheart, his wife of 54 years, that in approximately three months, he would be dead.

Story's Inspiration:

This was created from another of Tracy's assignments where we had to write a short story around the lyrics of a Jimmy Buffet song about taking a walkabout. It inspired something slightly different in me.

Q&A:

1. After 54 years of marriage, why did George have to be so hurtful in his reply to her—"I don't want your company today."?

    It was more of a reaction to the strain of the secret he was hiding, than to intentionally hurt her. As the story progresses, we learn how completely in love he is with his wife.

2. Why had he not shared this devastating news with someone he loved for so long?

    Although he'd been hiding the stomach pains from his wife, so that she wouldn't worry about him, he only found out it was due to cancer during that morning's appointment. This fact was insinuated and not clearly stated.

3. Did he feel that giving her roses would help lessen the blow or was it to give him the extra strength needed to share this terrible news?

    Neither. It's a gesture he often made while in the doghouse. Plus he truly loved to surprise his wife with roses.

Mike

Heaven's Hiding Place

If only he could return to those wondrous, fulfilling days of ministering to his congregation, the gun beside his hand would not be necessary. He sat at his desk and crumpled another letter from parents informing him of legal action. Out on the rectory lawn a scant few children played tag. There once was a day when joys and shouts and imaginings overflowed the courtyard.

My life is over. I know suicide flies in the face of God Himself but I can no longer pretend this will ever end.   I pray that God, in His infinite mercy, will forgive me. Please pray for me and know that I never, not even once, was guilty of the shameful acts for which I am accused.

Father Bill O'Flanagan

The priest lay down his pen with a soft, practiced motion, took a deep, cleansing breath and pushed his chair from the desk. He secured the gun under his robe, tiptoed to the door and turned the knob. As the door opened, he ventured one last glance over the office where he'd labored for forty short years. He remembered the scuffed knees and tearful epiphanies of parishioners of all ages.

Now, he slunk out of the very room that defined him. His academic achievements, posted on pristine walls, spoke of a man of the cloth who was devoted to his life's work. Pictures that once held the favor of all who entered – the ones of him with various adults and children throughout the years – now silently accused him. Fingers pointed and whispers stabbed at a man whose sole purpose in life had been to serve.

Troubled boys who grew into vengeful men accused him of inappropriate advances and acts many decades ago. Rather than speak first to him, or even the church, they opted to contact lawyers and the media. Immediately, good parents and good boys – past and present – questioned every conversation, every honest hug and every heartfelt expression.

An arm around the shoulders of a graduating high-school student fifteen years ago when the lad had won a scholarship to a prestigious school is now called 'inappropriate touch'. Bouncing a toddler on his knee ten years ago is 'prelude to molestation' today. Forgotten histories that should define a priest's love, now flipped upside down as convictions, destroyed the fabric of his faith.

"Love" is even a dirty word now. He stood accused by the acts of others who committed atrocities with boys entrusted to them; he fought a losing battle of legitimacy. People he prayed over and helped through virtually insurmountable personal devastations turned against him.

He no longer possessed the capacity to fight back. He was not a confrontational man. His ministry's definition hung on peace, love and understanding. He patterned his life on these ideals and knew no other path. Anger, an emotion mostly foreign to him, churned and gnawed at his soul.

The priest tiptoed down the hallway – wary of every step, careful at corners. He slid out the back door into what once was his refuge for prayer and contemplation. His sanctuary no longer afforded protection from the evils of this world nor allowed him to sort out the troubles borne by his flock. His own trouble was upon him.

He knelt under the great oak, right hand crossing himself, left hand clutched to his escape. His prayer was silent, fervent and final. Two years of legal wrangling and a congregation dwindled to a husk of its former self made him ask – why? Had these two boys, now men, hated him so much that they had to carry this through? Or was the lure of money the stronger player?

He could not recall anything specific of the boys other than they loved to wreak havoc with the other children when in his care. Twenty years ago? Twenty-five?

Father O'Flanagan's eyes shot skyward when a young boy's voice asked, "Mister Father Bill, why are you cryin'?"

Little Tommy's feet were dangling six feet overhead. His blond curls shot out from his head like golden corkscrews and his blue eyes locked onto the priest's in solemn concern.

"Tommy my son," he began while he gathered himself up under his feet. "I didn't know you were up there." Father O'Flanagan wiped a telltale tear away with his free hand.

"That's 'cause I'm hidin'."

"And just who are you hiding from?" he asked. The gun poked the priest's side as he shifted his weight to his right foot.

"Myself."

"How in the world do you hide from yourself? I don't believe I've ever heard of anyone doing that."

"I heard momma tell dad that Aunty Rose was still tryin' to find herself. There's no one really to play with here, so I decided to hide from myself," Tommy replied.

"How's that working for you young man?"

Tommy shrugged. "It's not as easy as it looks. No matter where I go, I know who I am. Even worse, I know *where* I am. Even when I pretend, I'm still just *here*.

"Hmm. Sounds like quite a little problem you have there."

"No, not really."

"Oh? Why is that not a problem?"

"Well, it's kinda like this. While I'm runnin' round trying to hide and then find myself, I end up going to some really cool places. Like up here in this tree. Did you know you can see my house if you climb to the tippy top?"

"Tommy. You mean to tell me you climbed way up there?"

Tommy's face flushed. "Well, I thought if I could climb higher than my thinking maybe I'd lose myself. Even then, I found myself 'cause of seeing my house."

"Tommy, it's dangerous up there. If you were to fall you could get hurt very badly."

"Oh I don't think so."

"Why not?"

"Well, it's like you said last Sunday during mass. God protects us. And where do you think is the best place for Him to protect me?

"I don't know, tell me."

"Right here where he lives. I mean, if he's not gonna protect you here then how is he gonna to keep cars from runnin' over you when you cross the street?"

"Hmm. I'll have to think a little on that one. Why don't you come down from there? It would make me feel a lot better."

"Ok," Tommy said as he shimmied down the branch until he hung from it with both arms. Father O'Flanagan started to reach out to help. Simultaneously he remembered the lawsuit and the pistol and drew back. Tommy dropped to the ground.

"See? That was *sooo* easy."

"Nevertheless, son, let's not tempt God by climbing all the way to the top anymore. Sometimes He lets us get hurt to teach us a lesson." The priest bumped the gun under his robe with his wrist and felt a strong pang of guilt.

"You know Mister Father Bill? Momma told me I should pray for you at night in my prayers, but I told her you probably didn't need me to."

Father Bill's eyes flickered a moment. "Why, I need people's prayers just like everyone else. Why would you think I didn't need *your* prayer?"

"Well, it's like this. You don't ever do anything wrong and I figure, since you are so good, I should spend my prayer on someone who needs it – like Jason Long."

"I wish that were true Tommy. Just because it *looks* like I don't need your prayer, doesn't mean that's true. In fact, I need all the prayers I can get."

"What ever could you do wrong?"

"There are many, many things Tommy."

"Like what?"

Father William O'Flanagan stroked his chin, looked up through the branches of the great oak to the blue sky and said, "Well, for instance, I could think that I can no longer help anyone or teach anyone. Or I might think that my life is defined by how many I can help rather than how much."

"I don't understand that second part but you teach me all the time. So how could you think that?"

"Sometimes, Tommy, we can think bad things – like what I just said – until we believe them. That is why I need your prayers." The priest's cheeks moistened as he continued to look upward.

"Father, why are you crying?"

"Because, son, I just found myself."

Story's Inspiration:

Heaven's Hiding Place was written off of a "plotomatic" form an English professor gave her class in the autumn of 2007. I was auditing the class and drew the prompts; a priest feels misunderstood and is contemplating suicide. My thought was to take the Catholic Church's ongoing sexual molestation problems and turn them to the possibility of a priest being wrongfully accused. The use of a child to help the priest out was not by accident.

Q&A:

1. Do you find writing dialog difficult?

    Not really. I enjoy dialog if I can 'feel' it. In this instance I needed a child's voice to impart wisdom. That became quite tricky. A couple readers suggested Tommy sounded too grown up. I reworked and reworked the dialog until I was fairly satisfied. I believe I could go back now and do a better job, but I feel that way about all my writing.

2. Why don't you go back and address something you may be able to fix?

    One thing I've learned as a writer is that you must call it quits at some point and move on. Each piece of writing is a learning experience. Maybe one day I will have the luxury of sitting down endless hours reworking short stories, but for now, I must manage my time wisely. Sometimes you just have to call it 'close enough'.

3. How do you get to that 'close enough' call?

    It's different for different pieces. If I feel I can dramatically improve a piece with some extensive rewriting, I'll do it. If I look at the writing and say to myself, "You've already done eight rewrites and any more will be minor," then I have to step back and ask myself if I can justify moving forward. Some stories just seem to end themselves while others want to go on forever. I attempt to strike a median range and push the stories that want to end quick and reign in the ones that want to run long. Not very scientific, eh?

Tracy

Pieces of a Puzzle

I tell myself I don't need you, waiting for the day, I won't have to.
I ask myself not to need anyone, still waiting for the day to come.
Caught in between now and what used to be, waiting for me, looking for fantasy, stuck in the reality.
I tell myself when I'm ready it won't be so much fantasy with no reality, I ask myself one more time, not to need you, not anyone, it just takes time.
I focus aimlessly on yesterday, helping me to see myself where I am and need to be.
There goes the butterfly. He's following me, that's not a fantasy.
Probably?
I tell myself I don't need you, I'll be fine.
I wake myself every time.
I make up some excuse to drift back in my mind, it makes me feel better to steal that time.
Searching, hoping for gray days that truly shine.
There's that dream again and it's appearing the same. The images I see aren't making any sense compared to the feelings so intense.
I see myself creating a dream, dreaming myself out of what shouldn't be, my intuition tells me not to search, I'll find . . .
Time has taught me not to hurry, not kill.
Time is teaching me not to worry.
I will.
I ask myself not to bother, what's supposed to be isn't forgotten, there is a plan, way in the bottom, planted inside.
Pieces of a puzzle buried alive.
I tell myself to pick a part, but it exposes itself for a start, coming in closer to the picture, I suppose it's my heart.
I can't tell you how many times I have said never or enough or no more please it's just too much.
It picks us.
To all degrees
It doesn't make it any better.
I keep going back to where I ask myself what was that?
Please.
I find myself each and every time, pondering the shape of the pieces to find …

Rebekah

Baptism by Fire

Harold stood in the aisle, a can in each hand. Should he go with the industrial strength or the regular formula? The ingredients were similar, but the phrase 'industrial strength' implied that it might be too strong. He couldn't decide.

"Can I help you?"

Harold jumped, almost dropping both cans. He turned to see a young woman looking up at him with wide brown eyes.

"Well," Harold felt his face flush. "I'm just trying to decide here what strength to buy."

The woman glanced at the cans, then scanned the shelf where the rest sat in a neat, gleaming row. "What is it you're gluing?"

"Uh…." He had no intention of telling her the truth. "It's for my son. He's got an art project."

"Oh, well, if it's just for paper or cardboard, I'd go with the regular strength." The woman gestured to the can in his right hand.

"Actually," Harold cleared his throat, "his project might get wet."

"I'm sorry?"

"I mean, it…it needs to be waterproof. The glue."

"Oh," the woman frowned. "In that case, you might want to try this." She reached up for a third kind of spray adhesive. "Here, this stuff should do the trick."

Harold took the can from her and tilted his head back to study the label through the bottom half of his bifocals. "Water resistant," he murmured.

"Just be careful," the woman said, replacing Harold's other cans on the shelf. "I think that might stain fabric."

"Thanks," Harold said. He wasn't worried about that. As long as it didn't stain skin, he'd be fine.

***

That night, Harold stood in his bathroom armed with his can of glue, the timer from the kitchen, and a comb. The harsh bulb over the sink reflected light off the top of his smooth, pink head. Harold grimaced as he read the warnings printed on the back of the can. Use in a well-ventilated area. Allow glue to dry for one hour before introducing to water. Flammable.

He sighed as he flipped on the bathroom exhaust fan. He took a deep breath and held it, spraying the glue in a circular motion on his head. The glue was cold and wet, and gave him a chill like a crab scuttling down his back. With his comb, he carefully pulled what few strands of hair he had across his scalp, feeling them stick to his head with a tenacity he never experienced with hairspray.

Once he was satisfied that the hairs were perfectly positioned, he gave his entire head another blast from the can. Then he set the timer to sixty minutes and left the bathroom quickly, expelling his breath in a whoosh. He had nothing to do now but wait and reflect on the events that had brought him here.

Harold had recently been offered a teaching job at a Christian school in Georgia. The school was affiliated with a soaring Baptist church—the kind that televised its services, the pastor wearing more spackle on his face than the cracked walls in Harold's kitchen—and baptism was mandatory for all new employees. The pastor had assured him that it would be quick and painless, and that he would even hold Harold's nose for him so he wouldn't feel the burn of chlorinated water in his sinuses. Harold was grateful for that; he'd always had sinus problems.

What he was worried about was his hair. Harold wasn't a vain person, but now that he was eligible for senior citizen discounts at restaurants, he knew his looks were fading faster. Thick bifocals, sagging jowls, teeth that were yellowed from years of coffee—he accepted all these things. But ever since he'd begun losing his hair, Harold had been cripplingly self-conscious about it. Because he stood in front of a classroom all day, Harold was particularly sensitive about how he looked from behind.

Now he was going to be in front of an entire congregation, and who knows how many viewers in the television audience. More eyes would be on him tomorrow than had ever been in his entire life. To top it off, he was going underwater. Ever since he'd learned that he was to be completely submersed, Harold had been having nightmares about surfacing from the baptism with his matted comb-over clinging to the side of his face like a frightened rat.

Hence, the glue. He paced his small townhouse, popping in and out of rooms and flipping distractedly through his lesson plans as he waited for the timer to ring. He didn't want anything to ruin his chance of making a good impression on his church. Harold saw this baptism as an opportunity to start over. He hadn't always followed the straight and narrow; his twenties and thirties were fraught with questionable deeds and sketchy characters. After his mother had passed away, Harold decided it was time to grow up. He'd finished college, rebuilt his shattered credit, and made himself somewhat presentable to the opposite sex. Maybe someday he would break down and buy a hairpiece, but for now, his comb-over was sufficient.

Harold returned to the bathroom and eyed the timer. Only two minutes to go. He plugged the sink drain and turned on the tap. Time to simulate the baptism. As he waited for the sink to fill, he studied his hair in the mirror. It didn't look bad. Maybe a bit helmet-like, but the casual observer wouldn't notice it was glued in place. He was glad he'd gone with the waterproof glue and not the industrial strength after all; he might have had a hard time prying his hair from his head once the baptism was over.

He wrapped a towel around his neck and shut off the faucet, listening to the final drip-drip. When the timer dinged, Harold took one last look in the mirror, drew a breath and plunged headfirst into the sink.

He emerged a second later and wiped his eyes, then leaned forward to examine the results. His hair was still in place, and to his surprise, he saw that droplets of water hadn't even penetrated the layer of glue. They beaded on his glistening hair, and slid toward his forehead as if his comb-over were a freshly waxed car.

"Well, how about that?" Harold murmured, smiling at himself in the mirror. He was ready for tomorrow.

***

Harold woke up early the next morning. The baptism was scheduled to take place right after Bible class, and he wanted to make sure the glue had plenty of time to dry. He went through the ritual of spraying the glue on his head, then combing his hair over and spraying again. He coughed and tried not to inhale, but he could still taste the noxious fumes. It reminded him of the glue that came with the model airplanes he used to build as a child. He shook his head, sheepish that his child-self would be laughing at his adult-self, were they ever to meet. *Enjoy your hair while you've still got it, kid*, Harold thought, replacing the cap on his can of glue.

Harold sat in the back corner of the room during Bible class, paranoid that people would be able to smell the glue if he got too close. After class ended, Harold hurried past the coffee-hour table, forgoing the donuts and fellowship in order to get to the baptism tank before someone noticed the smell. He found Pastor Roberts behind the pulpit and shook his hand.

"Good morning, Brother Harold," the pastor said. "Fine morning to be baptized."

"Yes it is."

The pastor grinned. "Miss Gale will show you where you can change, and then you can come back here and we'll start."

Harold blinked. "Change? I thought I wouldn't change until after I got baptized."

Pastor Roberts laughed. "You don't want to get your clothes all wet, now, do you? We have a special suit you can wear, down in the basement. Miss Gale will show you."

As if out of nowhere, a large, heavily perfumed woman appeared beside Harold.

"Good morning, Brother Harold," she said cheerfully. "Follow me."

Confused, Harold did as he was told.

Miss Gale took Harold down the plush carpeted steps to the church basement, which was busier and brighter than a casino. Harold nodded absently as he passed various church-goers streaming toward the stairs, barely registering the greetings aimed his way. All he could do was wonder what sort of suit the pastor had in mind for him to wear.

"Here we are," Miss Gale said, bringing Harold into what looked like gym locker room. "I wasn't sure if you were a large or an extra large, so you can take your pick."

Harold eyed the wall where two suits hung. They were maroon bodysuits, short-sleeved and knee-length and couldn't have looked more unflattering.

"You can change here and leave your clothes in one of these lockers, where you'll find a towel and a pair of shower slippers. I'll wait outside to bring you back up."

Miss Gale closed the door, leaving Harold to stare at the bodysuits as a new kind of panic seized him. He completely forgot about his glued hair as he realized that he was about to be a hundred times more embarrassed.

When he was twenty-three, Harold had wanted to do something daring and controversial, so he'd gotten tattoos—one on each leg. They were ugly and faded now, but at the time, they'd been glorious, colorful pieces of art Harold had loved to show off. He was fifty-six now, and each pale, hairless leg sported a picture of a naked lady, perky-breasted and big-bottomed, winking out at a world that hadn't seen them since the early eighties.

Harold looked at the clock over the door. The service would begin in ten minutes. He looked wildly around the room, hoping an idea, some way around the potential humiliation, would pop into his mind. He imagined the horrified faces of the proper Baptist wives and the uncomfortable coughs of God-fearing-Baptist husbands when they all saw the vulgar, voluptuous women on Harold's white legs.

Then Harold remembered the television cameras mounted throughout the sanctuary and his heart sank a few more degrees. His baptism would be broadcast to hundreds, perhaps thousands of homes. His scandalous legs would fill the living rooms of countless old ladies and homebound church members. He would never live down the shame.

What am I going to do? Harold thought as he went to the body suits and pulled the extra-large one from its hanger. He held it up to himself in front of the full-length mirror and saw that the legs reached just below his kneecaps. Not even the naked ladies' heads would be covered.

Maybe he could leave his socks on. They had holes in the toes, but if he pulled them all the way up, they might hide the tattoos. Hastily, Harold hiked up his right pant leg and tugged at his sock, pulling it as high as he could. Looking in the mirror, he saw that the sock only reached to just below the woman's breasts, almost accentuating them.

"Dagummit," Harold hissed.

"Brother Harold?" Miss Gale knocked on the door. "You about ready?"

Harold looked around the room, wondering if he could squeeze through the high, narrow windows that peeked into the flowerbeds outside. He was about to climb up on a chair and find out when suddenly an idea came.

He went to the door and found Miss Gale waiting in the empty hallway.

"Brother Harold, you need to change," she said, looking at her watch. "Service starts in three minutes."

"Miss Gale, I have a problem, and I think you're the only one who can help me." Harold eyed Miss Gale's tan legs, encased in opaque pantyhose he was certain would fit him.

Miss Gale followed Harold's gaze.

"I need your…your pantyhose," Harold said.

"Beg your pardon?"

Harold did his best to explain, opting to keep his tattoos hidden. He didn't want to offend her.

"I understand," Miss Gale said when he'd finished, "but I…I can't show my legs in public, either."

Harold nodded, though he was crushed.

"I have awful varicose veins," she continued. "And I haven't shaved in weeks. I always wear pantyhose, even with shorts."

"I see."

They both stood for a minute, even as the opening music was piped in through the speakers that lined the basement ceiling. Time was running out.

"Okay, fine," Miss Gale said suddenly, and stepped out of her beige high heels. "Get back in there and start changing. I'll hand them to you."

Harold ducked back in the locker room without a word. He was too uneasy about the entire situation to even thank her. Within minutes he was dressed in the pantyhose, body suit and shower shoes, the naked ladies reduced to vague shadows beneath the tinted nylon. From a distance, they were invisible.

With seconds to spare, Harold and Miss Gale made it behind the pulpit, where the baptism tank sat below them at the bottom of four rubber-lined steps. Four more steps sat opposite them – the ones Pastor Roberts would descend. A thin screen separated Harold and Miss Gale from the hundreds of people seated in pews. Harold removed his glasses and placed them on a ledge above the stairs.

"I'm going to hide out in the ladies' room until church is over," Miss Gale whispered. "I'll be able to hear the sermon from in there.

And congratulations." She squeezed his arm and left in a rose-scented cloud.

Harold realized that he hadn't even noticed her legs. He wondered if they were as bad as she thought. He was certainly uncomfortable in her pantyhose, which had been warm when he'd wriggled into them. Her legs must be pretty unsightly if she wore these things in the summertime.

He thought of her as the music ended and the pastor welcomed the congregation. She had a pretty face, and a sweet smell. He wondered how many other women would have relinquished their pantyhose to a veritable stranger. He thought of her smile as the pastor asked everyone to turn to the next hymn, signaling to Harold to descend the baptism steps and meet Pastor Roberts in the water. He did so, remembering the bounce of her curls and the swish of her round hips beneath her skirt. And as Pastor Roberts recited the baptism scripture, Harold thought of Miss Gale hiding out in the ladies room, embarrassed of her legs, and he smiled. Pastor Roberts held his nose and laid him backwards into the chilly water; Harold resurfaced with his hair intact, his tattoos disguised and his soul washed clean. He was reborn.

Story's Inspiration:

This story was inspired by my father, who has sported a comb-over his entire adult life. When we moved to Tallahassee, FL, my family joined a southern Baptist church, which required the traditional total-immersion baptism. My father, paranoid that his comb-over would fail, thus exposing his shiny, pink bald spot, decided to glue his hair in place to prevent any embarrassment. Let's just say that at 15 years old, I was still plenty embarrassed.

Q&A:

1. You say your father was the inspiration behind the story. Does he have the naked lady tattoos, too?

    No, that part is fiction. I got the idea for the tattoos from a friend who has Anna Nicole Smith tattooed on his leg. But my father's legs are definitely pale. They'd make a great canvas for some ink.

2. But the story of the hair glue is true?
    Yes. Very true. And it did keep his hair in place. Except his baptism was not broadcast on the TV program. Thankfully they did most baptisms during night church. I actually was baptized on the same night as my father. Those rubber suits we had to wear were pretty awful.

3. Do you often use family for character inspiration?

    Because my family is so big and filled with so many different personalities, it's hard not to drag an element of one of my siblings or parents into a story. They really are an interesting bunch…stranger than many fictional characters I've come across in books.

Jeff

An Anniversary Remembered

Eileen looked across the dinner table at Harold, her husband of almost sixty years. "Harry, you're not eating again—what's wrong?"

"I'm not that hungry. That's all."

"But you never seem to be hungry anymore. I keep wasting food with you."

"Ahhh, would you quit worrying?"

"Maybe I should take you to the doctor's."

"Oh, stop being such a worrywart, I'm fine."

"In all my years, Harry, I never thought I'd see the day when you wouldn't eat my meatloaf dinner."

"I'm sorry. I just have some stomach bug or something—it'll pass."

"Well, I hope it will pass by tomorrow evening—it's our anniversary, Harry."

"I know that doll, and not any anniversary, it's our 60th."

"It's times like these that I regret not having kids, though," Eileen said.

"Oh, none of that, now. You can't think like that, we've had a very rich and rewarding life together."

"Of course, I know that, but…never mind. Where should we go for our big dinner?" Eileen asked.

"Where we always go on our anniversary—Eugene's restaurant."

"I thought you might want to go somewhere different this year."

"But it's been our tradition for as long as I can remember. Besides, Eugene will be upset if we don't show," Harold said with a chuckle.

"I suppose you're right. We don't want to disappoint your good friend, now do we?"

"We always have a wonderful meal there too—let's not forget that."

"I just have a weird feeling about eating there this year."

"Nonsense. You and your premonitions. We'll have a great time there, as always."

"I know that, dear, I know we will. I'll make reservations tomorrow."

* * *

Eileen put on the television for Harold and began cleaning the dishes. When done, she made a pot of coffee and poured two cups. She brought them into the living room where Harold relaxed in his favorite recliner. After placing the coffees on the end table between the recliners, she sat down next to him, glancing over from time to time, admiring her husband.

"What are you watching, Harry?"

"Oh, I don't know. Whatever was on when you turned on the tube."

"That doesn't sound like you—no ballgame tonight?"

"Nah, I'm not interested."

Eileen focused on the program; it was a *60 Minutes* special on senility, and on the ever-increasing percentage of the elderly who suffer from it.

"Why watch this nonsense? Our minds are sharper than most youngsters, Harry."

"Oh, I know that. Like I said, just watching what was on, something to occupy my mind."

"You're not touching your coffee, Harry."

"Sorry. Don't think it would do me much good with my stomach acting up."

Eileen watched him with concern, but soon began to relax and watched TV with Harold until bedtime.

* * *

The next morning Eileen woke to a healthier Harold. He gave a huge smile.

"I love you, honey, more and more every day," he said. "I breathe every waking breath for you. My heart pounds out every heartbeat for our love. You are my life."

Giving her a big kiss, Harold pulled Eileen back to the bed and they held each other for what felt like hours. Throughout the day, they expressed their love by showing those little signs of affection that, at their age, were often neglected or taken for granted.

Eileen felt young again.

* * *

It was almost time for their big dinner. As Eileen put in her gold earrings, she felt the stirrings of excitement over their anniversary.

Harold stepped into the bedroom wearing his best suit. "Well, doll, I think not eating yesterday has really worked up my appetite."

"I'm glad, Harry. I was worried about that."

"You worry too much about me—I told you I'd be fine."

"And you were right, dear."

"You look beautiful in that dress."

"Ya think? This old thing?"

"Old? I guess it suits you then," he said and they laughed.

"Oh, Harry, you old bugger," she said and laughed some more.

"In all seriousness, you are as beautiful now as when I first laid eyes on you."

"Oh, Harry." They kissed and hugged and held each other. Tears welled in her eyes as sixty years of marriage flashed by.

* * *

They took the F-train into the city and cuddled up on a seat near the exit door. At the East Broadway stop, a large black man almost sat on Harold.

"Stop, stop, stop—what are you doing?" Eileen asked with urgency.

"Trying to sit down, lady."

"On my husband?!"

The man looked beside her and back to Eileen. "What are you talking about?"

"There's only room for me and my husband on this bench— you'll have to find another seat."

The man looked at her oddly and then scrambled up the train looking for another seat before the train took off.

"Crazy man," she said to Harold.

Harold laughed. "You almost had a pancake for a husband."

She laughed too. "What was he thinking?"

"You know, there are quite a few crazies in this city."

* * *

From their stop, it was a short walk to Eugene's. As they entered the restaurant, they were welcomed warmly by Eugene and his staff. Eugene shook Harold's hand and gave Eileen a hearty hug and a kiss on the cheek. They were led to a table set with flowers and a complementary bottle of champagne chilled in a bucket of ice.

"Congratulations, my friends! Sixty years and still madly in love. How do you do it, old pal?" Eugene said and patted Harold on the back. "I'll check up on you two lovebirds a little later. But please let me know if you need *any*thing at all. Enjoy your evening," he said as he walked away.

"This is so nice, Harry, isn't it? You were right about coming here."

"Eugene's always does things in style," Harold said.

"He sure does."

The waiter brought some bread and filled their glasses with champagne. He went over the specials and gave them time to ponder. Harold decided on the fish special and asked Eileen to order while he went to the restroom. The waiter came back right after Harold disappeared into the men's room down the hall. Eileen ordered Harold's special and requested the spaghetti dinner for herself. Then she sat back, relaxed, and soaked up the ambiance.

* * *

Eileen waited for Harold's return when a commotion erupted near the front of the restaurant. Two men wearing ski masks stormed into the restaurant waving guns at the people.

"Everyone remain calm," one of them yelled.

Eugene held out his arms and said, "I'm the owner here. We don't want anyone to get hurt."

"No one will be hurt if you do as I say. Empty the register into this bag." Eugene accepted the bag and hurried to the cash register.

"Everybody else, place your wallets, jewelry, and valuables at the edge of your tables, so I can come around and collect them. Cooperate with us, and we'll quickly be on our way."

The other gunman stood near the men's bathroom door when it opened.

Harold stepped out.

Eileen looked on in horror as the masked gunman whirled in fear and pulled the trigger.

"What'd you do, man?!"

"I don't know, I don't know. He surprised me—I didn't mean to."

"Let's go—we got to get out of here."

As the gunmen fled the restaurant, Eileen hurried to Harold's side. He lay motionless, spread-eagle on the floor, his blood everywhere. Eileen knelt down, cradled him in her arms, and wailed.

"Why, oh why?" she asked over and over again.

She felt a strong pair of hands grab her shoulders and help her up.

"Eileen, Eileen—it's okay. Let me help you back to your seat."

She closed her eyes for a moment, and when she opened them, the floor below was empty—no Harold, no blood. She looked around while stunned patrons looked on. As it all came back to her, she put her hand to her mouth and let Eugene assist her back to her booth.

Once she was seated, she asked, "I did the same thing last year, didn't I?"

Eugene nodded.

"And the year before that?"

He nodded again. "Every year since Harold was taken from us six years ago this night."

"Why do you keep putting up with me?"

"Harold was a great man and a wonderful friend. I can understand why you want to keep him alive. So I do what I can to help . . . I'd be dishonoring him if I didn't." Eugene rubbed her back. "Can I get you anything?"

She looked up and tried to smile. "A cold glass of water would be nice." And then she sat back, numb and stricken with grief. Like an inpatient after visiting hours, she felt terribly alone.

Tomorrow, she would begin the painstaking process of resurrecting Harold in her mind again, so they could live happily ever after, at least until their next anniversary.

Story's Inspiration:

I went to NYC for the first time in February of 2008. Many of my favorite movies and books are set in New York, so it was exciting to finally visit there. I had seen this sad old woman on the subway at one point, and she became my muse for a story about an old woman's state of mind in a fast-paced city.

Q&A:

1. Was she just preparing meals and coffee in her mind, or actually going through the motions of preparation?

    Yes, she was making the meals and coffee, which is why she's asking Harold why he's not eating his meatloaf dinner. I wanted to suggest that this could be a regular routine in her life, but she washes it from her mind every day or so. In her mind, this day was an exception; Harry's usually a good eater and likes his coffee in the evening.

2. Why a gunman and not just a death by natural causes, since they were so old?

    Part of the reason is for social commentary. The other is that had his death been from natural causes, it would not have been as traumatic to Eileen. She may have been prepared for it or accepted it as so. I needed something tragic to send Eileen into her alternate-universe.

3. Were you insinuating by the "60 Minutes" special on TV that she was senile?

    Yes, but it wasn't intended for the reader to really catch it at that point. It was more subliminal and setting up for later, something authors refer to as "foreshadowing," so when her mental state is revealed later in the story, it will make sense. The reader won't feel cheated by a complete surprise ending.

Mike

Turnabout

"What?!"

"Yeah man, I snuffed her."

"So, you're telling me there is no way you were in the tavern knocking back a few cold ones when you said you were? You're telling me your alibi hinged on an ex-girlfriend who now wants to have your baby? You're also telling me that all the witnesses I lined up off my initial interview with you lied? What the hell were you thinking?"

Gary looked up from cleaning his fingernails. "I don't have to think. I killed her. I wasn't thinking when I did it and I don't have to think now. If *she* had thought before she messed with my stash, she would still be here. Since *you* thought instead of reacted like this, you got me off. That is why I pay *you* to think. So I don't have to."

"But her head. Why did you have to cut off her head?"

"She snorted it. It should stay up there."

"What kind of answer is that?"

"An honest one."

"Honesty? You're sitting there talking to me about honesty? You don't know the meaning of the word! Everything you say is a lie or an evasion."

"Definitions are for thinking folk. Remember, I pay –"

"Yeah, yeah. You pay me to think. Why did you cut off her feet?"

"What difference does it make?"

"I need to know what I am dealing with here. Let's just say it helps me think, ok?"

"She tried to run."

"When?"

"When I was about to chop off her head."

"Hell, so would I. So would anyone."

"She wasn't just anyone. She was *my* woman. No woman of mine does that to me. I warned her she was making it difficult."

"You are a sadistic lowlife. Ok, she must have screamed because you cut out her tongue."

"No, she cursed me."

"What did you expect? 'Oh thank you darling for attempting to remove my head. Here let me lay still so you can get a clean shot.'"

"Precisely. That is exactly what I told her. She got all righteous and started telling me what to do with the coke, and then she called my mother some nasty names."

"Your mother! That must be it. You had a rough childhood. Lots of men in her life and abuse, right?"

"Hey! Watch it. She tried to say that about my momma and look where she's at. Pops was a good father and momma took care of all of us. She was the best cook in the world, and if there was ever anything we needed, she would find a way to get it. She made sure I got a good education. I had the best childhood a person could have."

"So what is your major malfunction? Why in the world did you do it? What possessed you? Hey! That's it! You were demon possessed, right?"

"Come on man, that stuff is crazy. I am as sane as can be."

"OK. You cut off her head, her feet and her tongue. Then you laid the body in bed and put everything back where it belonged. Was that due to remorse? You wanted to put it all back together again?"

"Man, where do you come up with this stuff? I just didn't want to trip over everything. Also, if the dog got a hold of anything, I might never find it again."

"You are sick; you know that? You and all your 'witnesses' had me convinced you were as innocent as a newborn baby. Now you tell me you are a cold, heartless murderer without remorse and without extenuating circumstances. Not only are you sick, you make me sick. You disgust me!"

"Is this supposed to be meaningful to me in any way?"

"I suppose there is nothing you really care about, so no, I am sure there is no meaning you can glean from my utter revulsion of your pitiful life."

"Good. So let's talk turkey. That half mil I slipped you on the sly so the IRS doesn't get most of it covers everything up to this point."

"Up to this point? Your alibi and every witness we have are not credible and you want to stick with it? You're nuts!"

"I need you for the civil trial. Her parents are going after my money."

"I can't do this! You are asking me to ignore the facts and pretend you are innocent."

"One million *after* expenses?"

"Deal."

Story's Inspiration:

Turnabout was an exercise in dialog. The goal was to use the bulk of the written text as dialog with minimal exposition. This one was a blast to write. With the exception of one sentence, the story is conveyed in total dialog. This exercise is an awesome challenge I recommend to all writers.

Q&A:

1. Are you a lawyer basher?

    No, not really, but you have to admit, they are easy prey. I felt a lawyer would be a great character to use in a virtually total dialog story. The banter and macabre setting just worked for me from the get-go.

2. Earlier you stated that you enjoyed writing dialog. Did that help in writing a dialog driven story?

    Of course it did. I was not sure I could carry a storyline solely on dialog. The writing simply flowed. I don't know that there were many rewrites on this one. I do believe I edited out a few lines of back and forth banter, but what survived is fairly pristine as I did not have to tweak it much. I really did get a kick out of writing this one.

3. The bad guy character, or should I say criminal, is sort of over the top and extreme. Why did you write him that way?

    I felt like sneaking some dark humor into this one. One way you do that is to create a 'larger-than-life' character. I wanted him to be extreme to reveal the corruption of the lawyer which allowed me the 'dark' punch line at the end.

Tracy

In Sync

We are inspired by moments that touch our soul,
they unfold and release its treasures.

For every moment is in sync with the next.

We are inspired to reveal our secrets harbored deep within,
for these are our gifts to be given.

For every gift is in sync with another.

We are inspired to be and to do as our energies were created,
for only they know their meanings.

For everything is in sync with duality of moments,
harbored secrets, inspirations and creative forces unseen.

I am truly inspired when time becomes non-existent and
space has no meaning and my life's force is in motion,
it is then true love is present.

For everything is in sync as it should be and the spirit in us is free to
soar,
for more than just now, but an eternity to explore.

Rebekah

Moped Girl

Al was a chubby chaser. He liked his women big—big breasts, big butts, big, squishy stomachs. Give him a woman who never missed a meal and wasn't afraid to take seconds. He liked the way they smelled—like cake, candy and sugar, all the things he wasn't allowed to eat growing up. He liked their personalities too, the sweet, giving, friendly women with an undercurrent of desperation and insecurity that manifested in self-deprecating humor and hugs that lasted a bit too long. Big women were comfortable and disarming—he always knew what he was getting into with them.

That was why when the large woman brushed against him with her stomach and made him drop the hotdog he'd just carefully decorated with ketchup, mustard and relish, Al couldn't resist asking her out for a drink.

The woman gaped at him. "Are you serious?"

"It's the least I could do," Al looked down. "Look, I got mustard all over your shoes."

The woman looked down too, though Al realized she couldn't see her shoes and would have to take his word for it. "But I'm the one who bumped into you," she said.

"Well then, I'll let you buy the second round." Al smiled, noting that even though the woman wasn't smiling back, he could see two very fetching dimples on her round, rosy cheeks.

"I can't right now," the woman said, looking at her watch. "I'm late for an appointment."

"Listen," Al reached into his pocket for his business card, "there's a bar called Mulligan's on the corner of Thirty-Ninth and Sixth." He handed the card to her. "I'll be there at seven."

The woman accepted his card as if expecting it to explode like a trick cigar.

"Albert Gordon," she read. "You're an attorney?"

"Guilty." Albert smiled even more broadly, hoping to coax one out of her. He especially loved it when big women smiled.

"I'm Brenda," the woman said, still looking unsure of the situation. "But you really don't have to do this. I'm sure the mustard will wipe right off."

"Please," Al said. "I won't take no for an answer." This particular line always worked. He doubted many women Brenda's size heard it very often.

Finally she gave him that dimpled smile he'd been hoping for. "All right then, Albert Gordon," she said. "I'll see you tonight."

Al watched her waddle away, her flowing skirt billowing out behind her like an open parachute. He imagined putting both hands on her soft behind and squeezing, and had to stop himself before his fantasy got away from him. He turned back to the cart and bought another hotdog, his mind flashing forward to that night.

Dating big women was like a drug addiction for Al. He hid his attraction to them from his friends, following the old adage that fat girls were like mopeds—they were fun to ride but you didn't want your friends to see you on one. He imagined himself a spy when he was with big women—always looking over his shoulder or ducking his head when they were in public. And if he did see someone he knew and suddenly had to hide his face or steer his date in another direction, the women always went along, thrilled to be taken on a ride with so many unexpected twists and turns.

Brenda would be no different.

***

"This is a nice place."

Brenda looked around her, almost in awe, and tugged at her cardigan, though the buttons were still miles away from their holes.

"Glad you like it," Al said. It actually wasn't that great of a place, just a half-step up from a dive. But it was cozy, and it was unlikely that he would run into anyone he knew here. It was where he always took his dates in the beginning.

"I think I'll just have a Diet Coke," Brenda said after scanning the drink menu. "I'm trying to cut back on…certain things."

"Two Diet Cokes," Al said when the waiter appeared. Then he turned his attention back to Brenda, taking in her blonde curls and her blue eyes twinkling like he used to imagine Santa's would. "You're very pretty," he said.

Brenda fidgeted with the sleeve of her sweater, and then looked up at him. "Did you lose a bet or something?"

Al shook his head. "Do you always respond to compliments that way?"

"I'm sorry," she sighed. "I don't get asked out very often, and the last time someone told me I was pretty was in grade school. Even then it was a line from a play I was in."

Ah, the humor! Al loved it.

"People think thin equals beauty," he said. "They never bother seeing what's inside."

Brenda groaned. "Please don't start up with that whole 'inner beauty' speech. Believe me, I've heard it a million times. If they ever had an inner beauty pageant, I'd be wearing the tiara."

Al glanced over his shoulder as a couple entered the bar; he didn't recognize them.

"Besides," Brenda said, "you asked me out and you don't even know me. I could be just as ugly on the inside as I am on the outside." She sipped the soda the waiter set before her. "So I'll ask you again, what's the deal? You lose a bet or what?"

"No bet," Al grinned. "Just saw a nice woman and took a chance."

She eyed him. "Was your mother fat?"

"No."

"Did *you* used to be fat?"

"Never. The guys in high school used to call me Bird-Chest."

"Did some big fat girl break your heart and now you're a serial killer who preys on women like me for revenge?"

Al laughed. "I promise you, there's no deep-seated ulterior motive here."

Brenda drummed her thick fingers on the scratched lacquer tabletop, her magenta nails clicking. "Well, I give up. If you're not planning to make me into a woman-suit, I guess you're just a normal guy."

"Thank you."

"So," said Brenda, placing her elbows on the table and resting her chins in her hand, "did you get another hotdog after I ruined your first one?"

"I did. That guy has the best hotdogs in the city. I walk all the way from Forty-Fourth just to get them."

"Every day? Wow. I wish I got that kind of exercise."

"Exercise is overrated," Al tried not to notice her giant bosom resting on the table. Whenever she moved, the table rocked on uneven legs and tilted toward her, anchored by her breasts.

"Well, it never did me any good anyway." Brenda drained her glass and licked her lips.

Good, Al thought. *More of you to love.*

"I just sit around in my office all day long," she continued. "Being an accountant isn't conducive to a healthy lifestyle, let me tell you."

As Al listened to her talk about herself, he pictured taking her back to his place and feeling those full, luscious lips on his neck, those creamy thighs around him, those meaty hands running through his thinning hair. That was another thing Al had discovered about big women—they were easy to get into bed. They took what they could get when they could get it, and because Al was a successful, decent-looking man, they took it from him pretty much right away. Over-eager, shy, aggressive or laid-back—he didn't care. He wined them, dined them, showered them with attention and showed them a good time. Eventually he sent them on their way, usually because they became too attached, started wanting marriage and kids and all the things every woman wants. The great thing about big women was that they always took the ending well. Gracious through the last date. No tearful phone calls for weeks afterward, no begging to come back, no shouting matches or angry threats. They treated the relationship like a good dream and accepted that all good dreams end eventually.

But first Al wanted to have his fun.

He called Brenda two days later and asked her to dinner. He hadn't thought it strange, asking an obese woman out to eat, but apparently Brenda did.

"Are you sure you want to eat with me?" she asked him.

"I wouldn't ask you if I weren't sure."

"No, I mean," she lowered her voice, "are you sure you won't be…embarrassed?"

"Embarrassed? Of course not." Al didn't bother adding that he'd make sure they steered clear of places where he might run into an acquaintance. "Trust me, there's no need for me to be embarrassed."

Finally Brenda seemed convinced. "Okay, Mister Confident. Let me just warn you that I'm not a cheap date."

"Good thing they just raised the credit limit on my MasterCard."

"I'm a meat and potatoes kind of gal, in case you haven't noticed."

"I plan on buying you dessert, too."

"And your own, I hope. I don't share."

"Neither do I."

She paused, then said, "You know, I'm usually bad at talking to men. I mean, in a dating sense. This whole situation is kind of new to me."

Al smiled to himself. He knew she would be putty in his hands after that night. Warm, doughy, sweet-smelling putty.

"You're doing fine," he said. "I'd never guess you were a novice."

"See you tonight."

***

Al was right about her. She was putty in his hands. A leisurely dinner: calamari, salad, steak, baked potato, creamed spinach, rolls, coffee, chocolate macadamia nut cheesecake, more coffee and a mint, all for Brenda, a nice stroll down Columbus, including a brief detour down a side street as Al saw one of his clients heading right for them, and a lengthy conversation in front of Brenda's building was all Al had to invest to be invited upstairs.

"Go slow," she'd whispered in his ear as he freed the buttons straining against the holes of her blouse.

"I will," he'd promised.

Al woke up the next morning to the sizzle of rain outside her bedroom window. He thought of skipping out early, but the rain begged him to cuddle up against the softness of her back, to reach around her and slip a hand into the crevice of her cleavage where it was warmest, and stay awhile. He thought of the night before, feeling the round, smooth curves, and listening to the gasps of a woman who had been without affection for a long time. He loved that he was the one to give her such pleasure, knowing that for the next few months, he would be the center of her universe. That he would be a god.

He felt her stir and he pressed his face to her neck, inhaling deeply. She smelled like the food tent at a carnival.

"You're still here," she said.

"Are you disappointed?" He found her hand and ran his thumb across the back of it.

"Just surprised."

"I'm not," he said. "I knew I'd still be here."

She turned her profile toward him. Al noticed that her nose was small and straight. Perfect, really. He kissed her cheek, wondering if she knew how perfect her nose was.

"Did you know you'd still be here when you met me?" she asked.

"What do you mean?"

She grunted this time and rolled onto her back so she could look at him. Al had to scoot out of the way to keep from being squashed.

"I mean, did you think that we'd end up sleeping together when I sent your hotdog flying?"

"You mean do I always date women who ruin my lunch?"

"I don't know." She sighed, the bed sheets rising with her body. "This all just seems too perfect to have started from an accidental food fight."

Al kissed her mouth this time.

"Not afraid of morning breath, are you?" she asked.

"If it means I'm waking up next to you, not at all." He knew the effect his words would have on her, that it meant she would probably fall in love with him, but he couldn't stop himself. Besides, it was mostly true. He loved being in a big woman's bed—like sleeping with a giant stuffed animal.

Brenda sighed again. The bed creaked. Al wondered if it would collapse, like it had with Corinne, who'd been pushing three hundred pounds when Al had dated her.

"I can't tell if you're full of it or not," Brenda said, "but it sure is nice to hear."

Al kissed her again, and as the rain continued to pelt the outside world, he decided that Brenda was the best thing he'd found in a long time.

***

After Al and Brenda had been seeing each other for a few weeks, Brenda dropped the bombshell.

"So, I'm thinking about starting Weight Watchers."

Al almost choked on the bite of swordfish he'd been enjoying. He coughed, his eyes watering, and couldn't speak for a minute.

"Drink some water," Brenda leaned forward, her chair groaning in protest. "Good grief, Al….Do you need the Heimlich?"

Al held up a finger and managed to swallow his mouthful. "Sorry. It's just…wow…are you, you know, sure that you want to do this?"

"Are you kidding?" She laughed. "I've been big my whole life. Believe me, I've tried Atkins, South Beach, Sugar Busters, I've eaten nothing but grapefruit and candy corn for a month, I've done every workout move, tried every pill and cream….Yes, I'm sure I want to do this."

"No, no, I meant, are you sure you want to be smaller?"

Brenda just stared at him. He should have known better than to ask her that, but he couldn't help it. He saw his attraction to her already fading as he pictured her svelte and healthy, a weak shadow of her present greatness. She would change—turn into a thin woman with all the arrogance and pretense that came along with it. A butterfly in reverse. Why would he need to hide her then? Why would she still need him at all?

"I'm sorry," Al said. "Of course you're sure. It's rude of me to even ask."

She sat for a minute before saying, "Everyone else has been so excited for me. Everyone's saying how great Weight Watchers is, how it teaches you to change your eating habits and how supportive the meetings are. My doctor says it's the healthiest thing I can do."

"Well…are you happy with your decision?"

"I am," she nodded. "I'm very happy."

"I guess that's all that matters then.

Brenda smiled again, her dimples deepening. Al smiled back, but inside he was miserable and he struggled to understand why. True, she had started out as just another big woman for him to play with. After spending time with her, though, he found himself anticipating her phone calls and emails, looking forward to holding her soft, warm hand as they decided where to have dinner. He'd begun ignoring the looks they received as they strolled down the street—the average, forty-something man hand-in-hand with the leviathan of a woman whose age was indeterminate because the fat in her face plumped out any wrinkles. He was even considering asking her to come with him upstate in a few weeks, to a place where he could bask in her glow without the rush of worrying that they would be discovered.

But now, now he knew the excitement would fade. As they left the restaurant and emerged into the chilly October evening, a sadness stole over Al that rendered him distant and annoyed the rest of the night. When Brenda reached for his hand, he barely felt her sausage fingers lace through his, and when she invited him up, he made up an excuse that he needed to get a head-start on a big deposition coming up the next day. He saw her face change from expectant to crestfallen. But the change was quick; in an instant she wiped all traces of it from her eyes and smiled understandingly, telling him she'd call him tomorrow, but Al still saw it.

***

A few days later, Brenda called him at his office. He tried to sound busy and harried on the phone as she went on about her upcoming Weight Watchers meeting and how nervous she was for it. When he hung up the phone, he berated himself for not ending things with her sooner. Now he'd have to listen to her go on and on about her diet and what she'd eaten that day, he'd have to watch her slowly waste away, shedding pounds like layers of dead skin. Perhaps he could bow out gracefully by inching his way toward the periphery until it was obvious to her that the relationship had run its course.

There was a small voice in the back of his head, however, that chimed in every once in a while, telling him that he'd already gotten too close. Despite his attempts to file her under the same category as the other women, Al had fallen in love. And by pushing her away, he was trying to spare himself the heartache of losing her. Maybe he was afraid that once she was thin, she would behave as every other thin woman in his life had and reject him. He was jumping ship before it went down like a brick.

Don't be silly, he told himself, irritated for even thinking he had an underbelly. Besides, life was too short to spend time dawdling over moped girls. He would find another one that was just as much fun to ride.

That afternoon, as Al was ducking down the steps to the subway, his cell phone rang. He stopped, glanced at the display, and saw Brenda's number flashing at him. His heart leaped at the sight of it, but he wished that he didn't *want* to answer. He wished he could ignore the call and keep walking down the steps. But he couldn't.

"Al?"

"Hey, babe, how'd the meeting go?"

Brenda's sigh was heavy with implied complications. Instantly Al was alarmed.

"Everything okay?" he asked.

"Well…no….." She sighed again. "Do you have time to talk?"

Warning…warning. Al couldn't remember the last time he'd been on the business end of that line. He knew what it meant. At least, he thought he did.

"Sure. You want to meet somewhere?"

"I'm at my place right now."

"I'll be there in ten minutes."

Al hung up and hailed a cab, his mind spinning. Could she be preparing to break up with him? If so, shouldn't he be relieved that it was over? Wasn't he planning to do the same thing to her eventually? Was his ego really so huge that he couldn't stand being dumped?

She buzzed him as soon as he rang the bell at her apartment building. He entered to find her sitting on her couch, hugging a throw pillow to her chest. She looked like she'd been crying, and she didn't offer her dimpled smile as Al dropped his coat and briefcase on an overstuffed chair.

"That was fast," she said. "I guess being small and agile has its advantages."

"What's going on?" he asked, her tear-streaked face making him uncomfortable. He didn't often see his girlfriends cry.

Brenda drew a shuddering breath. "Al, who's Corrine?"

The name hit Al right in the knees, which instantly weakened and threatened to send him sprawling onto her plush, beige rug.

"Corrine?"

"Yeah, Corrine," Brenda nodded. "Or how about Jamie? Or Beth? Or Larissa?"

Each name was like another blow.

"How do you know…." His voice sounded so weak and groveling that he let it die on its own.

"Could you believe that I wasn't the only woman in this city trying to shed some pounds?" Brenda glared at him. "And you know how it is when all us big-boned girls get together and gab. All kinds of personal information comes out."

Al pictured Brenda sitting on a tiny folding chair in a circle of other women her size and striking up what she thought was an innocent conversation with Corrine, the hefty red-head he'd dated a year before. Had they all been there, all of his past girlfriends? Jamie, the woman who'd boasted that she'd once won a pie-eating contest in college. And Beth, the quiet school teacher who'd confided to Al that she used to steal from her students' lunches when they were at recess. And even Larissa, who had gained ninety pounds with her first pregnancy and had never lost it. Each of these women had entered into their relationship with the same skeptical curiosity as Brenda, flattered by Al's apparent sincerity and intrigued by his sometimes suspicious behavior. And he'd broken up with each one gently, like releasing a rabbit into the wild after nursing it back to health. He hadn't heard from any of them since, and hadn't in a million years guessed that they'd ever cross paths in a city of ten million people.

Brenda was still glaring at him, waiting for him to explain himself. He rubbed the back of his hot neck with one icy hand, scrambling for a line.

"So, I uh…take it the meeting was informative?" he asked.

"You could say that." Brenda tossed the throw pillow aside. "Were you ever going to tell me about your fetish for fat girls?"

Al thought about running, about just turning and heading back through the door and hailing a cab back home and never thinking of Brenda again. But the voice he'd been ignoring for weeks was coming in loud and clear now; it was time to acknowledge how he really felt.

"Brenda," he took a deep breath, "I'm really sorry that you had to find out about my past this way. I only kept it from you because I knew how bad it sounded and I didn't want you to leave me. Because…I think I'm in love with you.

Brenda let out a laugh—not quite the reaction Al had hoped for.

"In *love* with me?" she shook her head. "Please, Al, spare me the gratuitous 'I did it for love,' crap. I may be a sap, but I'm not an idiot."

"Brenda, I mean it," he crossed the room and stood before her, but he was hesitant to sit. He felt like he was diffusing a bomb.

"I think you're a wonderful person," he said, reaching out to smooth her hair. "I think that we can get past this-"

"Don't," she shook her head.

Al's hand froze mid-stroke. "Don't what?"

She looked up at him, the disgust as obvious as spaghetti sauce on her face.

"Please, Al, you think I don't notice how you always look over your shoulder when we're together? How you practically jump out of your skin whenever someone walks through the door at a restaurant? How you've never wanted to introduce me to anyone in your life?"

Al took a step backwards, but the coffee table caught the backs of his knees and forced him to sit right on her TV remote. He felt it dig into his ass like an angry finger.

"You're so embarrassed by me you can hardly walk straight. You condescend to me like I'm some little girl you're babysitting. Don't tell me you love me when lately you've been acting like you can't wait to get away. I can tell you want out—you've been packing your emotions away like your vacation is about to end." She reached for a box of tissues on the end table.

Al felt blood sliding away from his heart, leaving it cold and useless. How could he tell to her that he wasn't embarrassed at all? How could he explain that he was initially attracted to the challenge of hiding her, like hiding an elephant behind a lamppost, but now he'd found himself truly wanting to be with her just because of who she was? He tried to think of a way to put it without sounding like a complete jerk.

"Listen, Brenda, maybe you're right, maybe I do have issues and I was afraid at first, but I'm not afraid now." He wanted to take her hand, but didn't think he could pry it from the tissue box.

Brenda shook her head, and managed a sad, half-smile. "Look, I appreciate you saying what you think I want to hear, but let's just call this what it is and be adults about it."

"Brenda, I'm not just saying anything." He stood up and began to pace.

"You can go, you know." She blew a honking sneeze into her tissue, her eyes red. "I've got friends and family out the ass. I don't need one more person in my life who doesn't want to be here anyway."

Al was at a loss. He wanted to shake her, to show her that in spite of everything, he really did care. But that chance had passed, and any attempt to refute her words now would seem insincere. He'd blown it.

"I really do like you," he said.

Brenda snorted and tossed her balled-up tissue onto the coffee table. "Yeah, I know. We're fun, aren't we? Us fatties?"

Al recoiled from a bite he knew he deserved. He saw his mother sitting there, bone-thin and stoic as she told him she was leaving. He saw his high school girlfriend sobbing after she told him she wanted to date other people, saw her angular shoulders heaving up and down, her knobby fingers wiping her pointy nose. He saw his college sweetheart resting her tiny chin in her hand as she sat across from him and listed the reasons why they should stop seeing each other. Yes, up until now, the fatties had been fun. But now the ride was over.

He left quietly and walked home with the deflated shuffle of a man who'd seen his future float away on the wind of blind arrogance.

***

Over the months that followed, Al made half-hearted attempts to date again. He tried to vary his tastes to include smaller-framed women, but he always found himself going back toward the large ones. And as the spring morphed into summer and then fall, Al found himself thinking of Brenda again, of their strolls through the park, crunching over golden leaves, watching their frozen breath curl together and dance off into the night, feeling the mattress sink from her weight and thinking how sexy it was to have someone so large be so passionate.

He began scanning the women bundled up in overcoats and scarves, trying to find that sweet-faced women with the blond curls. He wondered if he would even recognize her now, after almost a year of Weight Watchers. By now she'd probably dropped fifty pounds and not looked back. So instead of looking for big women, he began wondering if that thin women walking ahead of him was Brenda, or if that petite girl sitting across from him on the subway could be her. Sometimes when he got into a cab, if instead of smelling sweat and dandruff he smelled candy and sugar, he would turn to see if the person who'd just gotten out was Brenda. It never was.

Al wanted a wife. It killed him to know that he'd lost the one woman he could actually see himself marrying. Now he was just chasing after what could have been – a beautiful, funny woman with a new body and a wide, warm heart. He would chase her and chase her, and never catch her.

Story's Inspiration:

This story began from a writing prompt—a picture of a heavy woman on a couch. I'd always heard about regular-sized men who dated heavy women and wondered if there was something psychological at play in such relationships. I wanted to explore the mentality of a man who purposefully sought after big women, and what would happen if he fell in love with one in spite of himself.

Q&A:

1. It sounds like Al got what he deserved. Were you trying to create an unlikable character?

    Yes and no. I wanted Al to realize the he'd mistreated the moped girls he dated, but I did feel sorry for him that the one girl he really did love ended up leaving. He definitely deserved it, but at least he knew he'd been a jerk throughout his adult life.

2. It sounded like Brenda kind of lost out too. If Al really did love her, then she missed out on being with a man who could see past her physique, didn't she?

    Brenda is the kind of woman who can do better than that. She is driven, funny and determined to make her life better on her own terms. She's one of those people who don't need male validation to achieve happiness.

3. So we're to assume that Al never gets back together with his dream girl?

    No, this is one ending that I did spoon-feed. He learned from his mistakes too late. The last line pretty much seals his fate. Maybe next time he won't be so quick to hit on heavy women just because they're heavy.

Jeff

The Aftermath

Like every other day during the past few months, I felt depressed, broken, and defeated. The dirty dishes and laundry continued to pile up. Without intention, I was growing a beard.

I tried to locate my dog, Max. He was a Welsh Terrier officially registered by the name of Maxwell Snout Agent K9; my wife's idea. Stacy had been a huge *Get Smart* fan; we even had the pet names of 86 and 99 for each other. Lately Max had been curling up all day with one of Stacy's sweaters that had been abandoned on the living room couch.

But today, he wasn't there. I looked around the entire house, finally finding him in the den. He sat in my computer chair front paws on the desk in front of the keyboard.

"Max, what're you doing?"

He whimpered a response.

"Max, get down from there. Come on, boy." I walked over to pick him up, but he bared his teeth and growled a threat. He'd never done that before. "Geez. Okay, calm down, boy."

And then I caught a glimpse at what was on the screen. I left the room with a lump so large I thought my throat would split.

* * *

I couldn't find Max at dinnertime. Not that either of us had been eating much, but I wanted to try to get him to get *some* nourishment. Just a little food. I couldn't find him in his usual spots, so I checked the den.

Again, Max was on my computer chair, but this time standing with his hind legs on the chair, front paws on the desk, and going to town licking the screen.

"Max!" He looked over with guilt in his sad eyes. "That's enough. Get down." He commenced with the whimpering again, it seemed endless. I tried to pick him up, but he locked muscles and resisted. "Max—down—now!" I said with my deep daddy-means-business voice while raising my hand, feigning to smack his rear end. With that he jumped from the chair and scurried from the room.

I plopped into the chair and sighed. Big as life, I gazed at Stacy's beautiful face, a photo I took of her at the beach with the sun setting behind her, her skin aglow, blue eyes radiating love, life, and vigor. My fingers traced the digital outline of her face. "Damn it, Stacy. Why'd you have to leave?"

Max wasn't the only one having trouble accepting the truth. But I couldn't keep living in denial. I navigated to the desktop settings and changed the wallpaper back to the Windows default.

In the living room, I found Maxwell Snout again snuggled up with Stacy's sweater, and sat beside him and stroked his fur. I looked at his sad face and if I didn't know better, I would've sworn he was crying, but I couldn't see clearly through my own watery eyes.

Story's Inspiration:

This was based on a Rogues' writing assignment thought up by Tracy Panthera McDurmon. She sent us a comical picture of a Welsh Terrier staring at a computer screen to use as a visual writing prompt. I decided to go in a more sentimental direction with it.

Q&A:

1. It's not clear whether Stacy left him or died. Is this intentional in order to leave it up to one's imagination?

    In my original draft, I had explained what happened with his wife. But in doing so it really killed the momentum and flow of the story, and did not allow for a strong impact at the conclusion. Removing this explanation made the ending stronger and made the piece more minimalist in form, which yes, leaves the reader wondering what exactly happened, but may make them continue to think about the story long after they've read it. I do think I left enough clues, though, for the reader to understand her fate.

2. During the past few months, had he been working or was he so heart-broken that he just hung around the house?

In my mind, the narrator still went to work, but was probably performing poorly. Knowing the situation, his co-workers would've been sympathetic. The messy home and sloppy appearance was due to laziness from his depressed state.

3. Any way you could've expanded the story just a little bit?

Stories can always be expanded a little bit . . . or a lotta bit! But the writer has to know when his message has been conveyed. There are also times when writers like to experiment with different literary forms. This piece is more minimalist in style than some of my other stories. A lot less plot too, especially when you compare it against my next story in this collection, the much bulkier and plot-driven, "The Blue-Collar Blues."

Mike

The Man Who Could Not See the Moon

Straining to see the evening star, he rocked peacefully on the porch and sighed. Green grass waved to and fro, tickled by warm kisses from a spring breeze. Separated from this Earth by the green carpet of the horizon, the deep, brilliant blue sky began to reveal its possessions. Venus rose prominently, lording over the stars its ability to show up first, jealous of no one save Earth's nearest neighbor, the moon.

He remembered her, her Greek beauty evident even on her worst days. Her jet-black hair had known many incarnations: curled into cute swirls, allowing her a soft and gentle appearance (a lie), piled atop her head in a tight bun, bestowing a stately—even queenly— quality (a falsehood by all measure) but mostly allowed to fall straight, stretching to her mid-back in thin, smooth, black licorice strands that bespoke a no-nonsense woman (truth indeed).

He met Sylvia when she was young; at twenty she was vibrant and brazen—one of those women who could ooze sexuality without the slightest of effort. She strode olive-skinned legs; timeless, ageless, without blemish or imperfection, they embodied any man's dream of silken skin and tantalizing muscle. In keeping with her down-to-earth nature, she dressed in a style that was both revealing and plain.

Sighing once again at the mere thought of midriff shirts and short-shorts, he panned his sight across the graying heavens for that sliver that had grown recently to half a pie, knowing all the while it would not yet be visible. There was a sense of serenity in this search, with the warm breeze lightly brushing his white beard and the smell of flowers wafting about under his nose. Nothing was left of the turmoil surrounding his life, infesting it at times with loathing, and often deteriorating his view of her. Now, in his solitude, there was peace. Calm. Possibly, this evening would be the one that would show him the moon.

He could have married her at that young age, but he was young as well, foregoing good sense for a bout of perceived unworthiness. He had no right to consider himself within the context of such beauty. Who was he, anyway? Truly no one of consequence.

He wandered about in his head and to his parks, writing on any paper he could find. He strove to capture all that roiled within, all that vexed and plagued him, and all that allured and pleased him. No woman such as she would bore herself with him, or so he thought. He saw all the idealistic concepts and currents of his day, reveled in the complexities and virtual hopelessness of love, and cried onto white paper the red tears of loneliness, yet he could not see her love for him. He did not realize that underneath the model's curves, nestled in the lovely high cheekbones, and behind the piercing dark eyes a little girl longed to be loved. Yes, she could have been his, but it would take years for him to realize it.

He rose from his padded wooden rocker and strode through the screen door to the refrigerator. Plinking four crescents of ice into the depths of a glass, he drew a generous amount of lemonade from the tap on the dispenser. As he swirled the liquid around and around, he watched the half-moons clink against the rim and reflected on how they would melt away just as she.

His reality had been that he finally married Sylvia ten years later. She was a constant in his life: constantly critical, constantly negative, constantly busy, constantly stunning. Periodically throughout their life together, he glimpsed the little girl – playful, free, longing for love and peace in her life. The stretches of time between these observances were devastating, and they wore his patience thin. The woman clashed with his ideals, his dreams, and his whimsical notions of life and how it should be led. Over the decades, white-hot anger would boil behind the crumbling dam of his patience; it caused him to wonder that he never lashed out. Oh, he lashed out, but only verbally. Only? Oh, how his world darkened whenever he walked inside the house.

With a nearly visible start, he quickly turned on his heel and returned to the porch, taking up residence in his soft, welcoming chair. The night sky was winning its battle with the day; stars began to wake up on the horizon. The green of the meadow was fading to gray, and would soon be steeped in lazy blackness. He sensed that the object of his attention was overhead, but he waited patiently. Soon enough, it would slip below the wooden canopy over the porch. Soon enough, he would relax—not strain—to see it again.

She was always busy, running hither and yon, completing tasks, not completing tasks. More often late than on time, she was distracted by thousands of agendas, projects and family fires. She teased him with glimpses of the little girl, showing her just often enough to make him believe she was there.   The little beauty lived within the beauty— he was convinced of it! Throughout their life together, he arduously attended the premise of the incredible treasure within his Helen of Troy. He worked so very hard to be patient, and to bide his time until the little one came out to play.

Struggling with the constant criticism and accusatory questions that left him in damned-if-I-do, damned-if-I-don't situations, he persevered through the cold indifference that mauled his inner self-worth. All this was done in the hope that she would come full circle to a child-like love of life, and recognize the amazing thrill of viewing this world as something huge, complex, teeming with adventure, and worthy of attention to its minutiae as well as its grandeur.

He attempted to convince her of the need to look, smell, listen, and learn. Frustrated, at times he cursed her for her aloof indifference. Angrily, he would strike back at her snide, backbiting remarks and questions, realizing that, all the while, the little girl was slipping away.

Darkness now revealed the faint tinges of the Milky Way, its slow spiral a spectacle even at this late day in his life. Stars began to fill the void with camaraderie, a cheerful, collective voice, even though muted by incredible distance. Luna's light gave pale life to the grasses and flowers and revealed a more perfect world than daylight could ever show, devoid of blemish. Mysteries were born, and the soul was soothed by the rhythms of the night sounds as soft as the quiet landing of snowflakes on top of snowflakes.

But this was no time of shivering cold days. It was spring! There was no need for shelter, no need for brief forays into the bitter night, although some of those nights could make one forget the cold. No, now was a time of renewal, an ancient time handed down gracefully through the ages despite men's attempts to destroy all that is good. Spring. Warmth. Nurture. Life.

He had tried many means of turning her from her path of indifference to all that he held sacred. They took dance lessons; he sought to dance her into positivity by whirling her through waltzes and tangos, foxtrots and rumbas. They floated mere millimeters above the floor into another world where exquisite music and synchronized movement jelled with perfect harmony. At times his efforts seemed to work, for float they did. The little girl would then be lured from hiding only to retreat as quickly as she'd appeared: a phantom, a wisp, and a hope.

He would take her off alone, to woo her and strike boldly to her heart, yet he seldom found the mark. They would meld in bed, their passion furious and full of flavor, sating his need for the little girl within, who held the power and presence and knowledge of the woman. As time passed, the need for that girl would return. He devoted his life to his wife and their offspring, and gave of himself all that was humanly possible. At times he was contrite of his selfishness – or critical of his self-indulgence.

He gave her nothing that detracted from her natural beauty. The gifts were accents which drew attention to that which was apparent and needed no explanation. The hats she wore at his request lent her a graceful appearance. Her dresses – always demure – shrouded her beauty in mystery and focused her stunning looks into perfection. He had an eye for these things. He wished to please her in any way so he could reach into her heart, grasp the child's hand, and bring her forth into their lives.

The first peek of white curvature appeared under the rigid line of the darkened roof that covered the three steps to the porch. He ignored it and glanced lazily instead at the fading Milky Way. The light of the galaxy was being overwhelmed by the light reflected from an object that could generate none of its own.

"Isn't that life?" he thought. "We strive so very hard to make something that is our own, yet we only truly reflect that which has been taught to us and passed on through knowledge and experience. Oh, to be a star, to be someone of peculiar importance, to shine a singular and original light upon this world."

This longing cried out from his soul. Ah, a dreamer still! There were times in his life that he had been dismayed by his propensity to dream, to fight for ideals, and to believe in his fanciful views of life. But these traits were hard-wired into him, and once he realized that, he gladly gave in to creativity, enjoyment, and ignorance of that which plagued most men—day-to-day life.

Death left Sylvia's beauty untouched. He learned over the years that love did not change, it only beckoned without demand, and that little girls flourish when least expected. He had asked much of her: wife, mother, lover, friend, slave, free-bird, and soul mate. But the most demanding of all was his constant calling out to a waif—the child in her heart—to reveal herself.

Wisely, the girl flirted, revealed only enough to keep him looking, but not so much as to lose her charm. She played hide-and-seek with him over the decades, fearful of losing her innocence. She saved herself for those later moments when she helped him recall all that was beautiful in life. Without her, he surely would have lost sight of the beauty with all the war, death, poverty, political chaos, and the like surrounding them.

She anchored him to a view that was true to himself, the ideals he fought for, the dreams he believed in, and the life he desired. The girl took over when the woman was gone and reminded him of cherished moments splattered through the course of their years together.

A tear trickled and tickled his cheek. He slowly turned his gaze to the half-moon now fully exposed below the line of the porch roof. He endeavored to see it as a ball in the sky – not the flat, white surface he inevitably saw. Years and years ago, she had laughed joyously—exuberantly—at his wonderment during an eclipse. He had seen the moon as a spherical object in the sky for the first time that night, and he was amazed. For some reason, the moon had always manifested itself to him as a flat crescent, or an even flatter white pancake, two-dimensional and of little consequence. He had, infrequently, been able to drink in the sphere as a three dimensional, thrilling sight. Now, he focused nightly on reliving that experience – to see the moon in its regal splendor, devoid of its own light but ruling the night sky despite its barren lands.

Wiping his eyes, he relaxed for another chance to glimpse the night's grand beauty, just as he had throughout Sylvia's life.

Story's Inspiration:

The Man Who Could Not See the Moon was conceived one morning around 3:00am. I was driving up State Route A1A along the Florida coast when I looked up at the moon and saw it as a three dimensional sphere for the first time in my life. Prior to that moment, the moon had always looked to me like a flat crescent or pancake. I was amazed and pulled my van over just to stare. I wrote down the title on a piece of paper, and then I drove home and went to bed. The next morning, I wrote the story in two hours.

Q&A:

1. Do you write your stories that quickly on a typical writing session?

    In two hours? Sometimes. My writing times depend more on how long it takes me to get into the groove of writing. Not necessarily the 'muse' chick because if you wait on her you may never write again. Once I get rolling though, I can knock out a first draft in a couple hours.

2. This story is a very internalized piece of writing. Are you concerned about whether it will hold the reader?

    Ouch! Actually, yes. If I were to pick one story in this anthology I'd like to work significant hours on, this would be the one. I believe there is quite a bit more I could do with this to make it much stronger. My attempt to reach an 'internal dialog' with my main character will definitely make or break this story with the reader. I'm sure there are those who will not care for it. I've had enough feedback from others I respect that like it to put it out for consumption.

3. Everything a writer writes tends to contain aspects of the writer in the story. What portion or portions of this story ring true to who you are?

    As mentioned in the inspiration paragraph, I literally had never in my life seen the moon as a three dimensional orb. I pulled over in my van and dumbfounded is all I can come up with. I had no idea I would end up writing about my wife (who is still alive, of course). There are some accuracies between the couple in this story and my wife and me.

Tracy

In Her Field of Dreams

It's in the vast open fields, blanketed with wildflowers, where she
plays,
Where she lives, where she hopes.
The fields are covered in colors, aromas, and a secret spot, where time
stands still.
It's innocence, it's untamable, it's running free in a space that has no
boundaries.
This field is her reality left behind.
It's her future intertwined.
It's a place where she goes when things are wrong.
It's where she goes when things are wrong.
It's where she hides,
It's where she often dwells in pain, amongst the healing power in her
mind.
Here she is quite able to remain, be herself, all the time.
No more forced smiles,
No more broken hearts to mend,
No dissolution,
There isn't anything herein this magnificent field of imagination, she
can't do.
It's her field of wildflowers that have grown and given her peace and
pleasure.
It's her perfect breeze that's provided hopes and comforts, and dreams.
But yet the winds of change enter her field at times,
Change comes around her ever so often to gently remind.
The sadness is there for a reason,
Even in her imaginary fields of this kind.
In her field of Dreams, love she'll find.

Rebekah

Kevin, Take Two

If I didn't like whipped cream so much, my little brother would probably be dead.

***

Kevin came to us bug-eyed and sweaty, his things crammed against the windows of his dusty car: old sneakers, rumpled clothes, skateboards, empty CD cases. He was fresh out of California, clean out of money and five days off of cocaine. Hugging him was like hugging a bony, chain-smoking old lady.

I brought him inside, glad my husband James wasn't home yet. James had been against the whole thing, and cited all kinds of reasons why we didn't need an ex-cokehead around our six-month-old son. I'm not sure what made him come around. Maybe it was my optimism, my promise that Kevin would get a job and enroll in school and eventually find his own place to live. Or my argument that everyone deserved a second chance, and that twenty-three wasn't too late to start over.

"Here's your room," I gestured grandly to the Areobed I'd made up on the floor of our office.

"Thanks." Kevin dropped his bags and stretched out on the inflatable mattress.

I stared down at him, at his dirty, mismatched socks, his yellow-stained t-shirt, his smudged glasses and blonde stubble. I waited for him to say more, to thank me for allowing him to stay rent-free, for intervening so he wouldn't have to spend several miserable months with our parents at their retirement community. I waited for him to say something about looking for a job or applying for school. I waited for him to apologize for making us all sick with worry. If I'd been holding my breath waiting I would have passed out on the floor.

***

The first month slipped by without incident. Kevin found a job in the mall and started classes at the community college nearby. Every day he came home excited about his job and the people he was

meeting. Really excited. He talked a mile a minute. After only a few days at his job, he seemed pretty confident that he would move into management, claiming that his boss had zero people-skills. In the afternoons he'd barge into the house trumpeting about his latest "A" paper and how impressed his professors were with him.

I embraced his excitement, and encouraged him to go out with the new friends he was making, hoping that they were quality kids and not the sort he'd associated with back in California. He met up with them at skate parks and hung out with them after school. He never mentioned missing his old life or doing drugs. Why would he? He was different. He had changed.

***

"He should go to rehab," my sister warned over the phone. "People don't just quit cocaine cold-turkey like nothing happened."

"But he really seems to be okay," I said. "He's going to school and hanging out with some kids he met skateboarding. He seems happy."

"Just make sure you hide any prescription drugs you have around the house," she said.

Even though I thought she was being an alarmist, I dutifully removed my leftover prenatal vitamins and my dog's allergy medicine from the kitchen cabinet. But I told Kevin to help himself to the beer we kept stocked in the fridge. *He isn't an alcoholic*, I told myself. *He can handle beer*.

***

Kevin began forgetting things. He left lights on, and half-empty cans of soda around. He locked his keys in his car, lost his cell phone, his wallet, his homework. I gently reminded him to lock our front door when he left the house—gently because he seemed edgy lately and I didn't want to upset him. The front door remained unlocked. I suggested he buy a planner to keep track of everything, but he soon began to insist that his friends were stealing things from him—his money and his prescription Xanax and his CDs. And I felt sorry for him, thinking that maybe his new friends weren't so nice after all.

Then he broke his foot.

"How did you do that?" I asked him, holding Benny on my hip as I started dinner.

"I was trying to land a trick." He fumbled with a bottle opener, his hands shaking.

"That's a twist-off, Kevin."

"And I kicked the railing."

"Kevin, you broke your foot kicking a railing?"

Kevin looked sheepish, as if it had just occurred to him how idiotic that was.

"Yeah, well, I didn't know it was made out of metal."

"What did you think it was made out of, marshmallows?"

He took a swig of beer in reply.

"Well, how do you know it's broken?" I asked.

"It's all swollen and bruised." He proceeded to pull off his disgusting sock and reveal his foot, which was indeed swollen like a dead armadillo and purple as a thundercloud.

"That's so gross," I said.

"I'm getting x-rays tomorrow."

I didn't ask who was going to pay for that. I knew he would send the bill to my parents. My parents, who thought his biggest vice was pot, and who were more than willing to help him get back on his feet. Make that foot.

"He probably did it on purpose," James said later, in bed.

"Why would he do that?"

"To get pain pills."

I snorted in disagreement. "He doesn't do drugs anymore."

"How do you know?"

"Because he told me so and I trust him."

"Why? Has he done anything to prove that he's being honest?"

"He got a job. He's going to school. He *is* trying."

James ran his fingers through my hair. He was used to me defending my family. He knew better than to push me.

***

The next week, I lost a hundred dollars.

"Last time I saw it, it was on the counter," I said. I stood in the kitchen making coffee. Kevin sat shirtless at the breakfast table, noisily slurping a bowl of Captain Crunch.

"Mmm," he mumbled.

"I thought I put it back in my wallet," I said. "But when I went to deposit it at the bank, it was gone."

Kevin's spoon clinked against his bowl.

"Maybe I threw it away," I said. "It was near a bunch of junk mail I threw out." I bit my lip, annoyed with myself for being such a dumb-ass.

"I didn't take it."

I looked over at Kevin, who'd stopped eating and now stared out the window. It hadn't occurred to me that he might have taken it.

"Oh, I know," I said.

"I know what it's like when people steal from you. I wouldn't do that."

"Well, I'm not worried about it. If I threw it away there's nothing I can do about it, and if I didn't then I guess it'll turn up."

"People who steal, suck."

I studied the back of his bed-head, and it dawned on me that maybe Kevin's wallet and CDs hadn't been stolen. Maybe he had simply left them somewhere and forgotten about them. As I stared at his bony back, at his angular shoulder blades and jutting vertebrae, I wondered why he was such a scatterbrain.

"Do you want some coffee for the road?" I asked to quiet my wondering.

"Yeah."

I poured it into a travel mug and left it by the front door for him to grab on his way to school. It was still there when I left to run errands that afternoon.

***

Kevin stayed out late. Sometimes he didn't come home at all. And he avoided James whenever possible. He knew James had radar for deceit and was intolerant of nonsense, and so he disappeared from the house around six every night, just as James was getting home. Which left me to explain Kevin's behavior and to clarify his intentions.

"When's he moving out?" James asked almost nightly.

"I don't know."

"Has he saved any money?"

"I think so."

"How's his credit?"

"How should I know? It can't be that bad. I don't think he has any debt."

"Who are these people he hangs out with?"

"Just some kids he met skating."

"How old are they?"

"I don't know…his age, I guess."

Then James set his mouth in a thin line and shook his head. "Why can't he go live with your parents?"

"I can't just kick him out. Besides, he's already established here."

"Tell him he needs to have a plan."

"*You* tell him. I don't want to be in the middle."

"He's *your* brother. You are in the middle."

"Let's talk about something else."

That was the ritual for the next two months—I put up with Kevin when he was around but secretly wished he'd move out or move away or had never come at all. The more I ducked and dodged the issue, the worse it got. The elephant was getting bigger, gaining weight. Soon it would take up the whole house and trample us all to death.

So instead of wishing Kevin would move out, I began wishing he'd simply vanish.

***

I heard the quiet thud of the front door shutting. It was two in the morning, and I was sitting in the rocking chair feeding Benny. The door to the nursery was cracked, and through the opening I saw Kevin pass in a blur, headed for the bathroom. I tried not to listen, but still heard the obvious sounds of puking. My stomach clenched in anger.

A few minutes later I looked up and saw Kevin walk by the door, then stop and peer inside.

"Hey," he said loudly.

"Hey," I whispered. "You all right?"

"Yeah." He pushed the door open, flooding the room with yellow light from the hallway. "I hung out with J.J. and some kids from the skate park. I can land this awesome trick now. There's this concrete thing that's shaped like a Twinkie, and I go up one side-" he demonstrated with a trembling hand "-and do a kick-flip off the top-"

Is he out of his mind? I thought. Didn't he see that I was in the middle of breast-feeding in the middle of the night? Did I really look like I was interested in hearing about his latest skateboarding trick?

"-and then I land reverse, which is with my left foot leading instead of my right. It's totally hard to do but I've gotten awesome at it."

"You're skating on your broken foot?"

Kevin shrugged. "It doesn't hurt anymore."

"That's because you're taking pain killers."

"It looks much better." He plopped on the floor and started to unwrap the ace bandage from his foot. I could see his long toenails silhouetted against the hall light.

"That's okay, Kevin. I don't need to see it."

He looked disappointed but wrapped his foot back up.

"You drove home drunk?" I asked it as a question, though I meant for it to sound more accusatory.

"It wasn't far."

"Where were you?"

"J.J.'s house. He had some people over. There were these crazy kids who pulled up in a car they'd just stolen."

"Oh, that's great." I wanted to say more, but realized that not only did I have a semi-conscious baby in my lap and I didn't need to get all worked up, but worse, I was beginning to sound just like my mother. Our mother.

"I left before the cops came." He said this like he'd done something incredibly responsible.

I sighed and moved to the changing table, wishing Kevin would just leave.

"Wake me up at eight, will you?" he asked from behind me. "I have to work tomorrow morning."

"Don't you have an alarm clock?"

"I haven't figured out how to set it."

I pressed my lips together as I unfastened Benny's diaper. "Fine."

He said good night and retreated to his room. A few minutes later I heard the clicking of keys as Kevin settled in behind our computer and began his nightly ritual of instant messaging, emailing, and updating his Myspace page. I didn't know how he was able to stay up after puking like that. I would have passed out the minute the toilet had flushed.

Benny woke up at five a.m. When I passed by the office I still heard the *click click* of keys, still saw the sliver of light beneath the door. I soothed Benny back to sleep, but found myself tossing and turning when I returned to bed. A silent seed of anger hardened inside me, burning its way through its shell of denial.

At eight o'clock, the office was silent and dark. I knocked on the door.

"Kevin?"

No response.

Knock knock knock. "Kevin? You awake?"

Nothing.

I thought about breaking in. I'd become an expert at it after sharing a room with a sister who made it a habit of locking me out. But no. He was an adult. It wasn't up to me to wake him. If he missed work and got fired, that was his own fault.

At nine, I heard a weird static sound coming from the office. I pressed my ear to the door and realized it was Kevin's clock radio. I guessed he had figured out how to set it after all. When the sound went on for a minute or two, I knocked on the door again.

"Kevin?"

No reply.

"Kevin, your alarm is going off."

Nothing.

Fuck it, I thought. I returned to the family room, where Benny sat among his scattered toys and looked at me with smiley blue eyes. I turned up the stereo and danced around the room, focused on my son's giggles instead of my brother's silence.

In the afternoon the sky grew gray and stormy. I watched the wind whip our queen palm around in the backyard; our lake rippled and shuddered with the cold rolling in from the west. I pulled on a sweater and made hot chocolate, happy that it was finally getting cold, happy that Thanksgiving and Christmas were coming, happy that soon our house would return to normal.

I hummed as I opened the fridge and pulled out a can of whipped cream for my hot chocolate. I shook the can, held it over my mug, and pressed the nozzle. The whipped cream came out in a lifeless ooze. Frowning, I shook the can again, held it at a more severe angle and hoped gravity would help. Still the whipped cream was watery and flat.

I checked the expiration date, but I knew that I'd just bought the whipped cream the other day. I examined the nozzle. I shook the can again, pushing aside the voice that was now screaming at me that shaking wouldn't help. I knew what was wrong, but I shook the can vigorously, tears now coming. I pressed the nozzle harder, harder, until it snapped off the can and went flying across the kitchen.

"*Goddammit!*" I shrieked.

I threw the can in the sink and stormed down the hall.

"Kevin!" I banged on the door this time.

All I heard was that stupid alarm clock playing a station of static.

I yanked a bobby pin from my hair and rammed it through the little hole on the doorknob. A few twists and jiggles and the lock turned. I had to shove the door open; a mountain of clothes pushed against the other side.

I noticed the smell first. The room reeked of sweat and recycled breath and cigarettes and pot. Littered on the floor were empty fast food wrappers, packs of smokes, CDs, papers and clothes.

Protruding from beneath the same sheets I'd put on the Aerobed three months ago was my brother's bandaged foot. I wanted to kick it. Instead, I stood over the bed and glared at the giant slumbering lump, my anger boiling.

"*Hey,*" I said. I stomped on the mattress, missing Kevin's foot by inches.

Kevin didn't budge.

"Thanks a lot for ruining my whipped cream, you dick. Are you really that desperate for a high? I've got some glue, wanna sniff that, too? How about some Nyquil? What the fuck, Kevin? Can't stand to be sober for two seconds?"

The radio kept on playing, static interrupted by talk interrupted by static. It was three-forty-three. With one arm I swept the radio off the computer desk and onto the floor. It landed upside down and abruptly went silent.

"*Kevin!*" I couldn't believe he wasn't moving. "You need to find somewhere else to live, you know. I said you could stay if you got your shit together and obviously that isn't happening."

That's when I noticed his breathing. It was slow. Really slow. I paused and counted the seconds between breaths. When I got to fifteen, I grabbed the sheet and pulled. His limp body was wrapped in it, but I managed to get it off his head. He was face-down on the mattress. I shook him by the shoulder, hard enough to roll him to the side. His face was completely slack, his mouth crusty with drool that had dried a while ago. I could see the whites of his eyes beneath lids only partway closed.

"Kevin?" I said one last time. Then I called 911.

***

I held Benny on my lap, in a daze. I didn't remember driving to the emergency room, yet there I was, staring at the vending machine across from me. A chubby little girl carefully counted out quarters and dimes and nickels and slid them through the thin slot one at a time. I heard the coins clink home, watched the digital display add them up—twenty-five, thirty-five, forty-five. She stood before the machine, hands on her undeveloped hips, before selecting her candy. I watched the lazy metal spiral spin out her Snickers bar, watched her bend and push the flap open to take it.

I remembered when Kevin was young and chubby and obsessed with sweets. I remembered discovering his Halloween candy stash and laughing as he squealed at me to give it back. I remembered wrestling with him over the TV remote and the last can of soda, and always winning because I was bigger. I remembered ignoring him as I floated through the house, a teenager with more important things to do. I remembered ignoring him now, ignoring his forgetfulness, his mania, his skeletal appearance and the collection of beer bottles in the garbage I knew weren't James's or mine. I remembered ignoring him last night, ignoring his behavior, his lies, his cries for attention and help. Almost ignoring the runny whipped cream and the alarm clock that went on unanswered. I hated him for making me feel like a terrible sister, and I hated myself for being one.

The 911 dispatcher had asked what I thought Kevin had taken. I'd told her that he used to use cocaine, but I didn't think he still did. Even as I said this, I felt like a liar. Then I had run into the bathroom to check for her and found his empty pill bottles. Hydrocodone, Adderall, Xanex, Loratab. I had no idea if he'd emptied the bottles slowly or all at once, but I told the paramedics about them, and about Kevin drinking the night before. They'd swarmed into the office, big guys in matching blue outfits, firemen with boots that tracked dirt into the house. Instead of watching them coax my brother back to life, I'd stood at the front window and pointed out the fire engine to Benny, repeating *red truck, red truck*, over and over like a crazy person.

James met me at the hospital—as soon as I saw him I cried. He asked me for details but I shook my head, so he sought out a nurse for answers. When he returned he told me Kevin was stable but we couldn't see him. I asked if he was going to have brain damage and before he could stop himself James said, "Too late for that." I burst into tears again.

Back at home, James vacuumed the dirt from the firemen as I sat on the couch and watched Benny crawl after the vacuum cleaner. I knew better than to blame myself for Kevin's downward spiral, but I still couldn't shake the guilt. Like a bad dream, it promised to stay with me for a long time.

"It was his choice to do drugs again," James said that night.

"I know, but still, I should have known."

"You have too much going on in your own life to supervise him."

"Still, I feel like I knew in the back of my mind he was in trouble but just ignored it all."

"It's not up to you to save him."

I just sighed and drank my beer. I couldn't explain to someone who had no siblings how it feels to see your little brother fall. All I could do now was help Kevin get back up.

***

Kevin and I sat across from each other at my kitchen table; the morning light poured in from the huge window and set his blonde hair on fire. The IV needle marks were still on the back of his hand, his eyes were still blood-shot from puking his guts out, and his voice was still hoarse from the stomach pump tube forced down his throat. But he sat across from me, a ghost back from the dead, pale and thin and subdued.

"How about this one?" I asked as I studied my laptop screen. "New Horizons Treatment Center."

Kevin shrugged. "Sounds like a ride at Epcot."

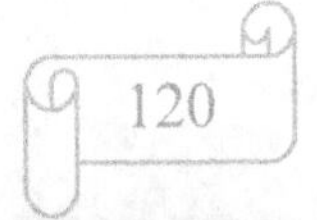

"So that should be fun, then, yeah?"

He looked at the table and picked at the frayed edge of a placemat.

"Okay. Well, there's one just called Challenges. How fun does that sound?"

"Not very."

I looked back at the screen. "How about Born Anew Foundation?"

Kevin wrinkled his nose. "What is that, like, a church?"

"I don't think so. It's in Jupiter."

"That might be cool. Being close to a beach."

I clicked on the link and studied the homepage. "It looks nice. You can walk to the beach. I mean, if they let you."

Kevin shrugged again. He looked miserable.

"You can do this," I said quietly. "Just think about how glad you'll be once you're done." I knew I was sounding like a public service announcement, but I didn't care.

He thumbed tears from his eyes and took a long swallow of root beer—the only kind of beer I'd let him drink until he left for rehab.

"It takes a lot of balls to admit you need help," I said.

He snorted. "Yeah, or an overdose and a trip to the emergency room."

"Well, either way, I'm proud of you. You're going to get better…I guess because you couldn't possibly get any worse."

Kevin shot me a withering look, but instead of retorting, he shook his head.

"I'm sorry," he said. "For all of this bullshit."

I looked at my little brother, and saw the same kid I used to shove around the house and tease and buy alcohol for and laugh with. I wanted to tell him he'd been forgiven, but he hadn't been yet. All the hurt, the suspicions, the aching frustration I'd swallowed for months— it was all as palpable as an entity sitting next to me at the table. But I knew that eventually I would forgive him, and myself, for everything that had happened.

I felt my breath catch as I said, "I know you are, Kev."

Story's Inspiration:

This story is loosely based on my experience living with my younger brother, an ex-addict. It was probably the most difficult thing I'd written, but because of the raw reality I was forced to face during the time and the healing that has taken place since, it is probably my favorite.

Q&A:

1. Here's another story based on a family member. How much of this is true?

    Almost all of it. He probably should have died at least once over the course of the last ten years. And his stay at my house was the end of a long road of drug and alcohol abuse. But it was more difficult for me to capture the real state of denial I was in than his behavior while living in my house. Writing it out really brought to light how obvious it was that he had a huge problem, and how awful it was for me to ignore it for as long as I did.

2. So was the breaking point with you the whipped cream incident?

    I think that was just one more thing on the list of clues. I think what actually did it for me was a picture I took of him with my digital camera that I was planning to email my dad, until I looked at the picture and realized that 'Kevin' looked emaciated—I couldn't send the picture to my dad. That was the 'Whoa' moment for me. The Whipped Cream incident happened later, and that was the last piece of evidence I felt I needed to approach my brother and say, "You have a problem."

3. So where is your brother now?

    He'll be three years sober in November of 2010. He is working full time and still going to AA meetings almost every day. He has sponsees now—other people recovering from addiction who come to him for support. And he's writing a book, sort of a memoir, cautionary tale for addicts and ex-addicts: Addiction Is Easy. I'm so proud of him.

Jeff

The Blue-Collar Blues

Her body was my addiction, and I had to get sober. My pale lips kissed her soft cheek knowing that tears would soon stream down it.

"Are you leaving?" She tried to fight off drowsiness and propped herself up on one elbow.

"Yes."

"Why?" she asked like a disappointed child.

I gave her a look. "You know why."

"But we're supposed to spend the whole weekend together."

"That was *your* idea—you didn't even ask me how I felt about it. You can't just show up and say, 'pack—I have plans for us'."

"I thought you would like the surprise." The hurt on her face kept growing. "Besides, you followed me here on your own."

I put my bag down. "Look, honey, this has to end," I said with my arms stretched out.

Despite the blasting hotel furnace, it suddenly felt as cold inside as it did out.

"What do you mean? *Why?*"

"Sorry, I gotta go." I grabbed my bag and left the motel room. For one exhilarating moment, everything froze—car headlights along the nearby highway, tiny white crystals in the dark early morning sky, steamy carbon dioxide from my long exhalation—and then sped up to a frightening pace.

The door to our room flew open, but I ignored it.

"Wait," she hollered.

I eased around to face her. She stood barefoot in the snow with her arms crossed. She wore nothing more than a pink shiny camisole and matching thong. Her platinum hair dripped over her shoulders.

"Get inside—you're gonna get sick."

"Won't you at least tell me why you're leaving?"

She shivered and squeezed her forearms against her healthy breasts.

"You know why. You have a husband. You have two children at home. What we're doing—is so *wrong*. I can't do this anymore."

"You can't *do this* anymore? And just what am I supposed to do?"

"Go home to your family, Karli."

"You son-of-a-bitch!"

Lights to the room next door came on.

"Would you *please* keep it down?" I asked.

"No, I *won't* keep it down!"

I grabbed her arm, forced her back into the room, and shut the door behind us. "Now look," I began, but she jumped on me wrapping her arms around my neck and legs around my waist. She began planting kisses all over my face.

"I knew you couldn't leave me," she said.

"I was only trying to get you out of the cold. Besides, did you really want all the other guests to see your ass?"

"Oh please, I don't care what they think."

"What's with you? You're crazy—ya know that?"

"Just crazy for you, Terry."

"Well you better get over it."

Her grip loosened.

"Why do you say such horrible things?"

"Look—it's over, okay? Get that through your *thick, fucking skull*. It's over!"

She slid down my body and onto her knees. "No-o," she whined and grabbed at my waistband. In one motion, she unbuttoned and unzipped my jeans, and then grabbed hold of my penis.

"What are you *doing?*"

I held her head away from my crotch, but I couldn't help looking at the way her narrow waist swelled up into a perfectly shaped apple of an ass. An apple that I wanted to bite into. And just beyond her ass, since her legs were tucked under it, the bottoms of her feet, pink from the snow, peaked out. And the thought of her standing barefoot out there, risking health and humiliation, all because of me, was arousing.

"See," she said while stroking me. "You can't resist me, baby. I'll let you do anything you want to me, you know that. And how many women can promise you that?"

* * *

She was curled up in the fetal position. Just dead weight, but she had a smile on her face. I took my time, got a shower and changed.

When I came out of the bathroom for the last time, she rolled my way and said, "Why did you clean up already? I wanted to lay around in bed all morning and play."

"Look . . . we had our fun, our last hoorah or what-have-you, but enough is enough. It's over. Take care of yourself."

I grabbed my bag and hurried from the room. Down the stairs and into the parking lot. I pictured the look of shock on her face. It transformed into pain, and then anger. But I made it to my car, a Ford Mustang, without her yelling at me from behind. Inside, I could not see through the windshield because inches of dry snow coated it. Sounding like an old man fighting to catch his breath, the car took its time to start. The wipers cracked, then slowly moved, and blew most of the snow from my vision. I lit a cigarette, looked behind me, and began to ease from the parking space. And that's when I heard it—the loud thud.

I whirled my head around to see Karli clinging to the hood of my car. This time she had enough sense to throw on her coat and boots before coming out; but still, she was hardly dressed for the weather.

"What are you *doing*? Are you *crazy*?"

"I'm not letting go . . . I'm not letting go!"

"Fine," I said. I punched the gas, did reverse donuts in the snowy parking lot, and laughed hysterically the entire time. She hung on for a while like she was riding a mechanical bull, but eventually the centrifugal force got the best of her and flung her from the car. She rolled to a stop.

My laughter stopped instantly and so did my car. She could have been seriously injured. All because of me.

I was about to get out of the car and go to her aid when she popped up and ran toward the car with chunks of snow falling at her side.

"Don't you *dare* le-eave me-e!"

I gunned it. Got the hell away and didn't look back.

* * *

It was foolish of me to drive home after that fiasco. But I didn't know where else to go. A couple hours after I settled in and crashed out on the couch, there was frantic knocking against my front door.

I opened the door the few inches the security chain would allow.

"What do you want, Karli?"

"I want a second chance."

"You can't have one."

Question marks formed in her eyes.

"And don't say, 'why not'."

"Why not?"

"What'd I just say?"

"Can I have a cigarette?"

"I quit."

"Since when?"

"Goodbye, Karli." I shut the door.

"Don't you think it'll be awkward?" She shouted from the other side.

"Awkward?"

"Yeah, you know, like as in the next time we see each other?"

"There won't be a next time . . . we're not going to see each other any more!"

"Of course there will be a next time. My *God,* you can be so *stupid,* Terry."

And then the realization hit me.

I unchained the door and opened it. This time I noticed that her nose was red and her face was flushed. There were shiny patches under and around her eyes half-ready to crystallize. She wore a faux fur coat with earmuffs and mittens. Yet she was shivering like she was naked and wet.

"You want some coffee?"

She came in and I shut the door.

"That would be nice."

"By the way," I said, "I'm sorry about the uh . . . the whole parking lot incident."

I took two cigarettes from my flannel shirt pocket, put them both in my mouth and lit them. I handed one to Karli and motioned for her to have a seat.

"I don't know what got into me," I said.

"It's okay. Guess I deserved that for acting like such a maniac."

I made some coffee and Karli, with coat and all, sat on a recliner in the living room. She pulled off her boots and pulled her knees to her chest to keep warm.

A few silent minutes later, I joined her with two cups of coffee. I sat on the couch opposite her. She reached forward, sipped the coffee, and thanked me. Only then did I realize that my cigarette had been hanging unattended between my lips. I found an ashtray just in time to catch the long stem of ash.

"Why is life so complex?" she asked.

"It just is."

"Jesus, what are we going to do, Terry?"

"What all adults do—struggle."

"That's reassuring."

I took a couple gulps of coffee. "Do you want me to lie to you? Tell you that everything is going to be great, fine, and dandy? Well, it just isn't. Everything's fucked."

She sat back holding the coffee mug and took a couple drags off the cigarette.

"Yeah, it's fucked all right, and you're not big enough of a man to do anything about it."

"What are you talking about?"

"Come on. You know about his temper."

"Yeah. And?"

"He *beats me,* Terry."

"No, he *doesn't.* "

"Yes, he does!"

"I know for a fact that Paul would never harm a woman. In fact, he despises anyone who does. In seventh grade, three kids were pushing around this girl after school. They were making fun of her because she was different. But mainly because she wouldn't give them the time of day. Paul beat them senseless with a baseball bat in order to teach them to 'have respect for the female population.' His words. Each of them had at least one limb in a cast because of it. The girl fell in love with him. And nobody ever messed with her again."

"Nice story, but you didn't let me finish."

"Please go on."

"He beats me with words. Ew, the stuff that comes out of his mouth."

"And I'm sure you don't provoke any of that."

"I can't stand being with him anymore. He's a big unloving monster. He knows nothing about compassion or romance. Or anything a girl wants or needs."

"He's a good father to your children."

"No he's not. He smacks them around."

"He *does not.*"

"With insults. Tells them that they'll never amount to nothin'."

"I don't believe that."

"The kids can't stand him. The big ruffian. Hey, I know," she said as she gleamed. "I'll get the kids and we can leave this Godforsaken town . . . and we can finally be together. You and me, Terry, what do ya think? We can get a fresh start. Nathan has fun with you. And Sarah adores you too. We'll be good as a family."

"You're going to take your kids away from their *father?*"

"Yeah, why not?"

"Your kids would hate you if you did that. And they'd always blame and resent me for it. Besides, Paul would hunt me down and slaughter me. You're not thinking clearly. You can't run away from your problems. They have a way of finding you. You're just going through a bad period with Paul. That's all. He's your husband. You've built this whole life together. You have a long history. With us, it was just a fling. I'm sure that deep down you still love him."

"But I don't love him. I love you."

"Don't say that. You don't mean it."

"Yes I do."

A tense period of silence followed with her gazing at me and me looking everywhere but at her. When she was ready, she put the coffee down on the table, snubbed out the cigarette, and let out a pleasant sigh.

"Remember the first time we had sex?"

"Yeah."

A glimmer came across her eyes. "It was so exciting. Paul and the kids were playing in the backyard and we went at it right on the kitchen floor. We were drenched from the summer heat. And at any moment, Paul or the kids could have just—"

"I remember!"

She acted hurt for a minute. But it never lasted much longer than that with her.

"Terry?"

"What?"

"Let's have sex."

"No."

"Can't you at least massage my ass? It's sore from when you hurled me off your car."

"Look—it's time for you to leave and go back to your family. And we're going to pretend that this affair never happened. And we'll still be all good and chummy around Paul. Like the good ol' times."

She got up in a hurry and put her boots back on. "You know . . . everything's not fucked like you had said. You're the only thing that's fucked, Terry. *You're* fucked."

She left the apartment without looking back.

* * *

After nine oil changes, three tune-ups, two battery replacements, about a half-dozen tire rotations, and some other fun, I had to stop off at Larry's Bar after work. Actually, it wasn't the work as much as the constant phone calls from Karli claiming to be my Mom. Every time she called, my manager, Mr. Dolton, and his assistant snickered as they sang over the intercom, "Ter-ry, it's your mom-my again." And they knew damn well that it wasn't my mother. At first, I quietly told her off. The next couple of times I hung up without saying a word. After that, I wouldn't even go to the phone.

Larry's overlooked the partially frozen, brown Allegheny River. The riverbanks were covered in white with black trimmings. Bare trees showered the hillsides as the final reminder that everything was dead.

Larry, or at least the old bartender whom I believed to be Larry, served me a draft beer. As I lifted the mug, I noticed the dark smudges on my hands. Despite ten minutes of hand washing with powdered soap and scalding hot water, I couldn't remove the grease from my skin or from underneath my fingernails. Plus, I smelled like oil.

After I gulped down half of my beer, I heard a familiar voice.

"Terry! Hey man, I was hopin' that you'd be here."

"Hey, Paul," my voice quavered. "What's goin' on?"

Paul Herse sat his big sturdy frame down next to me and ordered a draft. He was solid as granite. His brown mullet curled around his ears and his thick muscular neck.

"Not much. How 'bout you?"

"Same ol' same."

"Oh come on. Don't you have any stories for your good friend, here?"

"Remember Rhonda?"

"No, can't say I do."

"Well, I've been shacking up with her for a while. Spent the weekend with her."

"Is she a gamer?"

"Oh, is she. Damn if that girl doesn't know when to quit. She has the energy of a Jack Russell terrier."

"Goddamn, I bet she does."

"So what about you? Got any stories for me?"

"Come on. Nothing too exciting about the family life."

"How is the family?"

"They're good, ya know. Couldn't be better. Me and the wife . . . it's like we're on a second honeymoon."

"Really?"

"Yeah." Paul guzzled some beer. "Aw hell, who am I kiddin'? Honestly, Terry, things have been a mess for a while now. Don't know what's gotten into Karli. It's somethin' different every day.

"She's been cold and bitter towards me for months now. Not very patient with the kids. And lately, she comes and goes without any explanation . . . This past Friday, I come home from work and Karli's not there. No note, no call. The kids were all by them damn selves. I called all her friends, but nobody knows where she is. I was up all night. Even took the kids out driving with me looking around for her car. Nothing."

"Jesus." I said, finding it hard to swallow my beer.

"And she didn't show up until late Saturday evening drunk as a wino and she wouldn't tell me shit. I asked her where she was, and she said, 'none of your goddamned business.' She locked herself in the bathroom for hours. Now is that any way for a lady to act?"

"What do you think's going on?"

"Aw, hell if I know. She's too young to be having a mid-life crisis. I don't know what to think. Maybe you can talk to her."

"Me?"

"Sure, you know Karli as well as anyone—"

"No, Paul, I don't know her that well. Really."

"Oh, come on, you two get along just fine . . . like a couple of ol' pals."

"Yeah, guess so. We seem to have a rapport."

"A rapport?" He said wide-eyed.

"Yeah, well, like you said, we get along."

"Right. Well, that's why I want you to talk with her. I mean, well, it's a crazy thought, but what if she is cheating on me? Not that she's going to let on to you about that, but maybe you can, you know, figure it out. See how she responds to your questions. Tell if she is lying about anything.

"Christ," Paul continued, "If I thought she was sleeping with another man, I can't tell you what I would do to him. It would be slow. It would be excruciatingly painful. Remember what I did to that guy years back at the Fourth of July party? The one who kept running his lips and flirting with Karli?"

"Oh God, yeah. He had to have his jaw replaced. Among other things."

"That's the one. That was nothing. That would be warm-ups for what I'd do to someone who was sleeping with my wife. I would take him somewhere quiet and remote. Somewhere where no one could hear his screams. I would take my toolset and go to work on him. I'd probably end up having to kill the bastard. Well, I don't want to think about that. Just crazy speculation. I'm sure Karli's just going through some personal shit. Or I screwed up somehow and she just won't forgive me."

I realized that I'd been staring at my beer for minutes afraid to look him in the eyes.

"What's the matter? You're lookin' a little green. You alright?"

"Just a long day at the garage. I guess I inhaled a little too much of the exhaust fumes."

"Yeah, you need to unwind. Here I am battering you with all of my burdens."

"It's not a problem."

"Thank God I have a friend like you, Terry. Hey, let's play some pool."

"I-I don't know. I should get going."

"Oh come on. Just a few games. Loser pays for the table and a pitcher of beer."

Normally I whopped his ass on a consistent basis. But I knew at once that I was going to let him win the bet.

* * *

I made a stop before heading home. After almost falling on my ass from a patch of ice in the alley, I staggered up the front steps and wrapped on the aluminum screen door. She opened the door barefoot wearing her uniform from J. J.'s Diner. A forest green collared shirt with tiny white pinstripes and a tan skirt. A white nametag was pinned to the shirt, saying nothing but 'RHONDA' in black letters. A cordless phone was in her hand.

"Terry? What're you doing here?"

"Jus' checkin' on ya."

"Drunk?"

"Can't I come in?"

She looked at me strangely then sighed. Her long silky brown hair was pulled back, and she played with it. "Do you have anywhere to be later?"

"No. Why?"

"Alright, come on in then."

It seemed too warm in her apartment. The alcohol heated my blood making it feel better outside in the freezing cold than indoors. I took off my coat.

"My babysitter cancelled on me and I need to get over to the diner. Can you watch Charlie?"

"You want me to baby-sit?"

"Why are you checking on me if you can't help?"

"No, yeah, I came to help. I can help."

"Are you sure? Are you capable of that? Are you capable of *any*thing?"

"What's with all the hostility?"

"Why do you even come by here, Terry?"

"Is this the thanks I get for checkin' on your well-being? I was thinking about you, that's all. Wanted to see how you were doing, since it's been a while."

"I'll say it's been a while—haven't seen you in months."

"I know. I'm sorry about that."

"You don't need to apologize to me."

I looked around. Her place was spotless. She always took care of her things. And everything felt and looked warm. Wood furniture, burgundy drapes and rugs, red throw pillows on a burnt orange couch. There was the smell of pine and potpourri in the air.

"Did you come from Stew's?" she asked.

"No, Larry's. I ran into . . . ."

"Who?"

". . . um, Paul."

"Paul."

"Yeah."

She straightened her skirt while looking around. "How's he doing?"

"Same ol' Paul. We were playing pool. We were on our last game, the tiebreaker, loser had to pay. I set him up for the game winning shot, but some guy bumped him. Paul scratched and lost the game.

"So Paul chased him around the table and broke the pool cue over the guy's head. Things were getting ugly. The guy he hit had a bunch of friends nearby. Of course Paul wanted a piece of them too, but I convinced him to get out of there . . . fuckin' Paul . . . Of course, I know some people just love that side of Paul," I said while grinning.

"Yeah, well, I need to get to work. Charlie's in his crib in the bedroom. He just had his dinner and should be asleep by now. Do you remember where everything is?"

"Of course, I do."

"Call the diner, if you need me."

"Will do."

She walked over to the closet looking fantastic even in the boring server's outfit. She had been a high school cheerleader. She had tall, slender legs that would force guys to stare at until they tripped over themselves. And Rhonda's smile would make your heart flutter. She had only improved over time. She put on her coat and boots, but stopped halfway out the door.

"Does he ever ask about me?"

"Paul?"

"Yeah."

"He doesn't even recall your name."

She left and I wandered around the apartment wanting to turn on the TV, but afraid it would wake her boy. I raided the refrigerator; found a bottle of beer and stuff to make a sandwich. After the long day plus all the alcohol, my body began to slow down. I went into the bedroom. Charlie was fast asleep; his eyes were shut tight and his hands were curled into fists. He was about five months old. Wisps of blonde hair sprouted from his smooth head.

On Rhonda's dresser was a framed picture of her and Paul as homecoming queen and king. She wore a huge smile and a pink gown. Paul gave his usual scowl and wore a gray suit that was a couple inches too small.

Beside the picture was a scrapbook. Different pictures of her and Paul throughout grade school and high school. I was in a few of the pictures with them. Looking at them made me sad. So I shut it before too long.

I opened her top drawer. A waft of sweet perfume hit me and I looked through her sensual underpants. The drawer below it held silky and lacy lingerie. I held some of the articles out and envisioned her in them. And then I took those visions with me as I lay down on the side of the bed farthest from the crib.

* * *

I heard the creek of the bedroom door. "He-ey."

Through the alcohol and deep sleep haze, I saw Rhonda's tall, athletic frame walk into the bedroom.

"Did he give you any trouble?"

"No, he's been sound asleep all night. He must have had a busy day with mommy."

"Yeah, we did have fun playing today."

Rhonda stood above his crib for a few moments admiring her child and then leaned down and kissed his forehead.

"How was work?" I asked.

"Slow. People have been staying in ever since this cold front came through."

"Can't say I blame them. It's miserable out there. Well . . . ." I began to get up with a groan. "I better get on the road."

"Don't. I mean . . . you can stay here if you want."

"Really?" I asked sitting at the edge of the bed.

"Sure."

"Thanks. There's nothing worse than feeling that cold air when you're already groggy as hell. Guess I'll move over to the couch."

She laughed. "Don't be silly. You can share the bed with me." She turned back to her son. "Goodnight little man."

I lay back down.

"I should have said this earlier, but thank you, Terry. I do appreciate your helping out tonight." She slipped off her boots, crawled on to the bed beside me, and kissed my cheek.

"I didn't mind. Really."

"You would make a good father, ya know."

"Rhonnie?"

"Yeah?"

"Who is Charlie's father?"

"He's a bit of a mystery. Pretty unpredictable. And he drinks too much."

"Doesn't he ever help out?"

She laughed. "Occasionally, he does."

I was already falling back into a deep sleep. My dreams became a warped sense of reality, an extension from the current situation, but in a way that felt real and perfect. The way I had always envisioned things to be.

* * *

In the morning, Rhonda woke me up with breakfast: eggs, bacon, toast, and coffee. She also invited me over for dinner that evening to thank me for watching Charlie. I barely had enough time to eat and catch a quick shower, before throwing on the same clothes again and heading to work. Nobody seemed to notice when I got to work, so I quickly slipped into a clean pair of coveralls that were in my locker.

Around 10:30, I left the garage area to grab a snack. Cockroaches scattered as I walked down the hall towards the break room. Halfway there, I heard Dolton hollering at someone. Overhead, dull fluorescent lights flickered. I stopped and listened.

". . . You're a fuckin' bonehead, Sutton!"

"*Wha*-at?"

Mr. Dolton was always on Eric Sutton's case. It seemed like he had something against the guy, but no one knew why.

"How many times am I going to have to cover for your stupid mistakes? Mrs. Thompson just called. It seems that *some*one forgot to replace her drain plug after changing her oil this morning. She thinks she's been leaking oil all over town and now is afraid to drive it back. So we've got to tow her back at our expense and do it all over again.

Christ! Why is it that almost every time a customer calls to complain about our service, you're the one who performed it?"

"I didn't do that one."

"Your name's on the log."

"Harry did it at the last minute, because I got called over to help with—"

"Yeah, yeah, yeah. Always excuses with you. At least be man enough to admit when you've screwed up! I'm warning you, Sutton, one more mistake and I won't *need* to put up with your bullshit anymore."

I heard Dolton start to leave, so I continued walking while I fished for my wallet and pretended I hadn't overheard. I noticed the intensity in his eyes and acknowledged his presence with a head nod.

He stopped in my path. "And you! If I receive one more phone call from your so-called *mom,* I'm going to dock time from your pay!"

"If you did that, I'd probably owe *you* money."

"Smartass," he mumbled and left.

Sutton was alone in the break room looking pissed. "What's up his ass?" I said.

"I don't know, but I tell ya what. He's got it coming to him. And if I get a good opportunity, Terry, I'd be happy to be the one to do it."

"Well, don't let old *Dolt* get to ya. It's a shitty job, and there are better shops out there that would be happy to have you aboard."

"It's still not right of him. He shouldn't be able to get away with it."

Sutton left. I bought some snack cakes and soda from the vending machines and zoned out for a few.

* * *

Around 1:15, we were short-staffed because of lunch breaks, but it was dead in the shop. I went outside to face the cool, crisp air to have a smoke. After a few drags, she pulled up in her red minivan. She powered down the window.

"Where were you last night?"

"None of your goddamn business, Karli."

"I came by your place twice and you weren't there."

"I was out." I kicked a chunk of ice and it slid under her van.

"Why aren't you taking my calls?"

"Why do you think? I told you it's over."

"Were you with another woman last night?"

"Quite possibly."

Karli let out a deep animal cry, put her head against the steering wheel, and wept.

"What are you doing?"

I threw my cigarette in the slush and walked over. "Here," I said and pulled a handkerchief from my pocket. "It's clean."

"Thanks."

She wiped her tears between sobs. "Look," she began and took a moment to regain her composure. "I don't want to be any more of an inconvenience, but I really need to use the bathroom before I leave. Is that alright?"

"Of course. Pull into a parking space."

She parked and got out. Again, she wore the long fake fur coat but with knee high black boots. I led her inside, down the hall, and to the bathrooms.

No one was around.

She grabbed me by the waist of my coveralls and pulled me into the bathroom with her. I didn't resist too much—I wanted to find out how far she'd take it. She locked the door to the dingy little bathroom and undid her coat. She was completely naked underneath. Her fine smooth skin had goose bumps and her nipples were erect. She yanked off my coveralls, reached into my boxers, and found me already hard. Karli jumped up into my arms and wrapped her legs around me. She was already wet and I entered her easily. She moved feverishly and within moments was already about to come. I wasn't far behind.

In that instant, I realized that this affair would never stop unless I was strong enough to end it. Suddenly, I withdrew myself just before her climax. She thought I slipped out and tried to mount me again.

"No! Enough!" I let her go. She still had her arms and legs wrapped around me, but finally let go when she saw the look on my face.

"What the fuck is your *problem*?"

I dressed quickly.

"This game has got to stop, Karli. And it's got to stop now."

"Fine!" She buttoned up her coat, unlocked the bathroom door, and threw it open.

"Whoa," I heard someone say.

"You know, Terry—you're fucking pathetic! You're the biggest goddamn loser that I know! I was totally wrong about you! Good! Bye!"

She stormed down the hall. Shortly afterward the bells of the front door jingled as she left the garage.

Sutton was standing right in front of me with a suspicious grin on his face.

"Wow. That was intense," he said.

"I guess so."

"Your girlfriend?"

"No, just an old flame."

"Ya know, she kinda looks familiar."

"I guess she has one of those faces."

As I left, I could feel his eyes watching me. He was probably rubbing his chin, trying to remember where he'd seen her before.

* * *

After work, I went home and cleaned up. There was a flower shop on the way to Rhonda's so I picked up a nice arrangement in a vase. Rhonda answered her door with a beautiful, red lipstick smile. Her eyes lit up at the mixture of roses and lilies.

"You brought me flowers! That's so sweet of you."

Rhonnie wore a black sweater with a long white skirt and black suede boots. Her long brown hair was styled and wavy.

"You look stunning."

"Thanks. Come on in."

Her apartment smelled like a Thanksgiving feast, but she had roasted a whole chicken instead of a turkey. And she had mashed potatoes, glazed carrots, a garden salad, and French bread.

While she set the table, I fed Charlie his formula. His soft head rested in the crook of my arm as his long red fingers gripped the bottle. He sucked the thing down in minutes.

"Do you breast feed him?"

"I'm not going to let you watch, if that's why you're asking."

We both laughed.

She set the table with a burnt orange tablecloth and placemats. Cloth napkins, china, crystal, candles, the whole nine. She put the flowers I brought in the center.

"You didn't have to go through all this trouble for me."

"Are you complaining?"

"No-o. Of course not. I just haven't been treated like this in . . . longer than I care to remember."

"I baked apple pie, too."

"Do you have ice cream for it?"

"Sure do."

"Stop—you're killing me."

We were fairly quiet throughout dinner. Every once in a while, I would marvel at her cooking and she would let out this sexy grin and whisper a "Thank you." Even Charlie, who was in a crib beside the table, obeyed the peace of the occasion.

"He's a pleasant child." I said. "I don't think I've ever heard him cry."

"I know. I guess I got lucky."

"I think he takes after you."

Rhonda gave me a large, teary-eyed smile. "I sure hope so."

I looked down and continued eating.

"Terry?"

"Yeah?"

"I'm sorry."

"For what?" She gave me a look, and I knew what she meant.

"I'm not the same girl that I was. Even though I've obsessed over Paul for so long, I've come to realize something."

"What's that?"

"That you're the only person who's ever been there for me. The only one who has come to check on me and help me out when I've needed it. Not Paul. And not anyone else. Only you, Terry. And I won't ever, *ever* take it for granted again. I promise you."

After dinner, we had coffee with the apple pie à la mode and talked about old times. We laughed a lot, traded stories about strange encounters we've had at work. At the end of the evening, she gave me some food to go.

At the door, Rhonda gave me a quick kiss on the lips; hers were warm and juicy. And then she gave me an affectionate hug. We held each other for a while feeling the freezing air from the outside mix with the warm air from her apartment.

"You better get in," I said. "I don't want you catching a cold."

"Okay. I work the day shift tomorrow and my sitter's available in the evening . . . ."

"Would you like to go out?"

She smiled. "Give me a call."

* * *

It felt like I floated home and into my apartment. With a grin on my face, I walked through the dark into the kitchen and put the leftovers in the fridge. Suddenly, something in the air did not feel right. My grin faded. I turned around and, with the light of the refrigerator, I saw the silhouette of a tall, muscular man sitting in my living room on the recliner that Karli had curled up on only days ago.

It was Paul. He was looking up toward the ceiling.

I shut the fridge and turned the kitchen light on.

"Paul? What's going on?"

A shotgun rested across his lap.

"I got a call from Eric Sutton today."

"You know Sutton?"

"Yeah, I work with his wife over at the warehouse. We met at one of our company picnics. He's had me over to watch some games and such since."

"Oh."

"He only met Karli once—at the picnic. But he remembered her well enough." Paul continued to stare off into space, not looking at me. "He said she came by the shop today."

"Really?"

"Did she?"

"I-I'm not sure?"

Paul cocked the shotgun.

"Actually, I think she *was* there."

Paul looked at me for a second. Those eyes of his. They could stop your heart. After a long moment, he looked back towards the ceiling.

"Ya know, Karli and I haven't had the perfect marriage. But it hasn't been bad either. I mean, things could have been a lot worse. I've treated her well enough."

"I know you have."

"And to find out that my worst fears have come true . . . ."

"What do you mean?"

"Eric told me, Terry, so you don't need to hide it from me."

"Oh." My heart was in my throat, my flesh crawled. I looked down and froze, waiting for the inevitable lashing. Or maybe just the boom of the shotgun and then my soul being torn to bits in hell. But Paul remained seated in my recliner.

"Yeah, he told me that Karli's been sleeping with your boss. Some Mr. Dalton."

"Dolton." I said feeling a slight wave of relief. Sutton must have heard the stories or maybe had even seen what Paul Herse was capable of. That was his plan to get even with Dolton. To give Paul a reason to hate him.

"Yeah, that's it."

"I had no idea anything was going on until today, Paul. I would have told you."

Paul just nodded his head. On his cheeks were streaks of tears glistening against the moonlight that poked through my windows. I'd never seen Paul cry in my life.

"I need your help, Terry. You're my best friend, and the only one I would trust for this."

"Help? With what?"

* * *

We downed shots of vodka chased with cold beers as he told me his plan. So I suggested that we keep drinking. After midnight, we got into his car, an old Trans Am, and took off. We continued drinking during the trip. Halfway there, we ran out of alcohol and stopped off at a gas station.

Paul ran in while I had a smoke outside. There was a pay phone, so I put in some change and dialed her digits. The cold receiver stung my ear. She picked up after several rings.

"Rhonnie, it's me."

"Terry? It's late. What is it?"

"Well . . . something's about to happen . . . something's going on and I can't get out of it. Even though I want to so desperately."

"What do you mean? Where *are* you?" A sound of desperation forced its way from her throat. And it haunted me.

"It's Paul. I . . . I don't have much time . . . I better hang up."

"Paul? Oh God, Terry, what did he get you involved in?"

"It's uh, I don't think this is going to end well. He'll be out soon, I better go. I just needed to hear your voice first."

"Terry—wait! I need to tell you something!"

"I'm still listening."

"I think you need to hear this now." She sighed from panic. "I've come to realize—although maybe not soon enough—that . . . that I love you."

"You *do?* "

"Yes."

*"Real-*ly?"

"Yes. And I can only hope that it's not too late and that you still want to give it a chance. I can only apologize for all the times that I've turned you down. I know how much you cared for me. Emotionally, I wasn't there yet. But I am now. And I want to make it work with you."

"I'm really glad that you feel that way, Rhonnie. Can't wait to see you again . . . I wish I'd never left."

"Please be careful. And come over as soon as you can."

"I will. I promise." Paul came outside. My body jerked. "I gotta go."

"Wait—" I hung up.

Paul nodded at the phone.

"Shi-it. I was supposed to go over this chick's house tonight. Ya know, lay it to her. Figured I'd better let her know that I got tied up."

"This chick have a name?"

"Yeah, uh, Jenny."

"Jenny, huh? Sorry I screwed up your lay." Paul threw me a six-pack. "Let's go."

The inside of his car reeked of alcohol. We popped open a couple of cold ones and he floored it.

"Did you get any pantyhose?"

"Pantyhose?"

"Yeah, for masks."

He chuckled. "We don't need to wear masks."

"But that was part of your plan . . . to make sure he wouldn't be able to ID us."

"He's not going to ID us."

"Huh?"

Paul gave me a glance that said, "I know you're not *this* stupid."

"But you said we were only going to scare him."

"Look, Terry, once you make a decision to go down this road, you must go in with both feet. You knew damn well what this trip was about. Remember what I told you I'd do to someone sleeping with my wife?"

He didn't need my response.

"Well that's damn well what we're going to do, Goddamnit!"

"I'm going to throw up."

"Stop acting like a pussy. Have another drink and you'll be fine."

I leaned my spinning head against the cool window. The streetlights blurred into long streaks. Everything else became choppy.

Paul sighed. "Oh, don't worry so much, Terry." The words echoed in my head. "We're gonna get through this just fine. And you'll come out of it a better man. Trust me."

I dozed off and came to as Paul pulled his car behind some trees off a dirt road. "Where are we?"

"Dolton's address is a few blocks away. We'll walk."

"Paul, we better think about this again. You're not thinking clearly. This is a bad idea."

"I've thought about it plenty. This is how it's gotta go down. Now, the way I see it is that either you're with me or you're not. If you're not with me—that means you're against me."

"No, Paul." I said shaking.

"Shut up. And if you're against me . . . that would make me very angry. You're not against me, are you?"

"No, Paul. Of course not."

"Then get the fuck out of the car, because we're going to do this."

I wobbled from the car. Paul came around holding the shotgun in one hand and a toolbox in the other. He shoved the toolbox against my chest, and I grabbed it.

"Come on."

Paul jogged through yards and I followed. There was the occasional dog's bark, but no lights came on. Everyone was in a deep sleep. It was after two in the morning.

We stopped behind Dolton's place beside a tree. It was freezing. The wind picked up and snow flurries began to fall. My hands were ice and my ears froze. I didn't think to grab anything for the cold other than my bomber jacket.

"Fuck it's cold." I whispered, blowing into my hands.

"Stop being such a pussy." Paul wore a flannel shirt, jeans, and boots. The cold didn't seem to bother him much; his muscles kept him warm.

Paul grabbed the toolbox from me and removed a couple instruments. He crept to the backdoor and picked it open. He motioned for me to follow him in. I brought the toolbox.

Just inside the door was the kitchen. "I didn't know you knew how to do that."

"There're a lot of things that you don't know about me, buddy. All right, he's probably sleeping upstairs in his bedroom. You're going to stuff this cloth in his mouth while I duck tape him to the bed, so he can't react or scream."

"Then what?"

"What do you mean, 'then what'?" Paul sneered out of disgust. "Just follow my lead."

We passed through the kitchen into the living room. Paul pointed to the staircase on the far side of the room.

"Paul, wait," I hissed.

"*What?*"

"I don't know about this anymore. It's not right."

"Fuckin' pussy," he growled. "Stay down here then. I've got business to take care of with or without you. This man's getting what he deserves."

"But he doesn't deserve this."

"Of course he does."

"I mean . . . he didn't sleep with Karli."

His eyes became large and questioning. "How do you know?"

"Because I'm the one who's been sleeping with Karli. She came to see *me* at the garage."

I couldn't take those eyes of his, burning with hatred, so I lowered my head. I figured that he'd say, "Outside, now!" We'd leave this innocent man's house and go to an empty field where Paul would have it out with me. Throw me around like a rag doll, bash my head against the trees. But instead there was this loud snarl—I looked up just in time to see sharp teeth and a mullet that swayed like a lion's mane. He never moved so fast. I felt the wind leave my lungs as I hurled through the air. I landed on to a coffee table and broke it in half.

My back ached. I couldn't get up, but was soon lifted off my feet. Paul launched me through the air and into a china cabinet. My arm and ribs burst with pain. I got up to my knees in time to see the butt of Paul's shotgun coming at my face. I was too drunk, too disoriented to dodge it. He kicked me a few times in the stomach with his steel-toed boots. He grabbed the collar of my jacket with one hand and lifted me from the floor. I caught his punch square in the face. My eyes watered and my nose throbbed. He did this again and again until I was close to passing out.

He paused—still holding me up. I spit blood at him.

"I slept with Karli to get revenge, you piece of shit! So you can beat the life out of me if you want! But you'd only be finishing the job you started fifteen years ago!"

"Huh?"

"That's right! You took the girl I was in love with since grade school . . . and made her your drooling idiot."

"What in the hell are you *talking* about?"

"Rhonda!"

"Who?"

"Rhonda! You know, Rhonnie! You beat up three bullies with a bat for her in the seventh grade!" My voice softened. "The girl that has been head-over-heels in love with you ever since—despite how poorly you've treated her."

"Oh, her. You *loved* Rhonnie? Why didn't you ever say anything?"

"How could I tell you? She was obsessed with you . . . and I was infatuated with her . . . But, the sad thing is, you've never even realized she felt that way about you."

"Oh, no. I've realized it. Realized it plenty of times. She was always someone I could go and have fun with for a while because she felt that way about me. It didn't matter how many times I left, she was always ready for me to come back for more."

"What?"

"See. I told you there were a lot of things you didn't know about me. The only reason I kept leaving her is that I couldn't stay with someone who was that goddamn dependent and attached to me. It's pathetic. I no longer have use for that woman."

I had nothing to say to Paul. I began to touch my face in places that hurt; puddles of blood came away each time.

"In love, huh? Shi-it." He let me go and I crumpled to the floor. "I guess we're even." Paul let out a loud sigh. "Just one thing. If I *ever* see your face after tonight, I'll finish what I started here. That's a promise. You got that? Which doesn't leave you with much time to become invisible. You're already history in my mind, pal."

He turned from me. I looked up and saw Mr. Dolton crouched on the staircase—holding a bat. He stared at me for a while with a curious look on his face. I wondered how long he had been watching.

". . . Terry?" Somehow, he recognized me despite my face being a swollen, bloody mess.

"Hi boss."

"What the . . . ?" He stopped and stared at the huge form of Paul Herse approaching him with a shotgun.

"No need to worry, pops. I was just leaving." Paul picked up his toolbox where I dropped it and left the way we came. He didn't even look my way.

I got up slowly and winced from pain with every movement. Dolton remained on the staircase, the bat still clenched and poised to strike. I brushed some debris from my jacket and watched streams of blood pour onto it.

"What the hell was all this about?"

"Don't worry about it. It was just a misunderstanding."

"But my home! It's a fucking wreck! You're going to answer for this you little weasel!"

"Hold on a sec. You know that big motherfucker who just left? He came to your house with the intention of torturing and killing you."

"What?"

"Yeah, that's right. And I found out about it just in time. I came here and saved your life. So I think, at the very least, you could be thankful for that."

"Who is he?"

"Your worst fuckin' nightmare. And if you want my advice, I'd say to forget that anything even happened tonight. You won't ever have to see him again."

Dolton nodded in agreement.

"How about we call it a night?" I asked.

He nodded again.

"See ya tomorrow, boss. Bright and early, huh?"

He didn't answer. I turned and left knowing that I didn't have a job there, even if I wasn't planning to skip town.

* * *

Outside it was colder and snowing heavily. Great big gobs of fucking snow. I knelt down, scooped up a handful of snow, and applied it to my throbbing face. When I pulled my head away, it looked as though there was cherry slush in my hands. My bladder was about to burst, so I took a long beer piss that steamed while writing the letters "F-U-C-K" in the snow.

I walked aimlessly through the neighborhood and occasionally held snow to my face. My hands were numb, but there was nothing I could do. After nearly an hour, I approached a main road and found a convenience store with a pay phone outside. Fortunately, I had enough change to make one more call and ordered a cab.

There wasn't a bench, so I sat on the sidewalk and pulled out my pack of cigarettes. The remainders were all broke in half from being thrashed around by Paul, so I could only get a few drags out of each smoke before I hit the filter. The cab arrived 35 minutes later. My entire body was shaking from the cold.

"Mary, mother of God, what happened to you, son?" asked the old cabbie who wore thick glasses and had fat earlobes. The inside of his cab reeked of mothballs and I reeked of alcohol. Folk music blared from the shitty stereo.

"Had an accident."

"Need me to take you to the hospital?"

"No. That's not necessary." I gave him an address that was only a few blocks from my apartment. I didn't have any cash left on me, so when we got there, I bolted from the cab. Left him with one less fare and a bloody backseat.

In my apartment I brewed coffee, put on a hot shower, and got in. The majority of my body was bruised. Touching anything hurt. I must've lost my buzz somewhere during the shower; maybe the blood that swirled down the drain carried most of the alcohol with it. I was able to slow down the facial bleeding and tape up the cuts to the point where they only seeped. I drank a cup of coffee and began packing. It didn't take long. I didn't have much of value to pack. I didn't bother with the furniture; it was crap anyway. Just took my clothes, personal affects, and some small appliances.

I poured a coffee to go, packed up the car, and drove off. The sun hadn't shown its face yet, but it was light enough to see my surroundings. Bleak as usual. I had always known that I'd come to a point where I'd leave town for good. I just didn't know when or why. But I was ready. Hell, it was long overdue. But I had to make one stop before leaving.

When I pulled up, Rhonda was already standing at the doorway holding a mug—she must have been there for a while hoping that I would show up. I left the car in gear and she hurried down in a robe and slippers.

I couldn't even look at her. I kept my focus on the road ahead.

"Oh my God, what happened to you? Are you okay?"

"Honestly," I laughed. "I've never been better."

"I couldn't sleep at all. What the hell happened?"

She started to touch my face, but I jerked away.

Finally, I looked at her. "Charlie . . . he's Paul's son, isn't he?"

She retracted her hand and paused. "Yes. He is."

"You should have told me."

". . . I'm sorry, Terry . . . but you're the only one that I care—"

Before she could finish, I floored it. Kicked some slush up against her legs, but she didn't flinch. I slowed down and watched through the side mirror as her tired, fragile frame swayed. She continued to stare where our eyes had last met. Then she crumpled down to the wet curbside and dropped her head into her hands.

I cackled a demonic laugh as my eyes welled with tears. One lonely stream rolled down my cheek. I continued to watch until her image blurred and melted into a speck. Finally, she vanished from my sight.

Forever.

Story's Inspiration:

I had a vague concept of a scene set in a motel room; I realized it could be an exciting location to begin a story. I decided to have a pair of characters engaging in an affair and the man, the lead character, wanting to put an end to it. Aside from wanting a blue-collar theme, I did not plan or plot this story in advance; I just let my creativity run wild and let the story unfold naturally. It was the most fun I've ever had writing a story, and it is also my personal favorite of anything I've written.

Q&A:

1. Was Terry just as addicted to Karli as she was to him? Or was it that he just wasn't strong enough to end it?

    It started as his way to get even with Paul for not having a chance with Rhonnie, but over time, he became somewhat addicted to having intimacy with someone, anyone.

2. Why did Terry tell Paul, at his boss's house that he was the one sleeping with Karli, when he knew Paul would kill him? He had the chance to walk away before entering his boss's house.

    Even though he didn't care that much for Dolton, Terry didn't like the idea of being responsible for another person's death. Guilt took control and forced him to do the right thing.

3. Why did you end the story with Terry leaving without taking Rhonnie with him?

    I get this question a lot, although I thought the answer was obvious. Over time, Terry despised Paul so much and lived in his shadow for so long that the mere thought of raising Paul's baby made him sick. Also, he looked at Rhonnie differently after he found out that she'd been sleeping with Paul *and* had his child—she became weaker to Terry than he thought possible and he no longer respected or loved her the same way.

Mike

Characters of Silence

It always happened when the room was too quiet. Random phrases once again raced in and out of her mind.

Black forest, red velvet, white wine, blue cheese, hash browns...

Her hands tightened into fists. She shook her head furiously and tried to dispel the obsessive thoughts that assailed her daily.

She wiped her hands across her apron and turned to the pot that was boiling over. As she put the hot pan in the sink, she noticed a movement reflected in the window. She turned quickly, but her guests were still sitting motionless, exactly where she'd left them...

Tabletop chairs held them captive, staring at one another. *There should be conversation*, she thought. This was no way to conduct a party. In her younger days everyone would clamor over each other, spill things and have a raucous, great time.

There was the movement again. Something behind her watched over her shoulder. Watched to see if she did it right, perhaps? She noted it in the reflection off the old grandfather clock. She swatted the air behind her head just in case it was still there. Again she experienced the uneasy feeling of something amiss but she continued her quest.

She drained the water from the eggs, walked back into the dining room and laid one out in front of each guest. She admonished them to allow the steam to evaporate before cracking them. She walked back into the kitchen and the phrases bombarded the silence again.

Black forest, hood winked, snow drift, mouse trap, hot potato...

Rage built up inside her and she walked to the wall. Methodically, she pounded her head against it. She gradually increased the force – each blow a prayer to knock the words from her mind.

She jerked her head straight as memories of what happened the last time flooded her senses. She did not want to go away again. She felt edgy, ready to jump at the slightest noise. The silence must be filled. The phrases were about to begin again.

She spun on her heels and returned to her guests. She must have cleared her head longer than she thought – all the eggs were devoid of the steaming fog. She went to each plate, cracked shells and peeled the eggs with deliberate, dainty motions. Everything must be just right.

When all the eggs were properly hatched and the shells discarded, she remembered she needed to serve the drinks. She felt a tingle of excitement. Her temples pulsed; her breathe came faster. She filled each cup with the red elixir and placed them on a silver tray. She carried the tray with quick confidence back to the party and fully expected this act to be the key to set things off.

She served each guest with practiced movements, then stepped back. She waited with her back to the bay window that faced the family graveyard. When a shadow crossed the wall in front of her, she screamed out in alarm. She clasped her mouth with both hands; each shoulder tried to cover an ear. Fear rose to her throat. She was in trouble now.

She knew there were sounds to be heard other than those she made. She knew there was something she was missing, something she was ignoring. What wasn't she hearing?

She reasoned she was not hearing anything because she didn't want to.. Why, oh why did these things have to happen to her? All she wanted was a party.

Silence oozed around her. It seeped into the dining room, a thick invisible cloud intent on suffocating everyone. She saw her guests drowning in the silence. She ran back into the kitchen and grabbed the first knife she could find.

Black forest, wolf gang, dwarf star, mini skirt, removable parts…

The knife would be ineffective against silence. It was not silence that plagued this party. Silence was a good thing. But why? Why was the silence good? It provoked her, yet it was a lifeline. She never could remain silent. She always did something to thwart the ominous fear that hung in the air whenever the absence of sound invaded.

She would bang her head, shake her body, just to hear the sound of her clothing, but she never said anything. That is why when she finally called out, startled, in the dining room, her agitation escalated.

She lowered herself to her knees, inch-by-mortified-inch, and crawled on hands and knees just as slowly to the sink. She opened the cabinet doors, backed in and started to close them behind her. Before she could reach for the doors, the sounds began.

A loud, sharp noise. A scream. Running feet. Methodical steps. Her body shook. She closed the door on her right, but she did not dare reach for the one on the left.

The screaming got louder. Her mother's head struck the floor with a thud and red ooze flowed from her mouth. Deliberate steps searched the room. Meticulous. Certain. The feet knew she was there. She clutched the knife in her left hand, blade out.

Little Red Riding Hood, Snow White, Minnie Mouse and Mrs. Potato Head. . . She saw them sitting on the table in front of their feast, betraying her with their silence. A hand reached out and felt the top of an egg. *Of course it's warm,* she thought. *Now I am in big trouble.*

She wanted to cry but the sound would surely bring the feet. She placed her right hand over her left. *Robin Hood parried with the Sheriff of Nottingham.* She mustered the thought and held it tight in her mind. She was coiled – ready to unwind – yet she prayed for deliverance. She wished the feet would just go away.

Heels striking the floor, heading her direction, sent her into dizziness. She squeezed further behind the one closed door. The feet stopped in front of her. Her temples were a drum set, pounding furious rhythms she was sure the feet could hear.

The feet turned slowly. The left foot, directly in front of her, looked toward the tea party. She relaxed slightly. They did not see her. Silence roared in her ears. She wished her playmates would laugh or cry or make any noise to cover her breathing. No one would help her. She felt betrayed. Alone.

The feet stood there, listening. She knew they were listening for her. Fear jumped higher in her throat. Her hands shook uncontrollably.

The cuckoo clock called out its hourly song. The feet whirled around. She screamed. The door flung open and crushed her last hope. The evil smile appeared. With all her might she parried hard and straight and twisted the knife as she pulled it out. The evil smile clutched its throat and spurted red Kool-Aid all over the floor.

Enraged, she jumped up and turned as the cuckoo appeared one last time. She sliced the air with the red knife, severed bird from perch, and knocked the house to the floor. In the pile of rubble, the words "Made in Black Forest, Germany" stared up at her. She stared back. Silence settled around her.

She remembered now. She remembered the day Daddy killed Mommy. She looked down at the clean knife in her hand – now an old woman in her own kitchen haunted by memories.

She cried softly as she helped Minnie eat her egg.

Story's Inspiration:

This story came from a prompt given by Angela Hoy with the *24 Hour Short Story Contest*. I love this quarterly contest. The prompts are challenging, the word counts low, and the competition fierce. You have to use some of the prompt in your story. I remember the words "black forest" and "red velvet" were included in the prompt. While my story did not win the contest, I felt it came out pretty doggone good.

Q&A:

1. Another story written off of a *24 Hour Short Story Contest* prompt. What is it that you like about this contest?

   I love the contest because you don't have loads of time to doll up your work, make it all pretty and wow the world. You must use your raw talent. I also love the completion. There've been times I look at my story and compare it with the top three and find mine to be a shade better – in my mind. Competition helps stoke my creative juices. I tell people this contest is the most fun a writer can have for five bucks!

2. What have you found to be the most difficult aspect of writing for this contest.

   Without a doubt, titling the story. I always flash back to grade school when the teacher would make us read a story then come up with a title. I never felt comfortable doing it then and I still stumble. I want to create a title that wows, but also does not give away the plot or ending. This is not as easy as it sounds.

3. This story is very dark. Do you begin writing a story with a tone in mind or does it define itself as you write.

   Generally, I begin each story with a feeling or tone in my heart. This is not so analytical as it is emotional. One of my personal goals in a story is to evoke emotion. I do not feel I can properly evoke an emotion I am not feeling at the time of writing. This does complicate matters when I walk away from a piece of writing and then return and have to recapture the feeling. This is one of my quirks, I suppose.

Tracy

Crying Ache

I have felt the touch of love's warmth,

I felt its tantalizing,

Yet mesmerizing,

And deceitful ways of happiness.

I have felt the desires of a kiss so perfectly passionate,

I couldn't think or breathe,

Even when not being perfectly kissed by that love.

I still feel it now.

I still feel the arms around me that made me lose myself,

My cares and fears for theirs.

My energies increased for the day to day struggles,

Knowing they were there if needed.

I miss the arms that held me,

Caressed me just right, not to tight.

I miss the breath you breathed to me, for me.

My heart beat a little faster,

My days a little brighter and my nights a little quieter.

My troubles, not so many with you.

My desires for you still demands my attention,

And that secret spot in my heart,

Crying ache and pleasure too…

Rebekah

The Switch

Sometimes I wish I were a man.

I don't suffer from penis envy or wish I had a hairy chest or could push our lawnmower or anything like that. But in a way, I am jealous of my husband. I wish my brain were wired more like his. I wish I had The Switch.

I'm talking about The Sexual Switch. The ability to turn desire on and off like a garden hose. One minute you're watching TV, minding your own business, then you see a flash of flesh on a Victoria Secret commercial and suddenly you're ready to go. Your Fun Zone lights up like a pinball machine ready to knock around a few marbles. Screw making dinner, screw the kids sleeping in the next room, screw the blinds cracked just enough for a nosy neighbor to catch a show if he feels like peeping. You're randy and you're ready.

The closest I've come to having The Switch was way back in high school. Make-out parties. Getting geared up for a little first-base, second-base and so forth, only to have lights thrown on, coupled with the heavy, purposeful footsteps of an approaching parent down rickety basement stairs. If that doesn't wilt your lily, nothing will. But as soon as all was assumed well and kosher, as soon as the creak of the closing door reached your adolescent eardrums, the lights dimmed, music played on, and the baseball game continued without missing a play.

I think having kids has ruined any chance I ever had of recapturing The Switch.

Like the other day when I decided my husband and I should take a bath. The kids were finally asleep, the wine was red and the night was young. A picture began taking shape in my head: the two of us luxuriating beneath the warm, fuzzy blanket of a million tiny bubbles, feeling my husband's body resting against mine, sipping our wine as we talked. I turned the faucet on hot, and dumped a whole bottle of bubble bath into the burbling water. I even turned on our old lava lamp; after two kids, the glow from a blue, Spencer's novelty lamp is much more forgiving than the glare of eight naked bulbs screaming from the vanity.

My husband appeared, his iPhone set to a playlist of soft, sensuous songs, filling our bathroom with velvet music. We sank into the tub together, clinked glasses and let the hot water dissolve a week's worth of tension. I started to feel like a person again. A woman. And, dare I say, a bit frisky.

That is until the crackling monitor in the other room belted out the latest hit from our five-month-old daughter.

"Want me to get her?" my husband asked.

I sank lower in the tub and shook my head, determined not to let a few warbling cries upset my still-tentative libido. I focused on the music, the wine, my husband's scruffy face cast in a blue shadow, and tried like hell to block out my daughter's whimpers. Already I felt the painfully-narrow window of opportunity start to slip shut, as my modest sexual fantasies were replaced by my fantasy of climbing into bed and falling asleep to an episode of Bizarre Foods.

The cries escalated to somewhere between whining and wailing.

My husband, who had fished my foot out from beneath the bubbles and begun massaging it, looked at me.

"You sure you don't want me to get her?"

I was sure. Because I knew that, though he would try his darnedest to get our daughter to settle back down (he wanted to get busy more than I did), he would fail. I knew this because she was teething, and the only thing that *would* get her to settle down was to nurse. The reason I hadn't already leapt from the tub and beat a dripping, bubbly path to her door was that I knew once I'd transitioned to Mommy Mode, there was no going back.

The music stopped for a moment, and in that gap of silence came a huge, shuddering yowl of a baby who wasn't taking no for an answer.

"All right, all right," I muttered, and pulled myself from the tub.

"I'll just hang out here," my husband called after me.

I sat in the rocking chair for just under twenty minutes, nursing my darling daughter back to sleep. More than enough time for my visions of intimacy to swirl down the drain with my now lukewarm bathwater. By the time I made it to my bedroom, my husband had relocated our wine to our respective night stands, brought in the lava lamp, and lay on the bed in just his boxers, smiling as if welcoming me to a really hot party.

I almost burst into tears right there; the last thing I wanted now was to hop into bed and play a little naked rodeo. And my husband looked so sweet, so openly eager to get down to business. How was I supposed to tell him that I was ready to crash? That our daughter had sucked my mojo out through my nipples, and left me with the overwhelming urge to put on my most unflattering, wrinkled pajamas and call it a night? This was supposed to happen, dammit. The lava lamp was still on for crying out loud.

My husband is a very understanding, rational person, but sometimes even he finds it cruelly unfair that my maternal self and my sexual self cannot occupy the same body at the same time. And when my maternal self comes to roost, her fat ass doesn't leave for days. Sometimes weeks.

I've been assured that this won't last. That someday my body will be more than a couple feedbags attached to a jungle gym. That my husband and I will get an hour or two of private time without being interrupted by a crying baby or a toddler's nightmare.

So, as long as my husband understands that I don't mind giving without receiving, I'll get through this dry spell and emerge on the other side ready to be reciprocated. And maybe by then I'll have something resembling a switch of my own.

Story's Inspiration:

During one meeting I complained to my fellow Rogues that I sometimes find it difficult to separate my maternal self from my sexual self. It made for quite an interesting conversation, and the Rogues encouraged me to write about it. The result—The Switch.

Q&A:

1. This piece is a switch and obviously taken from a real-life event. Was it difficult to know how much personal information you wanted to share with your audience?

    Writing about a personal matter like sex and what goes on in your own bedroom is always going to be slightly taboo…I think I sort of went for it without being shy. It's not like things were wild and crazy at that time anyway, so I didn't have to tone down anything. Sadly.

2. Has your husband voiced any sort of trepidation at having an intimate part of your marriage revealed?

   My husband is a pretty good sport about it. He's used to me using our relationship for comedic or illustrative purposes. Part of the deal when you marry a writer, I suppose.

3. Is this kind of experience something all new moms have to look forward to?

   I don't know if I speak for every mom, although many moms who've read this piece already are telling me how refreshing it is to know they aren't the only ones who go through this sort of thing. The only solace I can offer is letting new moms know that things will get better! I think it's much easier to write about what goes on in my bedroom when nothing is going on…which is why I wouldn't be so revealing about my bedroom life right now!

Jeff

A Breath of Air

Air. It's the thing that sustains our existence, but we take it for granted. And now I realize how vital it is. Now I realize how much I need it. Crave it. Have to have it, but I can't get it. Not right now.

I'm like a heroine junkie in a straitjacket—what I need is near, but I'm incapable of reaching it.

His strong arms pull me from the tub of water and I gasp for breath. The wet cloth of the hood covering my head sticks to my face and vacuums against my gaping mouth as I suck oxygen in.

"Did that help your memory, smartass? Ready to start talking?"

"Go to hell."

I take a deep breath just before he plunges my head back into the tub of water. I hear the echo of the thug's laughter, the gasps of fear in my throat. I take a couple hard blows to my kidneys and nearly open my mouth and let the water pour in, but somehow I manage to keep control. Each time he keeps me under longer; I feel faint—almost ready to cave in.

The last time I remember this feeling of suffocation, I was with you. Staring like a love-smitten sucker into your emerald eyes, craving the brush of your glistening lips against my skin. Hoping like hell you'd run your fingers along my thigh, caress my chest. But it was only our first time together, and I was nervous like a Little League player during his first at bat. Would I strike out? Just the thought of being in the presence of such a beauty crippled my brainwaves.

But you played it cool and made it easy. You let me in. And I fell hard.

I'm hauled from the water again—this time sobbing. Almost at the breaking point.

"Do you think she would take this kind of abuse for you, dipshit? Do you?" He pauses long enough to let out an exasperated sigh. "Do you want to die? Do you want to die for this bitch? Come on—where's the girl?!"

Back underwater I have time to think about his questions. Would I die for her? Until I met Tina, my life had been long, miserable, and devoid of love. And now that I've finally found true love, he wants me to sell her out and hand her over to him? Fuck no!

Am I willing to die for her? Of course I am. These past months have been the happiest of my life. She stayed over for the first time last night, and we had an extraordinary, intimate night together. Barely slept a wink. We had breakfast in bed and laughed at the news before making love again. So if those are to be my last moments with her—my last moments spent with anyone, present company excluded—so be it. I'll have those memories of bliss to carry with me into the afterlife.

Tina disappeared while I was in the shower—never even told me she was leaving. I reasoned that she needed to return to her apartment in a hurry and didn't want to disturb me. I pray she stays there—doesn't return until these guys are long gone. I don't know why they would be after her, but it must be a mistake. A mix-up. Either way, I'll never betray her.

After another eternity, he pulls me out again. "She's conning you, pal. What name did she give you? Trudy, Trixie, Tina? Any one of those aliases?"

I say nothing.

"Last chance to save yourself. Are you going to talk?"

"Go fuck yourself."

"Have it your way."

I hear another man walk into the room. "Eh, Johnny, his wallet's been cleaned out. No cash, no credit cards. I got into his computer like you asked, and fifteen thousand was wired outta his savings this morning. She worked him. If he knows where she lives— she won't be there anymore. We lost her again."

"Fuck, fuck!" he hollers pounding a fist against my back each time. "Well . . . looks like you're no use to me anymore."

Before I can scream, "Wait," I'm shoved so hard into the tub that my head cracks against its bottom. Pain shoots through my skull. A shrill sound rings in my ears. But that agony is nothing compared to the truth. I should've known she was a whore disguised as an angel. How could a girl like her have fallen for me? Didn't it seem strange that she asked for my computer's password as I entered the shower? Christ, I'm such a fool!

Dying for our love seemed romantic, but dying over a scam is plain pathetic. I know that's to be my story now, because he won't be letting me back up for air this time. And as I feel the butt end of his gun cracking against the back of my skull, I realize I would trade all that time spent with Tina—that whole fake experience of love, all the false intimacy—for just one more breath of air.

Story's Inspiration:

This was based on another Rogues' writing assignment thought up by Tracy McDurmon. We had to write a story revolving around the precious and essential gift of air/oxygen. So I thought it would be cool to focus on a character being deprived of that gift.

Q&A:

1. "I hear the echo of the thug's laughter, the gasps of fear in my throat." Was the sensory described in that passage taken from any experiences of being underwater?

   Yes, we had an above ground pool when I was growing up and I spent a lot of time in it during summers. I was always seeing how long I could hold my breath under water and remember listening to the sounds the other kids made and the noises I would make when I couldn't hold my breath any longer.

2. Would you really consider dying for someone you only met a few months ago?

   It's hard to say—I hope I'm never in that position! I think if I truly loved someone—or believed I did—and they were in danger, I would put their lives before mine.

3. What made you come up with the idea of a bathtub scenario and having to come up repeatedly for air?

   First, I needed to keep with the theme of the assignment—the gift of air. Deprivation of air by water torture is not an uncommon means to extract information. Plus it seemed to be the most logical, least messy, and easiest way to torture someone in their own home.

Mike

Lavender Hour

I used to sit back and allow the night to fall with all its impending disaster. The colors of the day would fade into pale imitations of themselves, then into a pastel purple before crossing over into the grays of late evening and the blackness of night.

It was in one of these lavender hours, which truly lasted but mere moments, that I embraced the answer to all my problems. I considered rebellious thoughts of upsetting applecarts, toppling expectations and the like. This required the one small thing I did not possess. Courage.

Yet in that lavender hour, I peeked at courage. Its cold-steel confidence challenged me. I could stand up to him - I could actually rebel! I explored this possibility. Courage presented itself for my possession. But then, I could no more stand up and speak my mind than a log can stand up and be a tree again. The lavender oozed slowly into gray and I glimpsed courage once more. He never thought to hide it; why should I? I viewed this courage as a way out of madness.

I knew I would have to support myself for the first time in my life. There would be no more lovey-dovey after dark. No more hiding his deformity in the hopes of convincing himself - and me - that he was still the man he'd always been. He would have me no more once I stood and defied his pre-eminence.

He accused me of talking to myself these past few months. I knew what he was saying - I was insane. Courage whispered again. It tickled my ear. It held my fancy with its tale of conquest and freedom. I knew it lay there, waiting for me to grab it.

That night, I knew he would be naked in the ocean. He liked the thought of coming to me as a salty, seafaring brute. It was the latest of his fantasies I had to endure. I put up the best fight I could, fearing the sight of his patch-covered eye, which meant the night was about to begin. He was strong . . . too strong. I could never hope to hold him off.

* * *

Two years stretched our relationship thin. Our yacht had been dashed on the rocks along with our vacation and dreams. We wore tattered clothes and dirty faces; we no longer looked to the horizon for help.

Each night he doused himself in coconut oil. He thought the smell turned me on. It was better than his stinking sweat.

Courage. I could feel it growing in me. I sifted through the makeshift footlocker, pulled back the tattered sheets and stared at my hope for freedom. Quickly, I covered it up and stepped outside our ramshackle shelter.

Without him, I would be free to think, to feel, to breathe. I could weather the storms that loomed over my life. I could prepare my food the way I liked it. I could strip naked without fear of provoking him in the daylight.

I made that mistake once. About a year ago, I freed myself of the sand-laden scratchy clothes I wore. He took this as an invitation to tackle me in the surf.

When I saw what had become of him, I fought with every ounce of energy I possessed. I didn't want that thing in me. It was a lumpy stick that bent at an odd angle at the end. He must have been hiding it from me since the wreck. We hadn't messed around for months. He always explained that he was still hurting from the injuries he suffered during the crash. I guess he had been. It looked like it would be painful. It was.

My reaction angered him so he bruised my face. It felt like an apple that had been bounced around and left to sit for a week. He avoided me for a couple weeks after that, but then the real trouble began. He wanted to convince me that nothing had changed, that even though it looked deformed, it still performed the same.

I tried. I tried to let him have me like he used to back home. But the sand, the heat, the deformity and my healing face all screamed that life was unfair – that he was to blame. At first, I pretended, but I knew he knew. Then I just didn't care.

A week ago, he asked about my weight. He thought I was sneaking food on the sly, but the idiot couldn't see where anything was missing. He was so dull.

Then the night came when I wrapped my hands around the courage and felt its cold, penetrating confidence. I let my fingers caress it, feel its strength, see its wisdom – and I believed.

I thought the night should be special. I dressed in my most provocative outfit – the one he liked and I loathed. I made sure my breasts were apparent - exposed beyond the point of a tease, which these days was not all that difficult. I coiffed my matted hair as best I could. Most importantly, I dug out the smile I lost a year ago when he began beating me. Courage had me in its powerful grip. I was determined to ally myself with it rather than him. I opened the footlocker, slid my hand down deep and came up with what I needed.

I walked to meet him in the surf – before the stupid coconut was applied. I timed my walk to greet him in my lavender hour. There he was, washing himself as if the ocean were his own private bathtub. He was singing an old Glenn Miller tune – off key, of course. I spied from the trees. It was not yet time.

The receding tide caused him to lose footing as he sang. I would have laughed in another place and time – but that place and time had long since passed from us. I watched in contempt. Behind me, I felt the swirling lavender tide of evening approaching. With a confidence I had never known in my life, I strolled toward his back.

I strolled well. I tucked my little chin to my right shoulder and ogled him out of the left corners of my eyes. The excitement that tingled my nerves surprised me. I thrust my chest out in an open invitation to grope me, and I let my skirt fall on the beach. I knew he would like that. He was a minimalist that way. He, of course, was still singing and facing out to sea. I was just as glad. He didn't deserve to see all that excitement coursing through me.

Courage in tow, I kept it in my right hand behind my back. The tingles multiplied exponentially and I began to satisfy myself. It wasn't that I wanted to; I had to. I must have moaned because all of the sudden, he turned, took one wild-eyed look, and was flattened by a wave. As he stood back up, I made sure to continue my show.

Excitement splashed over his face. He just knew he was getting it, but good, tonight. He approached puppy-dog smile and all. He puffed out his chest and winked at me like he was Tarzan or something. I turned my chin to my left shoulder with an inquisitive glance that he took as an invitation to drop his tattered shorts and pose. That about killed it for me; seeing him profiling like I was craving it or something.

I took "courage" in my right hand and pointed it at his chest. Imagine the look! Hammer already cocked, my finger released my pain, my fear, my inhibitions. The blow knocked him onto his back. To my delight, he struggled back to his feet and looked at me with disbelief. I ripped the skimpy top from my breasts and threw it aside. I smiled a genuine smile for the first time in a long, long time. I walked my most erotic, tabletop walk to within three feet of him, cocked the hammer and pointed the gun at his pea brain.

He began to cry; that made me happy. I noted that the lavender hour, which truly only lasted a few moments, was fading to gray. Time to say goodbye.

He wanted to say something, but I needed the moment to be mine. I cut him off with, "Goodbye, warden," and pulled the trigger. With a satisfying splash of red, he flew backward with the tide. It made for a tidy cleanup, no pun intended.

* * *

It has been five months and I am as content as one could be in this situation. Now I sit naked at night and watch the moon rise as the evening breezes caress my body. When he was here I was all alone – isolated in a prison of sand and abused by its only guard. Now, I am free, and I am not alone.

The protrusion of my belly catches the last trickles of lavender as the moon wins its nightly battle. I wonder, is it insane to name your child after a color?

Story's Inspiration:

Lavender Hour was written off two words out of a magazine article on writing. A lady was describing how her group puts two to three words each meeting in a jar, and each member draws two words out of the jar and incorporates the two words into a story. She gave the example that she pulled the words lavender and hour out one day. These two words intrigued my imagination, and I simply let myself go from there. This was my first experiment with writing from a female point of view.

Q&A:

1. What was it like writing from a female perspective for the first time?

I was thrilled with the end product. I've told the Rogues many times that I do not care for a lot of my own writing. My writing never quite measures up to what I want it to be. This particular story, however, exceeds my expectations because I know I nailed a female perspective. That is very gratifying.

2. What makes you so confident about writing from a female perspective?

I have two older and one younger sister. Until I started grade school, my mother was a stay-at-home mom in the sixties. My father was a policeman always working crazy hours and I have no brothers. Basically I was raised by four females. I learned very quickly how they thought. I'm sure this translates into confidence.

3. You place that 'courage' carrot in front of the reader very early on. This appears to be a very key element of the story. How much of that was thought out in advance?

Oh, from the very beginning. I knew I wanted to write a story about an abused woman, but I didn't want the complications of society around. Then I asked myself what a woman would do if she had the ways and means to set her world right. Every time the word courage is used, in my writer's mind I substituted the gun. This woman was in an untenable situation and had to make a choice of whether to live her life out abused or not. One of a woman's strengths is she will take action if her offspring will be affected. I wanted to tie that all in to one story. I also had a lot of fun with the words lavender and hour. Of all the short stories I've written, this one is the most satisfying personally.

Tracy

Being Aware

Do you pay attention to the world you live in? the world around you.
Do you recognize how it makes you feel inside? that buzzing bee
circling constantly around, fills me with oddities of being alive.
That single blade of grass slightly bent to the ground suppresses my
abilities to get back up again.
To the wonder of the trees as they dance around.

To the brush of the wind and its enticing sound.
The sun's heat on your face, changes your mood and your pace.
Try and pay attention to the earth and its forces as she calls your name,
She's trying to tell you where your heart should remain.

The quiet has a voice with no sound of its own, but inside you that's
where it's known.
Listen carefully and you will hear your heart's desires coming clear.
Nearer and nearer they are found, pay attention to the world and what's
within you will surround.

Rebekah

Headlines

When Ray first saw the newspaper on the kitchen table, he nearly dropped his whiskey. He snatched the paper up and stared at the headline, blood roaring in his temples.

LOCAL MAN ACCUSED OF RAPE. The date was almost ten years ago, and plastered across the front page was his own face: younger, clean-shaven, and angry.

"Carla," he yelled toward the back of the house, "what the hell is this newspaper doing here?"

"I didn't do nothing with no newspaper," his girlfriend yelled back.

With shaking hands, Ray crumpled up the paper and threw it in the trash, then downed his whiskey to erase the sour taste of his past.

The next time, the newspaper was different. Ray came home from work, headed to the kitchen for a whiskey, and saw it in the same spot, right at the head of the table.

"What the hell?" he said as he grabbed the paper and read the headline. NOT GUILTY. In the picture this time his face was darkened with stubble, his hair was longer and his mouth was curled in the sneer of a man who'd gotten away with something evil.

"Damn that Carla," he said, and twisted the paper into a ball. Where was she even getting these old papers? Did she really think he wanted these yellowed mementos from his past? He'd let her have it once she got off her double-shift at the diner.

As he poured himself a whiskey, he thought about how lucky he was that his attorney had had no problem attacking the accuser.

"That lying little tramp has probably smoked enough pot to forget her own name," he'd told Ray. Ray knew he was wrong, but the jury did not. Sure, his name would never be fully clear as far as some locals were concerned, but at least he'd avoided jail time.

The next week, as Ray was heading off to bed, drink in hand, he passed the kitchen and saw a third newspaper on the table.

"For Chrissake, Carla, why are you leaving these out?" he shouted. Then he remembered that Carla was visiting her sister for the weekend. Ray picked up the paper.

TEEN'S DEATH RULED A SUICIDE. He studied the face of the girl whose sweetness he'd tasted all those years ago. He'd heard that she died back in '04…an overdose or something. After that, the girl's family seemed to give up. No more harassing phone calls or threats. Ray was a free man.

"It's over, goddammit," Ray said to the empty house. He balled up the newspaper and tossed it in the garbage.

The very next morning, another paper was waiting for Ray at the table. He read the headline through the fog of a hangover. CASTRO RESIGNS. The paper was dated that morning. Confused, he scanned the other headlines, but not one was about him. He dropped the paper and prowled the house, wondering who was leaving the newspapers on his kitchen table. Then he saw that the front door was cracked open. He threw it wide and shouted out into the neighborhood, "You keep breaking into my house, I'll kill you!"

Ray shuffled back to the kitchen and paged through the paper but couldn't find anything to do with him, not in the local section, the sports, or the classifieds. Irritated, he folded it back to the front page, where a little blurb toward the bottom caught his eye.

NEW MIDDLE SCHOOL APPROVED FOR DRAKE COUNTY. Beneath that was a map of the county with a little star depicting the intended location of the school. Ray realized then that it would be practically next door. Adolescent girls would be parading across his front yard to get to school.

"That's right."

Ray whirled around to see a figure standing in the darkened living room. The male voice sounded vaguely familiar, but Ray's pounding head kept him from thinking straight.

"What the hell are you doing in my house?" he growled. "Get out before I smash your face in."

The figure shuffled toward the sunlight filtering through Ray's dingy front windows. Ray squinted into the dimness. "Did you hear me?"

"Oh, I heard you," the man said. "I'll leave in a minute."

Ray watched as the weak sunlight fell across the face of his accuser's father, old now, lined with years of grief and rage. He held a revolver aimed at Ray's chest.

"You'll never touch a little girl again," the man said, and fired.

Story's Inspiration:

This story originated from a writing prompt where a person comes home to discover something on his kitchen table that is not supposed to be there. It ended up being a bit darker than what I normally write, but this story couldn't have ended any other way.

Q&A:

1. This is your shortest piece in the book; did the length make writing this a challenge?

   Yes, this piece I wrote for a 24 hour short story contest and the word limit was something like 700 words. The premise was provided for me – an object is discovered on the kitchen table that isn't normally there. That plus the word limit made this piece one of the most challenging. However, it was fun to pare down the word count and still be descriptive and poignant (at least I hope it was poignant!).

2. What usually ends up getting cut when paring down a piece based on word count?

   Word limits can be a great thing – they force you to tighten your writing and eliminate unnecessary words…something you might not have done if you could write as many words as you felt like. Sometimes I have a hard time of letting go of metaphors or other descriptive language I would have normally kept, for the sake of getting fundamentals across.

3. How did you come up with the object on the kitchen table being a newspaper?

   I have always wanted to play with the idea of someone using a newspaper to send a message…I wanted to do something about newspapers being from the future, but decided that sci-fi really isn't my genre. Then I decided on newspapers from the past, which I suppose is what newspapers are. I needed a reason for someone to leave newspapers on a table like that. I guess this story could almost tie back to *Incubation* (my first story in this book). If I'd changed the character's name to Morris…he would have definitely gotten what was coming to him.

Jeff

Between The Lines

My cell goes off. If only I could bottle that confused feeling when you're disturbed from a deep sleep I'd make a fortune. It's nearly two in the morning.

It's her.

The text message reads: "Thinking of you."

I text her back with the same message.

She returns with: "Call me now – it's an emergency!"

It's always an emergency with her.

I call her and she answers it before the first ring finishes.

"I can't sleep," she whispers.

"That makes, how many nights in a row now?"

"Fuck you."

"You already did."

She leaves me with some uncomfortable phone silence.

"Oh come on, I didn't mean anything by it," I say.

"That's the problem."

"What the fuck's that supposed to mean?"

"Fuck you."

Click. She hung up.

I was having a nice night's sleep for once, but now she's got my blood pumping. Now, I can't sleep either.

I call her back. Again, she picks up right away.

"What?" she asks.

"What do you mean, what?"

"What do you want?"

"I want to talk now that you've disrupted my sleep."

"Well, talk then."

"We're still hanging out tomorrow night, right? Actually, I guess it would technically be tonight."

"Yeah, of course we're gonna hang. We can have some fu-un."

I snicker and a glow comes over me. Over the phone, miniature voices squawk in the background.

"What are you watching?"

"*Two and a Half Men.*"

"It's on this late?"

"It's on my DVR."

I hear the laugh track erupt.

"I can't believe you watch that God-awful show."

"I think it's cute."

She makes the sound of blowing hair from her face.

"Lay down, Peanut. Good girl."

I picture Lori on her side leaning on one elbow, the same arm that's pressing the phone to her ear. The other hand strokes the fur coat of her fluffy little Maltese. Strands of Lori's long blonde hair drape across her cheek.

I begin to feel a tightening in my boxers imagining me laying the same way behind her, caressing her, kissing her.

There's something on her mind; I know it, but she just pretends to watch her show while we maintain radio silence. I turn on my TV with the remote and scan the cable stations. World news, infomercials, paid advertising, and dead air. I forgot that the time on my alarm clock is incorrect. It's really a bit past four a.m.

"Fuck!"

"What?" she asks.

"It's after four!"

"Yeah?"

"Have you slept at all?"

"Not really."

"Are you going to school?"

"Like I have a choice. Are you?"

"Uh, I don't know. Probably not."

"Must be nice."

"Yeah, right. You ought to try having alcoholics for parents some time. They forget that they even have a son."

I put my face straight into my pillow, suffocating myself.

"At least you can drink when you want."

"Oh yeah, some consolation."

I hear a buzzing sound from her end. She's getting another call or text message on her cell.

"I hear someone coming," she tells me. "I'll call you right back."

I'm guessing that some guy she likes was supposed to call her, but didn't. Which is why she can't sleep. It seems that he finally called.

She only cares for me when she's miserable.

Yet another consolation.

This is clinging onto someone for the shear sake of intimacy.

Ten excruciating minutes pass. Just as I begin to nod off, my phone rings.

"Hello."

"Hey you," she suddenly sounds so perky.

"So what's his name?"

"Who's name?"

"The guy who called you."

"Nobody called me. I said that someone was coming. My dad went in to the kitchen."

"Bullshit, I heard your cell buzz."

"That's because I bumped it."

"Yeah, right."

"Tell me what you're wearing," she says. "And be sexy about it."

"No."

"Well, I'm picturing you anyway. Naked. And it's making me horny. You wanna know where I'm touching myself?"

"Stop it."

"Too late, I can't stop, ba-by."

She's actually breathing hard and moaning into my ear.

"Tell me that you're touching yourself too," she says.

Whether she's really doing anything on the other line or not, I'm turned on.

"Yeah, I'm touching myself. You sound so sexy, how could I not?"

"Ah huh, I got ya. I was just playin'."

"Bitch." I'm still aroused.

She laughs, mocking me. My stimulation fades.

"Oh, I just remembered," she says. "I can't hang out tonight."

"What?"

"Yeah, I'm supposed to do something with my parents."

"When did they tell you this?"

"Tonight."

"Well, what is the special occasion?"

"Ah-h, we're going over to my cousin's house for dinner, and then we're all going out to the movies. Something gay like that."

I know that tone in her voice.

"You're lying," I say.

"No, I'm not."

"Yes, you are! You're going on a date tomorrow night, aren't you? With the guy who just called you."

"I don't need your fuckin' accusations, ya know. And even if I was going out on a date, you don't need to know about it. So just mind your goddamn business from now on."

"I'm really sick of this game you play with me. This on-again, off-again relationship. One day you can't stand to be apart from me, and then the next day you're going out and you won't tell me anything about it. People at school talk—I know what's going on. What's the matter? You can't control yourself? You can't be with one guy?"

"You know, I'm really wasting my time with you. You're becoming a burden to me. Just a waste of my fuckin' time." She sighs.

"You can't be serious," I say.

"I'm getting tired. Don't call me anymore."

I hear a click and then the silence of a lost connection. My temples throb, my blood pressure races. What is it about her that has this hold on me? I lie back in bed and stare at the ceiling. Forty, fifty minutes pass and not even a doze. I'll never get back to sleep, not until daylight.

My cell goes off. It's her, of course.

She texts, "I'm sorry."

She texts, "I love you."

It's too bad, I think as I pick up the phone to text her back, *I'll never hear those words come from her mouth.*

Story's Inspiration:

When I was a teenager, it wasn't as easy to make plans and communicate with friends like it is now. I was limited to the house phone but now with cell phones and computers, the options are unlimited. Using this concept, this story revolves around a late night conversation between a teenage couple where the exact nature of their relationship is fuzzy.

Q&A:

1. Why did you decide to give Lori sleeping issues?
    Insomnia is something that I had struggled with in my 20's, so sometimes I incorporate it into my fiction. It can be a serious and crippling disorder. Although there can be many possible causes of insomnia, in this story I am insinuating that stress and depression are the main factors being Lori's bout of insomnia.

2. Why the decision to make him have alcoholic parents?

    In my mind, it's a bit of an exaggeration. He calls them alcoholics, which was my way to show that his parents are more into partying and doing their own thing, than being disciplinarians. He has the freedom others teens his age *think* they want, when he would rather have parents who care.

3. Why does he cling to Lori if she constantly toys with his emotions?

    Probably has a lot to do with his parents. He needs the affection and attention that he is not getting from his parents, even if Lori's inconsistent with it.

Mike

Witch Moon

A forest weeps of amputated limbs and millennial brothers felled by mankind. In this valley sorcery brews in answer to the plight of trees. Whispered chants and incantations search out flesh and blood. In a glade within the woods stands a crumpled hut and a hag casting her spells.

A witch moon sneers through dark, locomotive clouds at the lovers. They stroll hand in hand thinking the windy night romantic. The lovers pause to kiss while distant thunder sends squalls of rumbled warnings.

Overhead the sky quickens to a roiling cauldron of slicing moonlight and piercing darkness. Lips part, hands rejoin and the lovers' previous pace hastens to a slow trot.

A frenzied wind weds the moon and clouds with an oak and willow along the lovers' path. The tentacled willow's writhing limbs perform a macabre dance with its oak neighbor; the lovers taste the first wet messages of impending doom.

Straining against a vengeful gust, the oak hurls spear-branches through skin and sinew. On his back, the man is now impaled like a collected butterfly. The willow lassoes and snaps his mate's neck as she is jerked to the heavens. Now a lifeless marionette, she dangles over her lover.

Oaken roots strain to be the first to taste seeping blood as the hag and willow laugh. Gales descend into swirling breezes that whisper their sinister secrets throughout the forest. Darkness wanes, the hag retires to her hut and trees anticipate the next witch moon.

Story's Inspiration:

Witch Moon was written for a Halloween Story Contest with a word count limit of 200. This sort of flash fiction is exceedingly difficult to write and is an excellent way to learn how to pare writing down to the bare bones. I attempted to personify the forest and particularly trees, in their desire for revenge against mankind for man's propensity to destroy. In the story, the trees find an ally in a witch.

Q&A:

1. You mention difficulty in writing flash fiction. How do you get a beginning middle and end in 200 words?

    Obviously that's the difficult part. Hemmingway wrote the shortest story ever. It reads like this: Baby shoes. For sale. Never used. If he can write a story (a sad one at that) in six words, 200 should be a bonanza! I don't think I captured much more than a vignette, but it worked for me.

2. Is an important criterion in your writing that it 'work for you'?

    Absolutely. In fact, I think every author has their own version of this. You must get your work to a point that you feel it to be worthwhile to the reading public. I often read and hear work that is nowhere near ready. Authors can tend to pull that trigger far too soon. You come to learn that feedback and critique is valuable. The more you invest in those activities, the stronger your work becomes. THEN you pull the trigger.

3. Is critique ever bad?

    No. Even a bad critique is good in my opinion. For example, a reader states, "Your story sucks." This is a horrible critique, one that gives you very little as an author to work with. It does tell you a few things though. Something about the story did not set well with this person. If you think the person has enough insight as to give you some valuable feedback, I'd ask, "What about it does not work for you?" Then I'd determine whether to give the complaint credence or file it in the mental wastebasket.

Tracy

Voices

Sara stood at the shore, each whisking/whispering wave brushed her feet and gently washed away the pains of the path she had just traveled.

She heard a voice from behind, a soft, caring voice say, "No more worries."

She had heard this voice many times and recognized its sincerity. She felt her road ahead would be less rocky. Sara focused on the horizon, its colors blending, melting into the water. It seemed as if it went on forever.

"At last a moment that means something, an image I shall never forget," she said to the image before her. Sara took a long, deep breath and it filled her heart with peace.

The voice spoke out again, "You are never alone." Comforted, she began to weep, releasing her fears.

Waves crashed around her, each signifying strength gained in momentum. She began to walk along the mesmerizing shore, going nowhere, going everywhere. Sara's feet glided on the sand. She felt as if she was floating above what used to hold her down. There was no ground beneath her, no barriers around her.

A new voice spoke to her at that moment, sending her into a different realm. This small voice was excited and anxious to explain its find.

"Look," said the wee voice as it pointed to the open water. "Do you think that boat has pirates on it?"

Sara replied, "if you want it to."

The wee voice smiled and hurried off to a new quest, saying as it left, "You're weird."

Sara smiled back, lowered her head and nodded.

The day is perfect filled with only smiles and laughter and new insights. The same as many others, but a new attitude of appreciation and thanks fills the air. The day is blissfully changing into what it should always have been.

For the days ahead will be, never the same and all the voices she hears now, especially the ones that come from the heart, are recognized and she finds them their place in her ever changing world.

"It'll all be worth it," her heart speaks.

Sara says "It already is."

She is surrounded by what most people only dream of and lives how most beings only desire to live. She searches for new ways of living, with a new fire, simplicity, understanding and acceptance.

Her feet aren't so weary now. The shore's relief whispers strength. The voices guide her in mysterious ways. Sara follows.

Not knowing Sara was listening, a stranger once said, "You become your thoughts."

Sara simply thought, *Careful what you think then,* not really understanding the true meaning of what she'd heard. Now she understands the stranger was right.

She'd once thought she was alone. She'd thought she was forgotten. She'd thought she didn't have the strength she needed for what she saw before her. Sara became what she thought; alone, invisible, weak.

Because of a series of events she had stumbled into that dragged her down, Sara started thinking differently. Each event had led her into her new way of being.

Her thoughts now transport her and make her life more pleasurable. She becomes her new thoughts. Thoughts of sweet caresses. Thoughts of less stresses. Thoughts of possibilities she could never even imagine. Sara thinks and dreams with an inspired purpose, to be better than before. Peace and joy and lots of silliness to explore.

Sara's thoughts consume her at times. She must simply just forget: Take herself to the shore and let the waves do their soul-cleansing magic. "It is what it is, nothing less, nothing more," says her heart's voice on her shore.

Rebekah

Mariachi Bandits

It all started when Ruben found out the music store was closing. "GOING OUT OF BUSINESS," the orange and white sign in the front window screamed at whoever would listen. Not that he made much money restringing guitars, stocking clarinet reeds and ordering sheet music, but when he added his paycheck to the money he got for playing random gigs, it was enough to get by. Most of the employees were either moving on to greener pastures, or were just punk kids and couldn't have cared less that the store was closing. Ruben was devastated.

"Why don't you just get another job?" his best friend Frankie Panetti asked him as they sat on Frankie's front step, drinking a couple of beers and watching the neighborhood carry on its evening rituals.

Ruben stared into his beer can. "Another job isn't the answer anymore, Frank."

Frankie blew a belch out of the corner of his mouth. "What's that supposed to mean?"

"It means, what good is another crappy job making eight bucks an hour gonna do me?

Frankie looked thoughtful. "You could always go on unemployment," he said.

Ruben tore at the paper bag wrapped around his beer. "Yeah, but even then, where's it gonna get me? Eventually I'll have to get a job that will pay almost nothing, and I'll still be in my stinking apartment, driving my POS car."

Frankie took a swallow of beer and then hit Ruben on the arm with his meaty hand. "I got it. Let's go to that dog track they got out there on Highway 59. I know a guy who won real big out there last month. Couple grand betting a super-fecta that came in, one two three. Only cost him two bucks."

Ruben considered this for a moment. A couple grand would be nice. He could get his car fixed, at least. Maybe buy that guitar he had his eye on at work and book some time a studio so he could send some demos out to record companies. It would give him that head start he'd been hoping for. But then, the money wouldn't go very far, not these days. If he really wanted to change his life, he would need more money. A couple grand wouldn't make much of a difference.

A couple *hundred* grand…well…that was a different story.

Frankie went on about the dog track, but Ruben was only half-listening. Deep within him, an idea was seeded.

A few days later, it blossomed.

Ruben was stopped at a red light when a marquee caught his eye:

Join us for Cinco De Mayo, Sign up for Free Checking!

He looked from the sign to the sprawling bank with white columns and a drive-through that could accommodate four cars at a time. He stared and stared until he heard a honk and saw an irate driver in his rearview mirror giving him the finger. Ruben drove on, feeling a smile creep across his face as the idea burst into full-bloom.

"You want to do *what*?"

Frankie gaped at him from over his double cheeseburger, his open mouth revealing the chewed-up meat inside.

"*Shhh*," Ruben leaned forward, glancing around the restaurant to make sure no one was listening. "I want to rob the Reliance Bank on 6th and Waycross."

Frankie shook his head. "Dude, you're kidding, right? You can't rob a bank. No one does that anymore."

"Well, then, no one will be expecting it."

"No one does it because it doesn't *work*. You'd get caught, or shot, or you'd get one of those special bags where the ink explodes all over the money so you can't use it. They've got all kinds of stuff like that now."

Ruben sighed and squeezed a ketchup packet, using it as stress-relief ball. He'd expected Frankie to go along with his idea unquestioningly, not to throw up a bunch of rational roadblocks.

"Fine," he said. "If you don't even want to hear my plan, that's fine." He pretended to be engrossed with the Monopoly game piece on his drink, but out of the corner of his eye he watched Frankie's face as his friend hosted a wrestling match between his intuition and his curiosity. His curiosity won out.

"Well, let's hear it," Frankie said. "But I'm telling you right now, no matter what it is, it'll never work."

Grinning, Ruben leaned forward again. "First of all, can you play the trumpet?"

On his last day at the music store, Ruben waited until his boss was busy with paperwork before sneaking to the back room and taking the items he would need for his plan. He stashed them behind the store until the manager wished him luck and handed him his final paycheck. Then Ruben pulled his car around back, popped the trunk, and loaded everything inside, slamming the trunk and peeling out before anyone noticed that a guitar, a trumpet, and a set of maracas were missing.

On his way home, Ruben stopped at Reliance Bank, ready to set the most important part of his plan into motion. He entered the bank, noting the guard at the door with his thumbs resting on his belt as he eyed the customers. The lobby was open and spacious, with a ceiling that stretched two stories high. The marble tile floor amplified the clatter of high heels and patter of voices. Lush potted plants and plush chairs and couches invited patrons to sit, relax, and enjoy the complimentary coffee and donuts.

Also in the lobby was a large, cardboard display, announcing a Cinco de Mayo celebration to take place the next Friday. Ruben stood beside the sign, watching customers cash checks and open accounts and take out car loans and second mortgages, until a slight, young man in a glasses and short-sleeved dress shirt approached him.

"Have you been helped, sir?"

"Not yet," Ruben smiled. "I was wondering if I could talk to a manager. I have a sort of…proposition for him." He nodded at the Cinco de Mayo sign.

The man smiled back. "I'll see if he's available."

Ruben waited, trying to take in as much around him as he could without being conspicuous. Behind the row of teller windows to his right he could see safety deposit boxes and several surveillance cameras mounted above them. Then a set of double doors to the left of the teller windows swung open, and Ruben caught a glimpse of a large safe door on the other side. Affixed to the safe was a large sign: *Manager Has Sole Access To Safe*.

Jackpot, Ruben thought. That was the target.

A man in a jacket and tie approached Ruben, his thinning hair in a severe part tamed by gel that looked like it could deflect blows from meteorites. He held out his hand, and Ruben noticed fingers that looked like they knew their way around a piano.

"I'm Mr. James," the man said. "I understand you wanted to see me."

Ruben drew a deep breath and launched into the story he'd rehearsed with Frankie.

"I'm the leader of a Mariachi band, and we're looking to book with someone for Cinco de Mayo. I saw your sign out front, and we were hoping that your bank would be interested in having us play for a few hours. That way we could get some exposure, and the music might bring in customers."

Mr. James looked at the cardboard sign as if an idea was starting to form. "You know, we were thinking of having some sort of incentive for people who come in and open an account with us. Customers might be lured in if we had a band."

"That's what I was thinking," Ruben said. "But I'm sure you'd want to hear us for yourself before you unleashed us on the public...sort of like an audition."

"That's true, that's true," Mr. James said, almost to himself. "I'm sure you're good, but we wouldn't want the customers covering their ears." He laughed.

Ruben nodded, trying to check his excitement. His plan was taking on a more beautiful shape than he'd hoped.

"Why don't you bring your band in on Thursday morning around seven?" Mr. James said. "Then you can audition before anyone gets here. Sound good?"

"Yes sir," Ruben said. "We'll be here at seven."

Wednesday night, Ruben assembled his team at Frankie's house to go over the details. He would play guitar, Frankie was on trumpet, a friend of a friend of Frankie's (a big, muscular guy who'd grunted that they called him El Lobo, and Ruben hadn't bothered asking him who "they" were or why "they" called him that), was on the other guitar. A girl Frankie used to date—Julia—was on the maracas. Of course, they weren't really *on* anything, since Ruben was the only who could actually play. But each one had a prop.

"It's pretty simple, really," Ruben said to his team. "We'll be there before anyone else arrives. The manager is the only one with access to the safe. We'll bring in our instruments, set up like we're going to play, and I'll say that we have to tune-up."

The magic phrase was 'tune-up.' As soon as Ruben said it, El Lobo would pull a gun out from the guitar case and keep it on anyone who might be at the bank early, while Ruben and Frankie forced the manager to open the safe. Julia would return to the car and start it up, ready to drive away as soon as the other three emerged, their instrument cases stuffed with the money. Ruben had instructed her to pump the gas pedal before turning the key, and to make sure the doors were all unlocked.

"Don't forget to open the left rear door yourself," Ruben said. "It doesn't open from the outside."

"What about cameras?" Julia asked. "Or guards?"

"I've been casing the place for a few days now," Ruben said. "The guard doesn't get there until seven-forty-five at the earliest. And we'll be wearing our hats the whole time—the cameras won't be able to see beneath the brims."

Ruben had gotten them all matching outfits from the thrift store down the block – black jackets with white piping, red dress shirts, and sombreros with brims two feet in diameter. He made them try on their costumes before going home for the night.

Ruben stood before Frankie's dingy bathroom mirror, buttoning up his shirt and shrugging into his jacket. He donned his hat, studied himself, and suddenly felt very idiotic.

What the hell am I doing? he thought. *I look like the lost member of The Three Amigos.* He imagined his poor mother, crossing herself and murmuring a prayer for his soul if she could see him now.

Someone knocked on the door.

"Ruben?" Frankie asked from the other side. "You in there, man?"

Ruben opened the door to see Frankie on the other side, stuffed into the shirt and jacket, the buttons looking like they could fly off any minute and take out an eye.

"Look at us," Ruben said, shaking his head at their reflections.

"What's wrong?" Frankie sucked in his gut, straining the buttons on his shirt even further. "I think we look sharp."

"We look like a couple of morons. Maybe we should just call it off."

"Call it off?"

"Yeah, just forget the whole thing. It's too half-assed. I don't even know how much money we're going to get."

"It's a bank, man. They've gotta have thousands and thousands of dollars in there."

"I guess," Ruben said. "Still…I just feel like I've left out some major detail."

"Yeah—how are we gonna split all that money? El Lobo wants to know his cut."

Ruben took off his hat and tossed in onto the counter; it completely covered the grimy sink. "Where did you find that guy, anyway? He's barely said two words all night."

Frankie shrugged. "Just some guy I know from around."

"Why does he call himself El Lobo?"

Frankie shrugged again. "Used to be El Loco, but the guy at the tattoo place screwed up the 'c'."

Wonderful, Ruben thought. *The Crazy is so much better than The Wolf.* "Tell El Lobo he gets twenty percent," he said. "He and Julia get twenty each, you and I get thirty. Fair?"

Frankie nodded, stuck his hat back on his head and left the bathroom. Ruben smoothed his hair and replaced his own hat, avoiding his reflection. He had no time for reflection. It was time to act.

The next morning they were parked in Ruben's car two blocks from the bank. Stashed inside the trunk were the four instruments and El Lobo's gun. Ruben had insisted El Lobo remove the bullets before hiding it inside his guitar case. He didn't want anyone to get hurt. This had to be as quick and painless as possible. He couldn't imagine what would happen if they were caught.

"Okay," Ruben said, "it's five after seven. Is everyone ready?"

The rest of them nodded, their sombreros swishing against the sides of the car.

Ruben sighed and started the car, listening to it protest and splutter to life. It was the final sign he needed to be convinced that he had no choice.

He pulled up in front of the bank and the four of them got out. As soon as they had shut their doors and moved to the trunk, the bank doors opened and the short man who'd initially helped Ruben headed toward them.

"You're here," he said as he approached. "Mr. James said to expect you." He smiled at them all and cleared his throat. "He's running late this morning, but he said to go ahead and let you guys come inside and warm up while you wait. A few of us came in early to hear you play. We've got coffee and donuts, too, if you guys want any. Come on in." He turned and walked back toward the front doors. Ruben watched him, feeling like that little man had just pulled the plug and sent his resolve down the drain.

"What do we do now, man?" Frankie whispered. "How are we supposed to control a bunch of people?"

"We've got a gun," Ruben whispered back. "Besides, the manager's got to be here any minute. As soon as he is, we can 'tune-up.'" He tried not to let uncertainty color his voice. Mr. James *had* to be there. He was the one with the keys to the safe. He was the one who would keep his employees calm and direct them to do whatever the robbers demanded. Nothing could happen until Mr. James arrived.

They pulled their instruments from Ruben's trunk and followed the young man through the lobby doors he held open. As they passed him and entered the bank, he pushed his glasses up his nose and said, "Those costumes are great."

"Thank you," El Lobo said. Ruben almost smiled. For such a brooding, intimidating guy, El Lobo's voice was oddly sweet.

But the almost smile died on Ruben's lips as soon as his eyes adjusted to bright lights inside. Milling around were about ten employees, drinking coffee and chatting as if they were at a party. Their merriment resounded throughout the lobby.

"So many people," Frankie said out of the corner of his mouth. "There weren't supposed to be so many *people*."

Ruben gave him a nudge. "Just be cool, man. Follow me."

He led the three other members across the lobby, where the short man stopped and held out his arms.

"You guys can set up here," he gestured to a spot in front of a large window. "You'll be auditioning first."

The word *first* hit Ruben in the gut like a cannonball.

"First?" Frankie said.

The man nodded. "We've got two other bands coming, too. They should be here soon." The man looked out the window. "I guess I should keep an eye out for them." And he scurried off.

Frankie, Julia and El Lobo stood holding their instrument cases. They stared at Ruben, waiting. Ruben realized that none of them even knew how to hold their instruments, much less play them.

"Okay, guys," he said as he set his guitar case down. "We're going to have to improvise here."

"What are we supposed to do when the other bands come?" Frankie asked. "Hold them hostage, too? We don't even have any bullets."

El Lobo grunted something, but Ruben was too preoccupied to interpret it.

"Listen, we just have to stall them all until the manager gets here. Then I'll say the magic words."

"But what if the guard shows up before the manager?" Julia's dark eyes were wide.

"Well, then we'll have to just add him in with the rest of the crowd," Ruben said. "Listen, this is our only chance to pull this off. Just trust me. Now pull out your instruments before someone thinks something is up."

Ruben retrieved his guitar from its case and slung it across his chest. Frankie pulled out the trumpet and stared at it like it was a strange creature from another planet.

"I don't even know which end to blow into," he said.

"You need to put the mouthpiece on first, jackass," Ruben told him, silently berating himself for not teaching any of them how to at least look like they knew what they were doing.

Julia and El Lobo had both taken their instruments out and held them awkwardly, looking as unnatural as elephants on ice skates.

"When are we going to just do this?" Julia asked.

"I told you, we have to wait."

"Why don't you ask when the manager will be in?" Frankie said.

Ruben threw up his hands. "All right, fine. Wait right here, and for God's sake, don't try to play anything."

Still wearing his guitar, Ruben sought out the short man with the glasses.

"Excuse me," he said. "But do you know when Mr. James is going to be in?"

The man opened his mouth to respond when a woman across the room called to him, holding a desk phone in the air.

"Be right back," the man said.

Ruben watched the activity all around him and finally realized that his plan wasn't going to work. Who in their right mind would ever try to rob a bank with four instruments and an empty gun? Wearing giant sombreros, no less. They would be the easiest robbers in the world to find. They might even end up on one of those shows that features the country's dumbest criminals. Ruben shuddered.

"Sorry about that," the short man returned. "That was Mr. James. Something's come up and he's not going to be in for at least another hour. He said to have the bands go ahead and audition—he trusts our judgment." The man smiled. "So, we should probably go ahead and get started."

Ruben just stood there, unsure of what to do. Should they even try to act like they could play anything at all? Or should they all just bolt out the door and not look back? Sure, the bank employees might be surprised and bewildered, but at least Ruben and the others wouldn't have broken any laws. Since when was looking like four idiots in matching costumes a crime?

Shaken, he returned to the other band members, trying to ignore the expectant faces of the bank employees who'd gathered around in a ragged semi-circle.

"Well, guys," he said under his breath, "it looks like this is it. Don't play too loudly…maybe they won't notice how badly we suck." He swung his guitar around, gripped the neck and began to play. Behind him he heard the feeble honks of Frankie's trumpet and the sporadic rattle of Julia's maracas. He couldn't tell if El Lobo was even bothering to strum his guitar. All he could do was close his eyes, play his heart out, and hope that he was good enough and loud enough to convince the audience that they were a legitimate, albeit terrible, Mariachi Band.

He played the first few bars of *Cielito Lindo* with his eyes squeezed shut. Then something amazing happened. From somewhere behind him came the most beautiful singing he'd ever heard. Ruben whirled around to see El Lobo, his face tender and earnest, singing the words to *Cielito Lindo* in a voice that rivaled Placido Domingo's. Ruben's heart soared as he strummed the chords instead of the melody, allowing El Lobo's voice to fill the marbled lobby. Suddenly Julia's maracas seemed to find the rhythm, and even Frankie's trumpet—while still pretty awful—didn't seem as noticeable with the dulcet vocals taking center stage.

Once the song was over, Ruben dared look out at the crowd. The bank employees all stared at the band in expressions ranging from enjoyment to polite amusement to downright confusion.

The man with the glasses stepped forward, looking decidedly uncomfortable.

"Well, guys….that was…nice."

Ruben offered a weak chuckle but couldn't think of a reply. He guessed that no singing, no matter how beautiful, could mask Frankie's playing.

As if reading Ruben's mind, the man leaned in close and whispered, "You might want to think of losing the trumpet player."

Ruben glanced at Frankie, whose lips were swollen and red.

"He's a little rusty," Ruben said. "Maybe a few more practice sessions would have been a good idea."

"Well, thanks for coming in, anyway," the man said. "Help yourself to some coffee. And you're welcome to stay while the next band auditions." He nodded toward the door, where Ruben saw that another band was already waiting, clad in similar costumes, armed with their own gleaming instruments. They looked smug.

"Come on, guys," Ruben said, pulling his guitar strap over his head. "Let's pack it up."

"We're not gonna tune-up, huh?" Frankie asked.

Ruben shook his head. "We're lucky they haven't called the police on us already." He replaced his guitar, feeling like a total failure. That is until he heard a woman talking behind him.

"You were *amazing*," the woman was saying. "Your voice almost made me cry."

Ruben peeked over his shoulder and saw a heavy-set woman gushing to El Lobo, who was ducking his head, the tips of his ears pink.

"Really, have you ever thought of recording an album or something?" the woman asked. "You and the guitar player could really make some money playing professionally."

El Lobo merely shook his head. "Never thought about it," he said quietly.

The woman dug through her large purse and pulled out a hefty wallet. "Here," she said, extracting a small card from its recesses. "My cousin owns a small recording studio off of Monroe. I'll let him know what I heard. I'm sure he'd be happy to let you record there."

Ruben saw El Lobo take the card from the woman and study it. Quickly Ruben snapped his case shut and hurried over to them.

"Seriously," the woman said, now addressing Ruben. "You make sure to call him. Even if they don't use you here, you shouldn't give up." Her smiled revealed a dimple on one chubby cheek, then she left them.

Ruben watched El Lobo stare at the business card.

"Where'd you learn to sing like that?" he asked.

El Lobo shrugged.

"Well, I could really use a singer for my gigs, if you're interested."

Finally El Lobo looked up at Ruben.

"Do you know any Jorge Negrete?" he asked.

Ruben smiled. He knew his mother would be proud.

Story's Inspiration:

This story began from a writing prompt—a picture of a man and a woman dressed in traditional Mariachi garb. I had originally intended it to be a love story, but my husband suggested a bank-heist for the sake of originality. Coming up with the plot-twist at the end was challenging but I think it paid off (pardon the pun).

Q&A:

1. Are you a believer in happy endings?

    I don't think endings should always be happy—that's not realistic. But since I'm a mostly positive person, it's inherent in me to see that the characters I like find some light at the end. Forcing a depressing ending just because you don't want to be too happy usually ends up being cheesy or contrived. So yeah, I usually like my endings somewhat optimistic.

2. What was the inspiration for El Lobo's character?

    At first I thought El Lobo was going to be the antagonist of the story. He was going to ruin it for everyone because he was the wild card, the suspicious, silent guy. But that was too obvious. He really helped me add the twist at the end. Who would have thought a crazy quiet-type could sing like an angel?

Jeff

Flying on Pixie Dust

"It's time for some pixie dust," I say with a yawn. After a night of tossing and turning, drenched in sweat from nightmares, I get up knowing that I have no intention of leaving the apartment. Twelve floors up and behind my front door, I feel safe, secure, isolated from the menacing world. I keep the thick window blinds closed; the lights stay off.

I find the remote and turn on the radio to a classic rock station. From the fridge, I fish out a beer while The Who is telling me to ride the *Magic Bus*.

I dig through my stash in the kitchen drawer. Sheila called it "pixie dust." Said it's because when on it she feels "like Tinker Bell flitting about leaving a comet-like trail of sparks." Flying off to Never Never Land or some such fantasy world.

That's why she liked it. "Anything to escape the real world," she would say.

But the real world wasn't so bad, at first. Sheila and I were happy; we planned a rich, rewarding life together. We wanted a big home filled with kids and grandkids. Spending entire days in bed, we looked into one another's eyes, whispered words of passion, and made love for hours.

"David," she'd say, "I hadn't begun living until we met. You brought me to life."

I'd pick daisies for her and sing ballads on my guitar. She'd give me backrubs and read poignant poetry to me. Occasionally we'd smoke pot and laugh for hours, order Chinese takeout, and eventually crash out in each other's arms. We didn't need anything else; we had all we needed in each other.

Pixie dust was Sheila's codename for angel dust. Also known as moon dust. Also known as PCP. Pixie dust sent Sheila off on a fantastical journey to Never Never Land.

In the kitchen, I take a good pinch of weed and sprinkle it with a healthy dose of magical pixie dust. I pack the pipe, grab the lighter, and head for the couch while swigging another beer. I turn the TV to a soccer match and keep the volume muted. Through my stereo speakers, Foghat takes me on a *Slow Ride*.

I light up, take a deep inhale, and let the smoke seep out. This is known as "getting wet." After a few more hits, I sink back into the sofa.

Our paradise shattered one day after an intense love-making session—Sheila told me her father had raped her throughout her childhood. Her mother told her to keep it quiet, that it was a normal thing. I was blind-sided; we were the perfect couple. Where did this come from? I struggled with it for days, weeks. My angel had opened her soul to me, shared her most painful secrets, such gut-wrenching truths, but all I could think about was me—how it made *me* feel.

Shortly after that incident, she brought home some PCP. A friend from work gave it to her. She said she needed something more than pot to help her forget.

As I watch the tube, my fingers and toes become numb. My scalp tingles and burns. My mouth turns pasty-dry; there's a bitter taste on my tongue.

PCP can alter your perceptions of reality. The images of the soccer players on the TV screen repeat themselves like instant replay— only it's the same angle and it reveals nothing of interest.

On the radio, Lou Reed's singing about his *Satellite of Love* and the room begins to spin.

In the weeks after Sheila revealed her past to me, she became increasingly distant. Stopped hanging out with me as much. I told her none of it mattered, that her past didn't bother me. But that was a lie. And she probably knew it. She told me she was damaged, wrecked, ruined—that she couldn't be trusted. That her life would never amount to shit with or without me.

Although I chose to use PCP for her sake, Sheila kept saying she wanted something more, something transcendental. That's when her co-worker introduced her to oxycontin, and I began seeing less and less of Sheila. Without her around, I stopped using PCP—even gave up on marijuana and alcohol. Probably because I thought it would bring her closer to me again. Or if I proved I could quit, then there would be hope for her as well.

Periodically, a CD or DVD of mine went missing. Pairs of shoes disappeared. My electric razor, my clock radio, my iPod—all gone. I searched for Sheila, but couldn't find her anywhere. She no longer showed up for work. I asked around and learned that oxycontin was highly addictive and often was a gateway to other, more dangerous drugs—especially heroin. The day I realized my gold watch—a family heirloom passed down from my great-grandfather—had vanished, I hired a locksmith to change the locks.

I didn't give up on Sheila, though. I pestered her old co-workers. One person told me that she had moved in with her friend from work—a guy named Rick. Rick no longer showed up for work either.

Through the speakers, Van Morrison croons out the words *And It Stoned Me*. I go to the kitchen, grab a couple more beers, and fix another batch for the pipe.

If taken in bold doses, PCP can make you hallucinate, even make you feel euphoric. You can have an out-of-the-body experience.

That's why I started using PCP, Sheila's pixie dust, again. When very high on PCP, my memories seem real, if even for a short period of time. I always went back to that early period when we were so lost in the moment. And sometimes—for only a few seconds—I even felt the warmth of her skin against mine, the sweetness of her breath, the taste of her saliva.

I found out where Rick lived and went for a visit. It was worse than I could've imagined—his apartment had become a crime scene. He'd been murdered, supposedly drug-related. No suspects. And no sign of Sheila.

Seven years ago, a rap artist named Big Lurch had murdered his friend's girlfriend while under the influence of PCP. The girl's chest had been torn open, a lung had been removed, and a three inch knife blade had been broken off in her shoulder. Teeth marks were found on her face and exposed lung. When the police found Big Lurch, he was naked, covered in blood, standing in the middle of the street and staring at the sky.

One can only imagine how far a troubled person could descend under the control of a powerful drug.

Soccer players come out of the TV and resume their game in my living room. The crowd goes wild. I get off the couch, join the action, and run after the ball. I kick over plants, knock down lamps, and feel alive for the first time in ages.

It's been many months since my visit to Rick's apartment, and I've yet to hear from Sheila.

Yesterday, I thought I saw Sheila on the street. I followed her, chased her for blocks, maybe miles, into a pharmacy. In an aisle in front of the pregnancy test kits, I grabbed her shoulder and spun her around. Fear flooded the girl's face. And it didn't look anything like Sheila's.

I knew I wouldn't get a good night's sleep.

My teammate feeds me a pass towards my balcony, the goal. I open the door and kick the ball through for a score. The crowd roars then cheers my name. The blinding sun beckons me. I venture outside and lean against the balcony railing. A few floors below, I hear a little bird chirping in the palm trees.

The bird keeps singing; the chirps are crisp in my ears. After a few moments, I can understand the bird's speech; I can make out words.

"David," it says. "It's me, Sheila!"

"Sheila? That's impossible. You're a bird?"

"Exactly. I found a way to escape my life—I'm now in the body of a beautiful bird."

"Oh, my God," I say and look closer. The image of the bird on the palm branch magnifies before my eyes; I can see Sheila's face on the little bird body. "It *is* you! That's amazing!"

"It is—it's so freeing. I can fly anywhere I want at any time."

"And you came to see me? Oh, how I've missed you," I say, as tears well up in my eyes.

"I've missed you too—much more than you can imagine. And I'm so sorry . . . for everything, for all the pain I've caused you."

"Don't worry about that. I forgive you. Just fly up here, so I can hold you again."

"Why don't you fly down to me?"

"Don't be silly," I say. "I can't fly—I don't even have wings."

"Yes, you do, sweetie. Take a look."

And wouldn't you know it, she's right. I have a huge set of wings. Like a picture of the angel Gabriel. Like the Hawkmen from the *Flash Gordon* movie.

I climb on top of the railing. Tom Petty is belting out *Free Fallin'*.

"Here I come, my love." I watch her part her wings to welcome me into her arms again.

I lean forward . . .

Begin to flap my wings . . .

And let the wind take me away.

Story's Inspiration:

Another great writing assignment from Tracy where a story had to be constructed around images of birds, trees, and pixie dust. I thought it would be interesting to use pixie dust as a woman's nickname for a drug.

Q&A:

1. Are you showing that through the use of drugs, one's mind can become so altered that you can harm and/or kill yourself?

    Absolutely. Much too often people—especially young adults—experiment with drugs in an uncontrolled environment without knowing what they're getting into. There have been many cases where seemingly harmless people do horrendous acts when under the influence (see the answer to question #3 for more on this.)

2. Why did Sheila wait until after their relationship was going so well to interject the childhood issues with her father?

    It's hard enough to reveal yourself to a partner when the secrets are not as painful. Sheila had to be at a point where she could completely trust her boyfriend before sharing information so traumatizing to her.

3. Do you think that the details of Big Lurch murdering his friend's girlfriend needed to be that gory?

    Ah, this is once again a case where fact is stranger than fiction. The facts relating to Big Lurch are 100% true. I decided to use these details to support the validity of the narrator's state of mind and to prove just how dangerous mind-altering drugs can be. So, yes, the details needed to be gory.

Mike

The Flashlight

Thirty barefoot assassins crouched in the dark woods bordering a small cluster of houses. All was quiet except for the occasional metallic clink of machetes, knives and various other instruments of their trade.

The moon peeked briefly into the night sky, then dove for cover below the horizon. Through their night-vision goggles, the men viewed the landscape – a surreal battlefield, uncorrupted as yet by human suffering. There was a sizzle in the air; anticipation set their hearts pounding, widened their eyes in expectation, and awakened the bloodlust true to each man's soul.

Trained for years just for this moment, these men would make a statement that the world could not ignore. However, the acts of violence they would perform meant more to them than did the statement.

Each had lost someone to the ravages of war, and was now left with only revenge to fuel their passions. With religious zeal, each strove to promote himself to the front line of the next evolution in reprisal attacks. These thirty had scrambled to the top of the heap – ready and more than willing to wreak their own brand of warfare on the unsuspecting infidels.

The proud label of terrorist was one they all aspired to, and now had opportunity to attain. Foreign media sources had long ago euphemized their line of work, upgrading them from murderers to terrorists, and now it had become an occupational title, like CEO or Vice President. The title carried punch, impressing those who heard it, and exhilarating those who attained it.

This war was as much a war of communication as of physical violence. The internet had become a powerful tool, second only to the media outlets that had long ago been purchased to lead the propaganda campaign. To make this skirmish a media event of planet-wide proportions, one black-haired, dark-eyed young man in his twenties carried cameras instead of weapons.

The cameras, night filters, zoom lenses, and super-sensitive recording devices were top-of-the-line; this was equipment he never dreamed he would hold, much less use. His directive was to capture as much of the action on video as possible, then revisit the carnage with a still camera to document the results. His work would be posted on internet websites for all to see.

Of all the combatants present, he was the only one who saw the bigger picture in the actions about to take place. Still, his motivation was based on personal revenge; every time he closed his eyes, he could see the bomb that had dismantled his little sister two years ago, right before his eyes.

He could feel the fever pitch rising in the crisp night air as they waited for the leader to drop his raised arm – the signal to begin the attack. There would be no explosions or gunfire; the silent assault would be carried out on the eighteen houses simultaneously so as to draw as little attention as possible from neighboring areas. This would also allow his audio equipment, carried in by several of the attackers, to be placed strategically in ten of the houses. He could record the screams of pain and agony with as little extraneous noise as possible.

The phone lines to all the houses would be cut at the same time on a signal from the leader. Then, once the assassins entered the houses, they would slit the fathers' throats and then follow with the murders of the children and the mothers. The entire operation was scheduled to take thirty minutes.

As the lone cameraman, he could only hope to get video footage of one or two actual assaults, so he felt pressured to select the right house in which to begin. After some consideration, he chose the white house, three down from the street corner. It was a two-story colonial which housed a husband, wife, and two children.

His blood ran cold when the raised arm went down. They were off and running in an instant. He glanced at his watch as he followed – two a.m. The streets were empty; traffic for many blocks had been monitored all evening and diverted as necessary; this particular phase of the attack was the most vulnerable. Eighteen pairs of wire cutters were held at the ready as the attackers listened for the nearly silent verbal command from the team leader. Within seconds, the command was given, and the night of terror had begun.

He followed two of his comrades onto the porch of the house he had chosen, their bare feet soundless on the boards. Using keys that had been made sometime during the past year to fit this particular lock and deadbolt, they were through the door in mere heartbeats. One assassin went upstairs to vent his bloodlust on the children; the cameraman followed the burlier of the two men through the living room and directly into a master bedroom to the left. He was astonished at the terrorist's incredible lack of hesitancy; he entered the slightly opened door without so much as a hiccup in his step. A man and a woman lay sleeping in the bed. The assassin brought his machete up high – nearly striking the ceiling – and came down in one violent swing that severed the sleeping man's head. The end of the razor-sharp blade caught part of the woman's arm, causing her to cry out, still unaware of what was about to take place.

Dropping his machete, the burly man leapt on top of the woman and placed a knife at her throat. A small stream of blood trickled down her neck. She awoke and sobbed as he stripped her nightgown off. The man slapped her to bring her into submission. Her blood, mixed with that of the corpse next to her, covered her left arm, and she turned her head to muffle her sobs into the pillow.

The cameraman chose to leave for the second house. Rape was not something he cared for and not what his superiors wanted the world to see. In many of the eighteen houses, the women would be raped, but to show that would put the terrorists in a bad light with their leaders. They expected a pure assault.

He made his way out the front door, checked the quiet street, and dashed across to a one-story ranch that was home to an elderly couple. He hoped the promised delay of five minutes had not elapsed. He entered the unlocked front door and was met by the sight of two people lashed to chairs. Blood streamed from the old man's face; the woman wept – a bruise formed around her swollen right eye. Wordlessly, he filmed the two as their torture continued, their chairs turned to face each other. While the old man watched, the attackers beheaded his wife of fifty years. With one clean swipe of the blade, he too met the same fate.

Quickly, the cameraman grabbed his digital camera and snapped stills of the scene. After ten quick shots from various angles, he bounded out the door to the next house. His meticulously planned route kept him moving. Each house contained corpses in predetermined rooms. Blood covered everything. He shot ten pictures of each affected room in every house.

In the next to last house on his route, a particularly attractive, wild-eyed woman fought and scratched as an attacker raped her. The cameraman entered the room, shot a few extra pictures and then tapped his watch. The rapist glanced at him, quickly grabbed his knife, leaned over the woman as if to kiss her, and slit her throat.

After photographing the last house, the cameraman collected his recorders from each of the ten houses. He had been disappointed in what he could hear of the attacks as they happened. He hoped the audio would come out better on tape.

As he picked up the recorder from the last house, he heard a noise. The sound signaled potential danger; he was working alone, all the infidels had been terminated, and even their pets had been eliminated during the controlled rampage.

He stiffened, reached for his small survival knife – the only thing he carried that even resembled a weapon – ready to move at the first sign of trouble. Again, he heard movement coming from the living room. He placed his night-vision goggles over his eyes and strode with confidence into the living room, his knife in his right hand.

A shadow separated itself from behind a tall wing chair; it was a dark-haired waif of about six. Fear contorted her small face. His sister! He knew it couldn't be her; his mind flashed back to the familiar vision of her running toward their house with explosions erupting all around her. The vision always ended as she exploded before his very eyes. Shaking his head to clear it, he looked again at the little one, and lowered his knife. Seeing this, she ran to him and hugged his leg, and began to cry, "I wanna go home! I wanna go home!"

"You don't live here, do you?" he asked.

She shook her head.

"Why are you here?"

"My mommy had to work late and I got to stay at Aunt Martha's. Will you take me home? I live two blocks that way in the house on the corner," she said, pointing. He knew the house; it was across the street diagonally from the first house he had videoed. That house had been unexpectedly empty.

With eyes wide as saucers, tears ran unchecked down her cheeks. She looked up at him – holding his leg, silently pleading. A light shining through the living room window startled them. She dove behind the chair; he flattened himself against a wall in the hallway. He barely heard the soft whisper of footsteps on the porch. The front door opened with a creak. The burly man that he had followed into the first house entered, spotted him, and walked quickly over.

"Your time is almost up! Move it!" he said, then exited just as quickly as he had entered.

Once the man was gone, the little girl pulled a suitcase from behind the chair and opened it. She crawled into it, lay down, and tried to close the lid. Without thinking, the cameraman walked over to help her. She held something small and silver in her hand; he bent over to investigate.

"It's my light-saber. It protects me from bad people!" she offered.

Unbidden, he remembered how his sister giggled in delight with the toy flashlight he'd bought her. She'd made him turn off all the lights, then flicked it about in the dark pretending it was a sword, fighting off enemies by the score. In the end it hadn't offered her much protection. Anger flashed through him. He straightened and started to step away.

"You're not gonna leave me here are you?"

He turned and noted the panic on her face. He walked back, softly lowered the lid and fastened the locks with two audible clicks. In that moment – in his heart and mind – this little girl became his sister. She gave him a second chance to save his sister's life. Leaving her locked in, he went to the bedroom where Aunt Martha lay in a congealing pool of blood, and gathered the last of his equipment into his bag. With his equipment bag in his left hand, he picked up the suitcase with his right. The luggage was heavy but manageable. Exiting the house, he left the front door open and headed up the street towards the little girl's home. Half a block away, he stopped, left his equipment bag on the sidewalk, strode quickly to the corner and trotted diagonally to her house. He carried his sister up the steps, placed her in front of the porch swing, unlocked the latches and jumped off the porch in one leap. He crossed the street at a dead run, barely losing stride as he grabbed his equipment bag.

He joined the burly man at the rendezvous point, just as everyone received final instructions.

"What took you so long? We were getting ready to go back for you!" the man demanded.

"I needed to make sure I didn't leave anything undone. I'll sleep much better for the effort," he said as he removed his goggles.

Story's Inspiration:

The Flashlight is a story where I was attempting to shed my "good boy" image. I wanted a piece that would be challenging to write and read as well. In this story I experiment with writing graphic scenes without the scenes deteriorating into graphic for graphic's sake. I feel the scenes all support the story arc and are necessary to move the reader forward, yes, even through appalling imagery. In fact, on subsequent reads, I think I probably took it a little too easy on the reader ...

Q&A:

1. You say you are trying to lose the "good boy" image. If so, why did you choose to let your character save the little girl?

   Even in the midst of tragic loss, I still desire good out of everyone, even my characters. I suppose this will be the bane of my attempt to break that image. Try as I might, some personal traits and instincts are much too ingrained in me.

2. Is that where the almost 'sympathetic' undercurrent of the main character comes from – your personal traits and instincts?

   Absolutely. Most all of us want a happy ending. I am realistic enough to know that life is not 'happy' per se. I attempt to reflect that fact in my stories. I feel there should always be a healthy dose of bittersweet to each tale.

3. Did you write this after 9/11?

   Yes. I wrote this story between one and two years later. While I am not too sympathetic to extremist's positions, I thought it would be interesting to portray a terrorist with some 'positive' trait.

Tracy

Gentle Nudges

He isn't a desperado,
He has imprisoned himself
From all the pain given from others and of others.
He's lost all his highs and all his lows.

Bet she knows he'll let somebody love him again.
Before it's too late.
For her it's never too late, in a dream,
And she is a dreamer.

He pretends he's unbreakable,
She knows the truth.
He's trying, he wanders aimlessly across the floor, pounding his
head
Trying to stop the voice, his ghosts . . .

Trying to stop the noise.
The noises need to go away.
He tries to lay in silence,
He has almost given in many times.

Afraid of his own emotions
Unsure how to go forward,
Assured he won't go back to what was not so long ago.
There's an unseen force that surrounds him,
Driving him and he has passion for passion.
This gently nudges him along,
To a higher ground
To love without bonds,
To love without restraints,
To love without fears.

She knows he'll stop denying himself, her smile and his own
happiness.
She tries to lay and dream,

She only tosses and turns.
She knows she's got to live and dream before he goes and gets
himself in love.

Because of his own ghosts, she sees them too.
She knows she's got to find her desires lost so long ago.
She was always on his side.
She was always on his mind.

She tries not to hide what she truly feels anymore,
As he does.
He tries not to keep it all inside.
But their hearts are guarded.

He lets go a little at a time,
He's going to sleep well one night and wake up stronger than
before.
Someday he will find her heart next to his.
The angels are waiting and they know for now this can't be all
there is …

Rebekah

Beating the Odds

Nick had considered himself a lucky guy, until now.

I should know—I married the bastard. Took me fourteen years to realize what a mistake that was. But by then Nick's luck had, as they say, already run out.

The other morning he came stumbling out of the bedroom, no shirt, hair crazy, eyes red, beard black and wiry as my Aunt Thelma's wig. His eggs were scrambled with peppers, onions and sausage, the same way they'd been since the morning after our wedding. His coffee was still steaming, his toast buttered on both sides, a jar of marmalade at the ready. Everything was just as Nick liked it.

"Morning, Sunshine," I said, watching him shuffle across the kitchen.

He rolled his bleary eyes in reply.

"The paper hasn't come yet," I said. "Paperboy must've had a wild night."

That was another thing—Nick's paper. Not that he kept up with current events; he couldn't give a rat's ass about the rest of the world. No, the only thing Nick read were the dog track odds. Every Saturday Nick went to the track with his buddy Amos, armed with the latest odds from the paper, and a pocket full of dollar bills. There he and Amos spent hours and hours betting on dogs with names like Bringing Home The Bacon, Peter Pumpkin Eater, and Flyboy, sometimes winning, sometimes losing, sometimes forgetting to bet altogether as they drank beer and flirted with the local track trash. Come Sunday, I wouldn't see Nick until well-past noon, which was why Sunday was my favorite day of the week.

"Those eggs still warm?" I asked, watching him shovel a forkful into his mouth, and spill some rubbery bits onto the table.

"Mmm."

"Supposed to be a hot one today," I said. For some reason, trying to make small talk seemed better than hearing the clink of his fork and the deep clearing of his throat like the last bit of milkshake through a straw. "Might break a record."

Nick slurped his coffee.

"I may go up to WalMart later. You need anything from there?"

"Socks," he grunted.

"What kind? Work socks or white ones?"

"Both."

I jotted this down on my mental notepad, wishing I could tell him to buy his own damn socks and that I was leaving. Better yet, I wished I could buy him socks, then later stuff them down his throat while he snored next to me in bed. I know it's not right having such thoughts, but that didn't stop me from fantasizing.

"What time you leaving for the track?" I asked.

Nick slopped marmalade on his toast. "Well if I had my damn paper I would know how things are looking, wouldn't I?"

"Well since you asked so nicely, I'll go have another look." I slipped through the kitchen and out the front door not expecting a reply.

The sun was low and orange, already searing through the humid air. It was gonna be one of those days when you see tar bubbles on the road and your hands melt to your steering wheel. We'd been getting rain about every day, and this day was already scheming to drop more in the afternoon. I stood on the front porch, eavesdropping on birds and the distant grumble of a lawnmower, watching Tommy Mavis from across the street climb into his pickup, that little girlfriend of his peeking through the blinds. Their cat leaped from the wheel-well of his truck just as the backup lights came on. One of these days that cat was gonna get it.

But still there was no paper.

Nick was not gonna be happy.

I went back inside and found him where I'd left him, his plate empty save for some crumbs, his napkin crumpled beside it.

"Sorry, Hon," I said. "No paper."

He looked up at me, his eyes tiny in his puffy face, like slits cut in the top crust of an apple pie.

"What the hell?" he growled. "What happened to that skinny kid who used to deliver it?"

"You want me to hunt him down and kill him for you?"

"Did anyone have a paper?"

"I don't think so."

"You don't think so or you don't know so?"

"I didn't really look, Sugarlips. If we didn't get it though, likely no one else did either."

"Well, why don't you go on outside and check? I gotta take a shower before Amos comes by. *Please*."

"There's that magic word."

He gulped down the last drops of coffee, then handed me his mug and pushed himself away from the table. If I'd have known that this would be the last time I saw him as he padded back toward the bedroom, his boxers sagging just enough for his buttcrack to peek out at the world, I'd have paid a little more attention. Instead I stood there wondering what had ever attracted me to Nick Golightly in the first place, and when the hell things started going sour.

Like I said, Nick had always considered himself lucky. God knows why, though. His momma died when he was twelve and his daddy used to get drunk and whip him with a fishing pole. He barely graduated high school—as soon as he did his daddy kicked him out. I met him while he was working at a grocery store that ended up burning to the ground after our second date.

When he first asked me out, I accepted out of pity. But as I got to know him, I found that I sort of enjoyed taking care of him. Kind of like having a pet monkey. He was lucky to have me—that's what he always said. And I whole-heartedly agreed.

Then he met Amos. Amos, that scamming, slimy kid with more pimples than an eighth-grade gym class. Amos was the one who introduced Nick to the dog track. The two of them went off one weekend with whatever money they could rustle up and came back big winners.

At first I couldn't believe it. With a shit-eating grin, Nick waltzed into our crappy little apartment and tossed fistfuls of money onto the kitchen table.

"Holy shit, Nick, what'd ya do?" I asked. "Knock over a Piggly Wiggly?"

"I won it at the dog track," he said proudly. "Amos made me put two bucks on the fourth race and told me to bet my favorite number. So I said one-five-seven-two, and that was the order the dogs came in. It won me over two thousand dollars."

January 5th, 1972. My birthday. I stared up at him, his eyes round and excited, his breath beery and his cheeks pink. I think that was when I fell in love with him, because he bet my fucking birthday at the dog track. How romantic.

Our wedding happened a month later (if you can call standing in front of a notary with Nick, his hound dog Elvis, and Amos in blue jeans and work boots a wedding). Two months later Nick had won over ten thousand dollars at the dog track. He made enough betting and working construction that we managed to buy our own house and even go on a vacation here and there. It was a decent life, though not quite what I'd pictured.

I taught myself to overlook Nick's shortcomings—his crudeness, his temper, his addiction to gambling, his smelly dog—and embrace the things about him I thought I loved. He was an earnest man, a simple man, he was loyal and had his moments of tenderness. And he used to make me laugh.

Now the only redeeming thing I can say about him is that at least he doesn't beat me. As if that should be a selling point.

"Anyone home?"

I heard Amos letting himself in the front door as usual and groaned.

"Go away," I said, just as his pimple-scarred face appeared around the corner.

"Morning, Pam." He sauntered through the kitchen to the fridge and helped himself to a beer, snapped it open and took a big swallow.

"Is it still morning?" I asked. "Your choice of drink kind of threw me."

Amos laughed, revealing his gray teeth, something caught between two of them.

"Ah Pam, always a riot."

"I'll be here all night."

"Where's your better half?"

"Hosing off somewhere."

Amos moseyed to our couch and threw himself on it, sighing like he'd just finished a hard day's work, something of which Amos has never known.

"He see the odds today?"

"No," I said, shoving a coaster at him. "We never got the paper."

Amos' blonde eyebrows shot up. "No kidding. You should've said so. I could have bought one on the way over."

"Well I would've tried to reach you telepathically, but my brainwaves don't go that slow."

Amos winked at me and swigged his beer.

"Can't you guys just get the odds at the track?" I asked.

"Yeah, but we gotta be prepared, Pammy. We gotta get a feel for the day's races before we go in there and start laying our money down."

"So luck's got nothing to do with it?"

"Luck always has *something* to do with it. But it's a skill that's gotta be learned. Like…like hunting…or knitting sweaters."

"What are you two yammering about in there?" Nick called from the back of the house.

"Nicki!" Amos called. "Where's your paper at, boy?"

"Gotta get us one on the way," Nick called back. "That Piggly Wiggly sells 'em."

"Good," I said. "Your problem is solved. Now please get your nasty-ass shoes off my coffee table."

"Your wife is sassing me, Nicki!" Amos winked again. I wanted to haul off and punch him.

"Women," Nick said. "Can't live with 'em, can't bury 'em in the backyard."

"Well you men have been a pleasure, but I've got errands to run." I walked past Amos, slapping his long legs with a dishrag as I went. "Don't wake me up when you jack-asses come home."

"Don't forget my socks," Nick called after me.

"Thanks for the beer, Missus." Amos held it up as if toasting my hospitality.

"Have fun at the track." I grabbed my purse and keys, and left the house.

Sometimes when a person gets into trouble, he's said to be in the wrong place at the wrong time. That always sounded kind of cruel to me, like the person brought it on himself somehow. But honestly, that's how it was with Nick.

According to Amos, the day started out fine. The two of them bought a paper from the Piggly Wiggly on their way to the track and poured over the odds like two hogs at a trough. I've been to that Piggly

Wiggly—the candy bars are coated in dust and the coffee could peel paint off a car. Apparently the storeowner doesn't sell many papers, and doesn't change out the ones on the stand. So that morning the paper was four weeks old, and the guys didn't have a clue. They'd read those odds for years—after a while they all kind of ran together.

The guys arrived at the track just before noon. The place was already hopping. Usually Nick and Amos were among the first to get there, but the stop along the way had set them back—they had to have their usual discussion of who they liked in what race and all that.

"Look at this one in the fifth," Nick said as they sat in Amos's car. "Mister Blister's got eight-to-one, but I got a feeling he's gonna pull away and win."

Of course he had a feeling Mister Blister was gonna win— Mister Blister had *already* won. Nick wasn't feeling lucky, he was just remembering the races from last month. I guess when you don't know it, you can mistake a decent memory and a strong cup of coffee for luck.

"I'm thinking Blister, then Jet-Settter to place," Amos said. "Then either Real Deal or Skin Of His Teeth to show. What do you think?"

Nick frowned. I could just picture him pulling on that rat's nest of a beard as he mulled over Amos' choices.

"Blister, Jet-Setter, then…" Nick scanned the odds for the fifth race again, "…how about Luck Be A Lady? Yeah, that's the one. Look, she took fourth last race, so she's ready to show this time. Trust me."

Amos numbered the dogs as Nick had said.

"I got a feeling today, Amos." Nick folded the paper under one arm as the guys headed toward the track. "I'm betting hard every race. We're gonna be richer'n hell after today."

They fought through the throng of people, women in cuts-offs, men in trucker caps, old ladies clutching their purses and trying to keep from getting mowed down. I've seen it before. It's ugly as a possum's ass down there. The floor is sticky and covered with cigarette butts and losing tickets and spilled beer. Some days you can just tell who has come straight from the check-cashing place, eager to drop their weekly pay on a bunch of dogs chasing an electric rabbit. Sometimes people even bring their kids. Little brats run wild down by the track, spooking the dogs, eating peanuts and throwing the shells at each other. Kids like that don't have a chance if you ask me. I'm glad Nick and I never bothered having any.

Nick and Amos got themselves a couple of beers, then went to the betting window. Armed with his picks, Nick glanced above the betting window at the marquee displaying the dogs and their odds for the first race.

"What the hell?"

"What's wrong?" Amos asked.

"Look here. These dogs don't line up with the ones up there." He pointed the marquee out to Amos.

"Bunny-Hop, Tanqueray, Regal Beagle?" Amos frowned. "That don't sound right."

"I know."

"Maybe the bookie knows what's up."

"Yeah, maybe. I'll ask him."

Nick was next in line, and after the man in front of him finished, Nick leaned on the window, his odds in one hand.

"What's going on with the marquee?" he asked the bookie.

"What do you mean? Nothing's going on with it."

"Why're the dogs different than the ones I got?"

"You must have the wrong ones. Whatever the marquee says is what's running."

"But I've got in all right here in the paper," Nick pulled out the odds page from the newspaper and slapped it on the counter. "Look. None of them jive with yours."

The bookie shrugged. "Looks like your paper's a couple weeks too late, son. Now you placing a bet or what?"

Before Nick could answer, there came a terrible groan from somewhere beneath them. Amos said it sounded like God's stomach growling. Amos felt the ground move, felt himself start to slip sideways, and he grabbed onto a nearby pillar to steady himself. He heard people shout 'earthquake,' but didn't think that was right. Earthquakes don't happen in Florida.

And that's when Amos saw the floor crack open, just split in front of him, a great big old mouth about to swallow him whole. People screamed and stumbled, and chunks of plaster started raining down on everyone. Amos ducked his head and began to pray, useless as nipples on a man.

When he finally got the balls to open his eyes, he saw a hole had opened up not five feet from where he was huddled up beside that pillar. It was jagged and dark, cracks in the floor like a dry creek bed. He got onto his hands and knees and crawled to the edge, not too close, but close enough to see that it went down pretty deep, and there was water rushing into the bottom of it.

"Well I'll be dog," Amos murmured. "A damn sinkhole. Hey Nicki, you gotta see this." He looked around. Nick was nowhere.

Amos stood then, brushing white powder from his jeans. He scanned the place—people getting to their feet, blinking like they were coming out of a dream. No one seemed to be hurt, though he could see one fat woman hyperventilating, another woman next to her, trying to get her to breathe into a McDonald's bag.

He looked back at the hole. It was about six feet across, and oblong, like a giant eye. He could see the layers beneath it, the cement floor, the foundation, some mud and dirt and rock, all different colored stripes of earth.

He side-stepped the hole, peering inside once more. That's when he saw Nick.

"Holy shit, *Nicki*!"

Nick had surfaced and was floating face down in the water. Amos could see the back of his head had been smashed in, *like a piñata* was how he described it. All busted open, his brain the candy spilling out. Even if Amos could swim, he wouldn't have jumped down after Nick. He was about as dead as you could get.

***

My attorney says I can sue the builder of the dog track. *Building on a geologically unsound area*, he says. Or I can sue the owner, if I'd rather. Or I can sue both. Either way, I could be a very rich lady.

I don't really miss Nick, so it seems kind of wrong to sue. I'm sure his family of buzzards will come calling as soon as they know about the money. A few of them are already being super-nice. Suing might be more of a headache than it's worth.

And while I don't blame Amos for what happened, I know that if Nick had never met him, he'd still be alive. But then again, maybe that's when you argue that Nick's number was up. I mean, what are the odds that a sinkhole is gonna open up right under your feet? Pretty slim, I imagine. It takes one lucky person to beat odds like that.

Story's Inspiration:

This story began from a writing prompt—"Nick had always considered himself a lucky guy." I had enjoyed the language and style of Five Easy Minutes so much that I sort of borrowed the neighborhood and shifted focus to another couple living on the same street. It is my intention to write several more pieces based on people from this fictitious neighborhood.

Q&A:

1. This is another story where the heroine is in a relationship with a less-than-desirable man. Is there something more to this than just fiction?

    That's an interesting point—I am actually married to man who is pretty much the exact opposite of the husband in this story and in Five Easy Minutes. I think that's why I'm drawn to working with characters who are so different from people I interact with every day. It's fascinating to me that some people live like this. I've never had to deal with this sort of 'Cave Man' mentality.

2. What gave you the sink hole idea?

    I just thought the irony of a sink hole opening up in a place where people are expecting to be lucky was kind of neat. Plus here in Florida sink holes make the news every once in a while. And because I opened the piece promising that things were not going to work out for Nick, I needed something dramatic to happen that sealed the promise for my readers.

3. During the sink hole scene you had to shift perspective because the narrator wasn't actually there—was that challenging to write?

It was kind of awkward at first—I wasn't sure how to present the scene without the narrator actually witnessing it, and because the person she receives the details from (Amos) isn't necessarily an intelligent man. But describing the scene through Amos's eyes was kind of fun, because the comparisons he had to come up with (God's stomach growling, Nick's head split like a piñata) were fun to come up with. So yes, it was challenging, but I like a writing challenge.

Jeff

A Window to Your Soul

You laughed in your sleep last night; it was quite exquisite. It reminded me of the time we visited Mills Pond and sat on the ledge as our toes swished in the warm July water. We plucked buttercups, held them under our chins, and laughed at the yellow glow against our skin. And then we blew the seeds of dandelions into the wind and watched them spread out drifting to their destinations.

Without turning, you said, "Dreams are the window to one's soul."

I'd like to believe that now, but I didn't even understand it then.

After a length of silence, you said, "I wish I were like one of those seeds and could just fly off to somewhere new."

In my heart, I believed that you would leave as soon as you were old enough. No matter the situation, you'd act so brave—unlike me. Sometimes it's hard to believe we're twins. We don't even look alike. Never have.

Remember Danny Bershum? The crush he had on you? He practically followed you around everywhere . . . I think you had a crush on him too but brushed him off because you knew I liked him.

But then one day he told you I was ugly and he couldn't understand how we could be related, let alone twins. You clobbered him on the head with your schoolbooks so hard that he lost three teeth and blacked out.

Yeah . . . how simple things seemed back then . . . how wondrous. How many times did we sneak through the cornfields at old man Watson's farm? You would lug around that sack full of smooth pebbles. Like a couple of boys, we hurled them at his aluminum awning; it sounded like a thousand firecrackers goin' off. Good Lord, would he be angry. He'd storm out every time, face as red as a hen's wattle! I never failed to panic, but you were fearless. Even the time I fell and hurt my knee while fleeing, you remained calm, came back and carried me away before he found us. Poor bugger never knew we were the ones. Thanks to you.

You constantly looked out for me. I guess it needed to be the other way too at times, but I was never strong enough. But that's going to change. Right now.

When the doctor comes in, I'll tell him about the laugh and maybe he'll agree that dreams *are* the window to one's soul. And your laugh last night means that your soul is happy. Happy enough to recover from this coma.

Happy enough that you'll never again do something so stupid.

Story's Inspiration:

I needed to write a sudden fiction piece for a creative writing class I took a few years back. I hadn't written anything so short and had no idea what to write about. Then one night, I was awakened by my girlfriend's laughter. When I turned over to ask her what was so funny, I saw that she was fast asleep. She was laughing in her sleep. That was the spark I needed to create this sudden fiction piece.

Q&A:

1. Why did you decide to have the characters in this piece be twins?

   I wanted there to be a link between the sisters beyond that of normal siblings. I wanted the narrator to have a strong emotional connection that only twins could have.

2. Were the buttercups and dandelion seeds taken from real life experience?

   Yes, these were some of the more innocent things we did as young children. We were always outside exploring; something that recent generations have lost with an over-abundance of technology and general parental paranoia over accidents and crime such as child abductions.

3. Were the pebbles hurled at the aluminum awning taken from a real life experience?

   Not sure if I'd ever tossed pebbles—maybe I did—but I definitely remember hurling handfuls of corn at aluminum awnings around Halloween.

Mike

Autumn Wind

An autumn wind blew red and gold leaves through the open front door. Uninvited foliage found corners and chairs and a couch to stop and rest on. The wind carried through to the kitchen where the refrigerator beckoned – its wares exposed to the world and that little light a beacon to intruding moths. Soap and water no longer tended the sink – just a few dirty dishes growing ever crustier with time.

There had been a night, one of many glorious nights, with lover's kisses and soft whispers that meshed a tangle of conversation and laughter. Music had played this particular night – smooth jazz serenades that had colored the background of their evening. The radio continued to sing to a world with no ears.

The lovers had sat at a bountiful table, now abandoned to mold and decay, a meal half finished in the course of two half-finished lives. A wineglass stood tall among the various tabletop dishes, its scent long since evaporated on the breeze. Its mate lay crumpled in a pile of crystalline shards – an innocent victim of circumstance.

High backed, fancy chairs kept vigil over the waiting table, stationary guards powerless to do anything but serve. The favored chair, the one he had sat in so long ago, was abandoned on its side – the cruel result of their frantic but futile departure.

Once, this old house had been the haven of inhabitants who were lovingly dedicated to its upkeep. Even now the dressers were stocked with pristinely folded clothing, closets coordinated with all manner of fine attire and shoes laid out neatly along the floor. The living room accumulated dust and cobwebs; nonetheless it displayed an orderly arrangement of furniture.

Outside, the lawn had gone to weed and the trees drooped for lack of trimming. The street – normally clean and well tended – lay littered with abandoned cars, trucks and decaying bodies. As the wind danced and tripped over dead foxes, squirrels and people, the insects and worms waged their wars; yet with them, there was no cataclysm, no mass destruction. Cruelty did not exist. Each combatant concerned itself only with survival, nothing more, and nothing less.

No petty arguments over politics, no religious fervor to stir the masses, no poverty to worry their soulless existence. Trees blazed with a glory the lovers would have envied, no longer bombarded by pollution and mistreatment. Flowers prospered outside their previous prisons – now bursting forth with one final blaze of glory before the impending frost sent them back to square one.

The lovers, and others of their kind would never again know "square one." They had squandered their opportunity to prove dominion over the flora and fauna. With them, they had taken all manner of beasts and included them in their global domestic disputes by way of blood. The world was now silent save the occasional radio or TV powered by the nuclear plants which still dispensed its product freely.

There had been untended fires from stoves left on and wiring that had decayed into sparks and flames. There had been tornadoes with no death tolls or financial devastation. There had been hurricanes and blizzards, but no one was left to measure the cost or damage. Birds had fallen from their lofty glides and crashed indelicately onto harsh pavements and deserted buildings.

Men had tried to run everywhere. The mountains. The sea. Underground. In sealed and protected bunkers with their supposed imperviousness to all attack. There were no more words to be spoken here save those remnants that had been given electronic life. Even they were dwindling now, an ever-more silent epitaph to a dead race.

***

These lovers, the ones who ran from their sacred home in panic and fear, had fallen in the trees behind their house. Their exposed bones were locked hand-in-hand, expressions long since melted from their faces. There had been no time for tears or good-byes – just the shock of knowing their last breath.

When the sun next rises on this quaint and once tidy home, silence will descend upon the radio. As with the beautiful lovers, its music will end as though it and they had never existed.

Story's Inspiration:

Sometimes I just get into these melancholy, apocalyptic moods where I want to write something sad and depressing. Ok, so it happens

a lot more than sometimes. This is similar to a short story from Ray Bradbury's *Martian Chronicles*. Bradbury is a writing hero of mine. I hope the story does him justice.

Q&A:

1. Did the issue of global warming have any influence on your insight for this writing?

   No, it was more the Ray Bradbury story along with the movie *The Omega Man* that starred Charlton Heston. I enjoy stories like this.

2. Were you influenced by man's continued misuse of the gifts God has given us?

   That certainly comes into play. As we get more and more frantic with life and continue to overrun what we have, the scenarios for drastic outcomes must increase.

3. So you are pessimistic about man's future?

   Pessimistic. Hmm. I'd prefer a guarded optimism, although this story certainly does not reflect that view. Mankind has faced many challenges and it seems as though we always rise above ourselves – only, of course, to fall right back into our own depravity. Maybe one day we'll actually get it together.

Tracy

Morning's Freshness

Morning's freshness, crisp, soft and fading.
Begins yet another of the same.

Why is this one any different,
Why does the beauty of this morning bring no ugly pain?

Hints of ambers streak the sky promising a new light.
Swirls of whipping whites bring on needed sighs to make it right.

Morning's freshness, crisp, soft and lingering.
Begins yet another of the same.

This one is different for the message it sings …

Hints of crimson and passionate pinks.
Swirls of defining blues, as she thinks.

Think of the feelings that the visions bring.

Why does this one differ from the rest?

Think of the visions, the feelings it brings.
This one differs because of the new meanings.

Morning's freshness, crisp, soft and amazing.
Never the same.

Hints of luminous silvers, each lining the gray.
Swirls of nothing make it all disappear.

Remembers those visions and feelings.
Come what may, until no more tears …

Rebekah

The Octopus

I realized I'd become someone else the day I watched my husband make himself a sandwich. I stood beside him at the counter as he lathered his bread with various condiments and piled on the cold cuts. Then he produced a knife and pressed down on the bread, severing the sandwich in two, its contents spilling out onto his plate.

"Wow," I said.

That was it. One word and suddenly I knew I'd become a stranger. The second I said it I started to laugh.

My husband looked up at me, bewildered.

"What's so funny?"

"Nothing," I said. "It's just…I wouldn't have cut my sandwich that way."

"What way?"

"Squishing it down like that." I laughed again. I laughed so hard I couldn't continue. I couldn't tell my husband the awful truth: The woman he'd married ten years ago, the one who used to drink him under the table and despised Disney World and watched shows about serial killers, was gone. And in her place was a mommy.

Within two years, I've given birth to a boy and a girl. I'm a mommy, officially. Every day I'm correcting behavior, teaching good manners and habits, kissing owies and wiping tears and tickling tummies. I spend more time interacting with a two-year-old and an infant than with any adult.

Naturally I would be quick to notice that my husband's sandwich halves looked gutted and cauterized. I've been reprogrammed to find ways to improve everything, to explain everything, to make everything better for everyone, like I'm some domestic superhero sent to the planet to make sure that sandwich is cut perfectly to maximize the eater's enjoyment. Wonderbread Woman to the rescue!

I used to be fun, carefree and uncritical. But lately it's like some cute, onesie-clad little disease has ravaged my brain, eaten up the important information I used to know—literature, equations, how to make a dirty martini—and replaced it with stuff like the cook time for chicken nuggets, which grocery store has those shopping carts shaped like cars, where my son stashed his favorite car (inside his new potty).

So my question is, is all the other stuff gone forever? Am I doomed to watch my husband slice a sandwich and think about how I would have done it and how I can coach him to do it correctly next time? If this is the case, I don't even like the person I've become.

Then I wondered, is it just me? Am I the only one who seems to have suffered from this pint-sized version of identity theft? Surely there have to be more out there, more women who wake up one morning and realize that they're more concerned with poop than politics, that they know the names of all three Wonderpets but only one or two Supreme Court Justices (Clarence Thomas and that woman….Ruth What's-Her-Name).

Take my sister Amy. She has three kids, 8, 6, and 2. After the birth of her second child, my husband nicknamed Amy "The Octopus." Apparently there is an octopus out there who lays eggs, and after she has done so, she sits around and blows on them. She devotes her entire existence to blowing on her eggs, keeping the current flowing around them just right until they hatch. And as soon as they do, she dies.

Amy wasn't always an octopus. She used to be fun. She used to dance on table tops and go hiking and picnicking and she has a Master's degree and has traveled to Europe and Mexico and India. But something happened with that first child and only got worse with kids two and three. Suddenly she was absent from family gatherings—I mean, she was there, but off in another room, bathing or feeding or soothing someone to sleep, always preoccupied with the general welfare and comfort of three other human beings. She could no longer play the drinking games that she herself had taught us all. She couldn't stay up late for karaoke or poker or Guitar Hero. Not when she knew she'd be awakened several times during the night to find a pacifier or change a diaper; not when she had to be up at 5:30 a.m. to pour the Lucky Charms.

It seemed cruel and unfair that kids could be so selfish and thieving. The truth is, kids don't even know what they've done. They don't realize they've created a monster. As far as they're concerned, Mommy has *always* spent her day meeting their every need. She's always been their personal chef, shopper, playmate, maid, teacher, chauffeur…you get the idea. They love the person she is, not the person she was. And really, what kind of mommy would any of us be if we *didn't* do these things? If we all weren't a bunch of Octopuses, blowing on our eggs?

And so, as I watch my husband eat his squished, sloppy sandwich, trying not to make a mental note of the crumbs falling onto the table, I know that I will accept my role as an Octopus for a while. It's not really such a bad gig. Not when I watch my son put his jump rope (which is really just a long piece of yarn) in time-out; not when I hear the happy coos of my daughter when she wakes up in the morning. And besides, after they go to bed and it's just my husband and me, I find my old self reawakening, begging to come out and play for a little while.

And when I let her out, I can appreciate her that much more, and let her know that someday I won't be The Octopus anymore.

And that's probably when I'll start to miss it.

Story's Inspiration:

I wrote this article after realizing that I was in danger of losing my Identity and becoming a short-haired, high-waisted-jean-wearing mommy. It is one in a series of articles I've written since becoming a mother wherein I address all sorts of problems and experiences most parents can relate to. Some have been published in my local newspaper, others I hope in include in a book about motherhood that has just been released.

Q&A:

1. This is the first piece here that is a major shift from fiction. Was that a difficult transition?

    It really wasn't. The non-fiction actually comes easier sometimes because I'm just reporting what happens in my own life now instead of trying to create a story for fictitious characters. And ever since I started the non-fiction, I've hardly written any fiction.

2. Do you prefer one over the other?

    I miss writing fiction. It was definitely a nice escape, which I could use every once in a while. But things happen in my life almost daily that is too good not to write down, so until life slows a bit, I think I'll be sticking to non-fiction. And it is rewarding to be able to record my children's lives for posterity or whatever. It would have been neat to have a record of my own childhood (although sometimes I am grateful that there isn't a more detailed account lying around!).

3. What prompted you to start writing non-fiction in the first place?

    That was a Rogues' decision. I think I was recounting a story about something my son did to the rest of the group, and one of them said I should start writing this stuff down. So I did, and started a blog, and eventually wrote an entire book (separate from the blog). More people have read my non-fiction than my short stories.

Jeff

Excursion

It's hard to breathe in here. Like an egg shoved into a carton with eleven others, I have no room to move. I'm stuck in a small submarine with three crew members and forty-seven additional observers plunging to the bottom of the sea.

This is the excursion I selected for the first port stop, which is the island of Aruba. The seven-day cruise-ship vacation to the West Caribbean Islands promised to be a relaxing break from the cramped cubicles and the day-to-day monotony of corporate society. But it won't be. I understand that now.

Before getting to Aruba, our eleven-deck, 74,000 ton cruise vessel rolled over the ocean's currents. With every swell, there was an overall sway before the stabilizers interrupted with a jolt followed by several large vibrations. This is necessary to keep the ship level, to stabilize it. Just like people need drugs to stabilize their lives.

At first I struggled to keep my balance, but as the hours passed, I adjusted to the motion and began to move with the ship. If only life was so easy to adjust to.

In this sub, I have a little round window that I'm forced to share with some married woman sitting to my left. I'm here alone, surrounded by strangers, yet I'm so close to this woman our cheeks are nearly touching. The glass is three inches thick to handle the varying pounds of water pressure based on our depth. If you want to take pictures of the sea life, flashes are no good. The light will reflect off the thick glass and ruin the photo. People keep doing it anyway.

I stare through this little window and remember sitting the same way on a bus two days ago approaching the cruise ship from San Juan's airport. Every time the driver hit the brakes, it sounded as if a bag full of bricks was being dragged under the bus. Several times, it seemed that our careless chauffeur was going to send us straight into oncoming traffic.

Looking out *that* window, I saw impoverished huts lining the unpaved streets. At one point, we passed by a poorly maintained apartment complex. Three stories up on a makeshift balcony, a young woman stood and shook dust from a spotted and tattered bedspread. The balcony lacked a railing or any other barrier to prevent a fall.

A sign posted to the bus's over-sized window read: *Emergency Exit: Lift this bar. Push this window open.*

Reality: In the event of an actual emergency, shove the person in front of you to the ground, use their head as a springboard, and then proceed on. Repeat when necessary.

At *that* moment, while wanting to knock out the bus window and jump, I flashed back to an evening two years earlier when I had tried to relax at home. From my bedroom window, I had a view of an overpass, and on it, a stressed businessman was threatening to jump to his death. The authorities arrived, the news teams swarmed, and the bystanders multiplied. It became an event that lasted many hours. It didn't help that he was surrounded by apartment buildings, and everyone stood out on their balconies partying on a Friday night. The crowd, drunk with excitement, urged him to: "J-u-ump! Do it, man! Jump!" Alleviate yourself of all life's pressures. Take the quick and easy route. Even though many times he arched forward with strained muscles, he didn't jump. He wasn't prepared to take *that* Emergency Exit.

But right now I'm surrounded by blue chromis and yellowhead wrasse and gray angelfish and black grouper and indint hamlet and so on. There's nearly 150 feet of water above my head. I feel a strain on the canals of my eardrums from the depth and the water pressure. The sub touches down on the ocean floor and the water looks oily. Depth affects color perception, so people once wearing red clothing now appear to be wearing purple. People smile and their lips are blue and their teeth are yellow. The illusion seems appropriate to me.

After only a few moments at the sea's bottom, our slow ascent begins.

Two young girls to my right have their bare feet up by their window. Amber, who is closest to me, is eight. Her sister, Megan, is eleven. I know this because Amber told me as we entered the submarine.

We pass a wrecked ship. Our guide tells us that it was no longer seaworthy, so his company bought it and sunk it just for this tour. Nobody tells the truth anymore—so why start now? At least give us the illusion of adventure. We want pirate stories, war disasters, and visions of treasure dancing through our heads.

No. They bought it and then sunk it. How imaginative.

The girls compare their feet. Megan says, "You better start taking better care of your feet. Look at your nasty bruise—that's no good."

"It's not?" her younger sister asks.

"No, you shouldn't have scrapes and blisters and cuts ... men don't like that."

A great barracuda swims across our path. Sea plants of different colors sway.

"They don't? Why does it matter?" Amber asks.

"Women's feet are a turn-on for men. Start using polish on your toe nails—like me."

Megan is eleven. Megan has shiny blue polish on her toenails.

A group of red snapper glides by.

"A turn-on?"

"Yeah, jewelry too. A gold anklet or toe rings. They're very sexy." Megan says with an air of authority that makes my arm hairs stand.

"I want to be sexy."

Amber is only eight.

Last night, I'd walked the length of one of the cabin hallways. Except for the late night partiers, almost everyone was behind closed doors. I wondered what type of sick perversions existed in the confines of those tiny rooms. A dominatrix fists her slave. A lesbian threesome commences battle with rubber and latex sexual weaponry.

Amber, who is eight, wants to be sexy.

I'd passed rooms that emitted loud grunts. Behind door number three, a man performs fellatio on a spider monkey. And somewhere, *somewhere,* in one of the cabins some old pervert is getting off to some young girl's cute little feet.

"What I really want is a tattoo around my ankle."

Megan is eleven.

"A tattoo of what?" Amber asks.

They continue to compare their feet while brushing them against each other's legs like little girls do. A game of sorts.

I'd continued the late night stroll to the lowest of the outer decks that wrap the ship. Alone at the stern, I stopped and leaned against the railing to reflect. As the grandiose propellers chewed the black sea far below, I wondered what it would be like to jettison myself, representing my silent farewell to this sick world.

If I stayed conscious after the leap, I would watch the only surrounding light source move steadily away. The fleeing vessel would create more and more distance between us, making its appearance seem less and less magnificent until it became nothing more than a faint glow. How long could I tread water in the cold sea before my numb legs would tire and feel like massive weights? After a couple of dips below the waterline, I'd finally slip below the sea's surface for good and leave a stream of bubbles caused by the final supply of oxygen as it's forced from my lungs. And after, there would be nothing ... but my unmarked grave.

A green moray eel waves past us, then dives straight down and brings up sand.

"A pattern. Nothing specific. Just all the way around the ankle. That's *really* sexy."

Megan is eleven and Amber is eight. They want to turn on men with their feet.

This is our world.

They try to turn *me* on with their feet. They flex and stretch their toes and giggle as Amber rubs up against me.

A group of scuba divers pass us as we pass schools of fish and the schools of fish try to escape from the scuba divers. The scuba divers wave to us. Sometimes you just can't get far enough away from humanity.

"But still not as sexy as toes."

"Why toes? What do they like about 'em?" Amber asks.

"They like to suck them."

"EEEWWWWW!"

"No-o-o," Megan says with a giggle, "it feels *go-o-od.*"

My God, she doesn't realize how men will want to take advantage of her body. She doesn't know how grossly they'll use her. Does she really, really want to grow up this fast?

"You let a boy—?"

"No," she interrupts. "It was Jessica. We were just messing around. That's not all we tried, but ... that's all I'm telling you."

If I wasn't already speechless ... if I wasn't already unable to breathe ...

"Does Jessica have sexy feet?"

Do *I* really, really want to grow up this fast?

Megan responds with a grin.

Where's my Emergency Exit now?

Surface. *Surface. SURFACE!*

Story's Inspiration:

Many years ago—just prior to 9/11-I went on my first family cruise. During one of the stops, I went on a submarine ride excursion where I sat beside two young girls. They were having a conversation that seemed way beyond their years. At that time, I was pretty jaded with society after back-to-back layoffs and other disappointments, and decided to make a dark, fictional satire from the whole experience.

Q&A:

1. Being down in the sub, did you feel claustrophobic at any time?

   Not in the traditional sense. It wasn't the confined or tiny space that bothered me—it was being jammed up in there with all these strangers. It may have been a different experience if I could've convinced some of my family to join me.

2. Did you think about saying anything to the two little girls as they discussed "sexy" toes and that men liked them?

   Since this story is semi-autobiographical, but greatly fictionalized, I had exaggerated their conversation to make the point of the ever-maturing society including the general acceptance of sexuality constantly being thrust in our face. You see it in person, in store windows, on television, on the Internet, etc. There is no mystery or sanctity concerning sex these days. Nothing is taboo.

3. As you looked out the porthole at the calming water, fish and scuba divers swimming by, did it give you a sense of calmness and serenity?

   Once I began to see some of the wonders of the ocean, yes—I was captured by the peace of it. But only for a moment. The camera flashes were a disruption, but the thing that ruined the experience was the group of scuba divers waving at us. They took me away from the serenity and the beauty of the underwater nature.

Mike

Little Girl Lost

"That's not fair." She frowned at the man as he clutched the item to his chest.

"This was never intended to find a little lady's hands. You just need to find something else."

The young girl's eyes squinted into Siamese slits as she glared up at the owner. "If you don't sell that to me, I'll make a ruckus like you've never seen."

"Little girl . . ."

"Sandra."

"Sandra, dear, this is not for you. Where did you find it? I know it wasn't on the shelves."

"It has a price tag on it and everything. You have to sell it to me."

"Look, I don't have to sell you anything. You can raise hell," the man realized people were beginning to look at them; "You can raise all the ruckus you want; this item is not for sale."

Sandra's sobs jerked more patrons' heads as she wailed, "Why can't I buy it mister? I saved up all my money just for this one thing and now you won't sell it to me."

Nearby mothers shot scornful looks at the owner. He whispered, "Sandra, do you know what this thing is?"

Now she was getting somewhere. "Of course I do," she whispered back. "It's a biomechanical, phase-lock time inverter. I need it."

"Yeah, you and half the connected galaxy."

"These people don't understand 'connected galaxy'". Hell, they're a century or two away from even peeking out of this little hole-in-the-wall galaxy they live in. Sell it to me, or I'll make life miserable for you."

"For your information, they'll be landing on their moon in four years."

"I want the inverter. I am sick of being trapped in this four-year-old body. I don't care what they're doing. I need to be a woman again."

The bells on the door rattled to life again. A portly old woman stepped into the shop as the other customers went back to their shopping. The black and white television sang the charms of Mr. Clean cleaning like a white tornado.

The man bent over, keeping his voice low. "You know these things were banned because of their inconsistent nature."

"No shit. I've been four years old now for at least thirty Earth years. Do you know how hard that is? I've forgotten what sex feels like. And just once, I'd like to be able to open a door without getting up on my tiptoes. Every time I find a place to stay, I have to run away before people realize I am not aging. That inverter is my only hope."

"You could end up in worse shape. I once saw a man age to a dried-up husk right before my eyes."

"I don't care. I'm sure everyone here would like to know what all you have back there in your storeroom, wouldn't they?"

"You can't expose me. You'll have the authorities after us. You know they monitor everyone stationed in foreign times and places."

"Just one shot, please. I'm on the verge of suicide. Even if I die, it will be a great mercy."

"You realize they'll detect the atomic signature and be here in minutes." The man carefully inspected every customer in his shop.

"It's not like I haven't had to run from them before. If I become an adult, at least I'll be on the same level. Does this mean you'll do it?"

"One shot. You have to leave immediately, no matter what. I don't want your biological signature around my shop. They'll be looking for you."

"I know, I'm not stupid. All I ask for is the chance to be an adult again."

"Make it quick. You can use the back room." The man placed the inverter on the counter to the appreciative nods of several mothers.

"Thank you," Sandra said out loud. She picked up the object and skipped to the back of the store. Once in the room, her hands flew over the device. She touched it in seemingly random places and kept at least one finger on it at all times. Within two minutes, it began to glow – a soft golden pulse which grew brighter with each touch of her fingers.

There are an infinite number of ways to touch the inverter and affect a different result each time. The inverter takes the sequence of touches, the intent of the mind, the time between multiple touches, from nanoseconds to days, and calculates the best response possible.

Sandra knew where she'd gone wrong the first time. She had been thinking about how she missed being a little girl when her fingers slipped off the device completely. This time, she would be more focused when she broke contact.

Before beginning the process, she stripped out of her clothes. She had packed adult clothing in her purse. Years ago, when she'd morphed into a little girl, she had gotten lost in her oversized clothing.

She focused on female beauty and all the wonderful aspects of adulthood. She filled her mind with nights of dancing and romance. Her fingers pulsed with the inverter as it changed color. When she could think of no more fantasies and desires, she focused on adulthood one last time and jerked her hands away.

***

As she inserted the last button on her blouse, Sandra smiled. Would Mr. Toyshop Owner be so pleased for her to leave once he saw her now? It might be entertaining to find out …

Story's Inspiration:

Little Girl Lost was written off a prompt given by the 24 Hour Short Story Contest, summer 2008. The word length was limited to 900 words, not including the title, of which I used all 900. With such a short word count, my thoughts were to tell as much story through dialog as possible. Dialog is a great way to show, not tell, a story in relatively short order.

Q&A:

1. A sci-fi story with a child/woman protagonist is an interesting twist. What lead you to go that direction?

When you write for contests like this you have to do something to set yourself apart from the competition. My hope was that this combination would prove interesting enough to catch the judges' eyes.

2. You stated earlier you struggle to write sci-fi plotted stories. You appear to have handled this one well enough. What helped you write this one?

    The short word length helped. I realized I could play on the brevity to force the reader to fill in some familiar sci-fi blanks. For instance, the crazy name I gave the inverter sounded like it came straight off the set of Star Trek. You can convey a lot in a crazy name…

3. You add a playful touch at the end of this story. Did anything in particular cause you to go that direction?

    Again, contest judges love happy endings. Lending them a little chuckle can't hurt. I also just 'felt' like ending it upbeat. "Trust your feelings Luke…"

Tracy

Replaced

Jenny had a way about her.

At times she could calm your mind and make you feel her warmth. With just a breath. Then there were times when Jenny was cold and heartless.

Today was one of those cold, freezing days when she made ice shiver. An arctic second place. It filled the room. Her eyes were piercing gazes of pain which sank into my bones. There was a mystery to her pain and passionless grace, for she had no reason to be this way. She had had a wonderful life, they say.

I watched Jenny open the window to let the snow blow in her face. She grinned just a little, and it seemed as if she liked the winter's bitter taste. Jenny flowed from the open window and sank into the chair. The chair was worn and tattered and its wood was bare. She loved that chair. She said it was comfortable and safe. I didn't understand that. She had riches stored in her safe. Jenny sat in her hard and rigid chair. She sat and sat and only stared. She stared at the ceiling. She stared at the walls. She stared at the empty room down the hall. There was a door at the end of the corridor. Its paint had faded. Its hinges rusted shut. She just stared and never spoke about the events that had taken place so many years ago. And wished me luck.

She just sat and stared and occasionally I would hear a mumble. There was no emotion. Not even a slight tear. I gathered Jenny's supplies and put them at her side. I pulled the curtains back and gave her space. I just wanted to cry. I filled her bowl with warm soup. Finally a smile showed on her face. Her eyes seemed to search mine for answers about why it was this way. I just gently touched her face and gave her a grin.

She returned the gesture and breathed in. Jenny was special. Special in a way that all other's burdens and wounds came to live in her place. She would wrap them in the light of the moon of winter's silence and give them her grace.

The years had taken a toll on Jenny. Her being this way. She needed the warmth of never-ending summers to take their place. I gave Jenny my hand and told her to rest as the light turned to darkness.

I could finally understand. Jenny pulled back the covers and basked in the moon's glow and revealed her wounded, healing soul. And the world was a better place. I have spent my days remembering Jenny and what she showed me. I never questioned why, I only pointed to the door and returned to the window and breathed in the coldness of the dark moonlit sky.

Freewrites

Freewrites occur when a writer sits down for a specified amount of time and writes only that which comes "off the top of his or her head." Freewrites often use prompts to get the creative juices flowing. Many times the writing is lame and of little value.

One of the advantages of freewriting is to get the "fluff" out of your brain. Sometimes, though, you hit on something special. Sometimes what comes straight out of your mind through your fingers to the page is full of gems. Often, even the worst freewrite material has some redeeming quality, some phrase, idea or concept that can be used later.

The following are some samples of freewrites by The Rogue's Gallery Writers. These are totally unedited. They were written in ten minutes (timed by a stopwatch), and were written from some sort of prompt whether it be a photograph, a word or an idea. Freewrites are enjoyable, creative and often a wellspring of stories waiting to be told. Enjoy.

Rebekah

Freewrite

I wonder if the roofies make the champagne taste weird. The last one didn't seem to notice, but hell, she was so slopping drunk that by the time I slipped them to her she probably wouldn't have noticed it I'd jizzed in her glass. This bitch is different. She's still pretty sober, still coherent, still probably expecting me to open another bottle of Cristal like the fucking stuff grows on trees.

But she still won't let me touch her ass, her tits, nothing. She wants conversation and eye-contact and this gay-ass slow-dancing thing out here on the balcony. Never mind that this is my parents' place and I still live in their basement and had to wait until they went on vacation to invite this snotty bitch over like some horny high school kid.

Never mind that this suit is second-hand and the cologne is from the sample counter at Sears and my socks don't match. No, this bitch sees what she wants to see, is so wrapped up in her idea of me as this rich bastard who's supposed to sweep her off her feet, all Prince Charming with white teeth and manicured nails and knowledge of poetry and theatre. God, how much more of this slow-dancing, Kenny G bullshit do I have to take? Drink the fucking champagne already!

Shit….Which glass is hers…?

Jeff

Freewrite

I look over at the slumbering mass of my husband and go over my mental list again.

Sleeping Pills—check.

I had crushed them up and stirred them into his nighttime cup of tea. Obviously they've worked because he's not even twitching when I flick his nose with my fingertip.

Rubber tubing—check.

I found ones long enough, so I used them to strap my husband to the bed.

One Dirty Sock—check.

I stuff it in his mouth so that no one will hear him scream. The fact that it's dirty only adds to my enjoyment.

Lighter Fluid—check.

I douse the bastard from head-to-toe, lingering in certain spots longer than others.

Cigarettes and Lighter—check and check.

I put a cigarette in my mouth, Marlboros, his favorite brand, and light it.

A Solid Alibi—check.

I'm at my best friend Cheryl's house this very moment having a girls' night out.

The last item on my list: Nerve . . .

At this I pause and think about another mental list . . . one that's been with me for a long, long time:

Slap, Punch, Kick.

Red, Black, Blue.

I go over the last item one last time:

Nerve—check.

And I fling the cigarette right between his legs.

Mike

Freewrite

I remember soft autumn days in WV walking up the alley behind my house, the golden red-brown leaves fluttering in the crisp fall air. We had five Lombardi poplars in the back yard, four of which stretched to the sky like colorful fingers. The fifth and middle one was stunted in its growth, a runt between towering adults. Facing them from the back stoop, they were a regimented military line protecting the back of the house. The one on the far right was by far the most majestic, stretching twenty feet above all the others. This was the one to climb.

My friends and I would scale the beanstalk, convinced we had the penthouse view over the entire town of Dunbar. Scrapes and near falls were adventures to embellish, but cresting the uppermost climbable branch was to enjoy supremacy – to rule the world. The leaves fluttering down could give you momentary vertigo, and yet you followed their haphazard path, color filled snowflakes that later would comprise the huge pile you would be diving into. There was also a maple tree in the middle of the yard, much too small to be considered more than practice fodder for the larger trees.

Rogues Gallery Writers Short Story Contest Winner!

As a pre-book promotion, the Rogues Gallery Writers held a contest in conjunction with ClearView Press Inc. to locate the best short story we could find and publish it in our *Writing is Easy* endeavor.

The winner, Amy Hunter Dutta, came through with this heartwarming little tale about a particularly interesting Christmas. We enjoyed the tale so much we felt it definitely should be included in the book.

The story had to be no more than 1500 words and could cover any topic, fiction or not, as long as it told a good story. We thank all the contestants that submitted work and encourage all writers to check for future contests at both www.roguesgallerywriters.com and www.clearviewpressinc.com.

Without further adieu, sit back and enjoy Amy's story…

Amy

A Christmas Tale

I burst into the house, threw down my book-bag with a loud thud, and sped into the kitchen. "Mom," I called. "The concert's tonight, remember? Where are you?"

"In here," a muffled voice called.

At the doorway to my parents' bedroom, I paused. My two younger sisters were there, clad in identical green velvet pinafores. They wore white puffy-sleeved blouses underneath, white tights, and black patent leather shoes. My mother's mouth was stuffed with bobby pins as she attempted to pin up Kori's poker-straight hair into a bun.

On the bed was a slightly larger version of the outfit worn by my sisters, identical down to the shoes. My eleven-year-old psyche engaged in a brief civil war with itself. Was I too old to be dressing like them?

As if reading my mind, which she probably could because there were six of us and by now she had crossed the threshold into superhero territory, my mom said, "Do you like them? They were on sale at Sears."

I bit my top lip. "Actually, I do." I went over to the bed and touched the smooth fabric. I began to picture myself tonight, hair piled atop my head, standing in place on the third riser. I pictured my current crush, Tim O'Brien, watching me from the audience. After the performance, he'd applaud as he realized not only was I gorgeous, but a great singer too.

I tried on the dress in my parents' bathroom and came out as my mom was finishing with Belinda's hair. "Now, make sure you two don't get dirty," she told them before they ran out of the room. She turned to me. "That looks very nice," she said. "Want me to do your hair now?"

I sat on the bed while she tugged at my long tangled curls. "You can even borrow my lipstick," she said, her voice giggly, like we were two conspiring teenagers. "The light pink would look really pretty on you."

"We practiced the 'Hallelujah Chorus' today," I told my mom. "Are you going to come up for it?"

She yanked my hair so hard I was sure some scalp came with it. "I always do," she said. "Did Mr. Weiskel make you all practice that part where it stops, right before the final 'Hallelujah'? Don't forget to pause in there."

"Yes, he told us."

Our town was so small that the middle and high schools were in the same building, and so their two choruses performed one Christmas concert together. A tradition ever since the school's founding had been to close the concert by singing the 'Hallelujah Chorus' from Handel's' *Messiah*, and everyone in the audience was invited up to join in. It was one of my favorite Christmas memories.

As my family piled out of the station wagon into the school parking lot, I inhaled the smell of wood fires from chimneys close by. The air was clear and the stars twinkled frostily.

We went through the entrance and down the echoing tile hallway. "Well, I'll see you all after the concert," I said, turning towards the chorus room.

"Can we go with you, just to see?" Kori pleaded.

"The chorus room sounds so neat!" Belinda added.

My mom nodded and took our coats. Like the reassembled insides of a Russian babushka doll, we skipped away down the corridor.

A group of kids were hanging out at the side entrance to the auditorium. It took me a moment to realize they were in my grade. And that Tim O'Brien was one of them. I felt my mouth go suddenly dry while my palms went suddenly wet. I tried to smile my most prim, ladylike smile.

I heard a small snicker from one of the girls. Then Tim's soft voice reached out to me. "Hi Laura."

My heart was in my throat, blocking my words. "Hi," I managed.

"You look nice," Tim added. I could see his dark eyes shining in the fluorescent overhead lights.

I nodded. "Thanks," I whispered.

Then it hit me, all at once, standing there in the hallway that stank of cleaning fluid, I was like a big, overgrown elf, wearing a little-girl dress and overly poufy blouse. And worse, that I was standing there with two miniaturized versions of myself, as if to further accentuate my dorkiness. My classmates were wearing jeans and corduroys and sweaters, looking totally cool and casual, like sixth-graders instead of Santa's helpers.

My cheeks burned, and I fled but not before I heard the laughter. I hurried to the noisy warmth of the chorus room, where girls and a few brave boys were scurrying around, checking each other's hair, adjusting stockings and ties, smoothing skirts and pants. Mr. Weiskel, immaculate as always in a pale green oxford shirt and red-and-green-striped bowtie, was giving instructions as to who was to line up where on the way to the auditorium.

During the concert, I focused on Mr. Weiskel, immaculate as always in a pale green oxford and equally festive bowtie, as he conducted us. I didn't want to look into the crowd and see Tim, possibly holding hands with one of the corduroy-pants-clad girls. I just wanted this miserable night to be over.

Following our songs, there was an intermission, and then we sat in the audience while the high school chorus took the stage. I enjoyed listening to their trills of *Gloria,* but I didn't dare look around to see who else might be scoffing at my clothes.

Before the last number, the middle school chorus filed onstage to join the high schoolers, and then Mr. Weiskel gave the familiar invitation: "In true Greenville Christmas tradition, we invite you to join us onstage to sing the 'Hallelujah Chorus'." Some older students handed out music to the audience members, ranging from grandmothers to young children, who were climbing the steps to join us. There was an excited hubbub as everyone grouped themselves together according to their voice range.

Finally, Mr. Weiskel stood in front of the much enlarged chorus, raised his hands until everyone was quiet and looking at him, and began conducting the opening notes. Ms. Glowes' piano accompaniment was drowned out by two hundred or so of Greenville's finest voices raised in song.

"Haaaa-llelujah! Haaaa-llelujah! Hallelujah! Hallelujah! Halleeee-lu-jah!"

I forgot my earlier humiliation, swept away by the overwhelming joy of the music. I was singing with the sopranos, not far from my mother and two sisters. Kori and Belinda were bent over the sheet music, while my mother pointed to the words so they could follow along. But my mother did not need to look; her voice rang out pure and true, I could hear it even above the warbling around me.

"And He shall reign forever and ever…."

Incredibly, my eye caught Tim's in the audience. He was…watching me! I suddenly lost my place on the page I was sharing. I glanced again to make sure, and it was true. He was watching me, and there was a small, secret smile on his face. I smiled back, warmth spreading from my cheeks over the rest of my body.

"King of kings! And lord of lords! King of kings! And lord of lords!"

The crescendo of voices rose louder and louder. I didn't bother looking at the music in front of me anymore. I didn't need it either.

"Hallelujah! Hallelujah! Hallelujah! Hallelujah!"

Then it happened. After fifty-plus years of Greenville tradition, someone messed up the Famous Pause. And that someone…was me.

I saw heads snap around to look, saw eyes searching, heard the barely suppressed laughter of my neighbors. Head held high, I belted out the last word along with everyone else. I was damned if I'd let on that I was the one who had missed the pause, who in their eagerness had rushed forward, marring an otherwise perfect Greenville performance.

After a standing ovation from the remaining audience members, we filed offstage. I considered going back to the chorus room, but was unsure of the reception I'd receive there from my fellow singers. Equally unappealing was the thought of facing my family. My mother had been steps away, and being a superhero, she could easily pick my voice out of two hundred. I stood lost for a minute.

A step beside me made me look up. There was Tim O'Brien in all his preadolescent glory. A shy smile hovered on his lips, and when they parted to reveal his braces-bedecked teeth, I thought I would surely faint.

"I really liked the concert," he said, shoving one hand into the pocket of his Wranglers. "Do you want to come with me and my parents to get some ice cream at Friendly's?"

I found my voice in less than a second. "Sure, that'd be great."

And I walked out of the school into the starry night, hand in hand with the man of all my Christmas dreams.

Hallelujah! Hallelujah! Hallelujah! Hallelujah! (PAUSE) Haaallleeeeeluuuuujaaaah!

Last Word

We, the Rogues Gallery Writers, sincerely hope you enjoyed this book. We hope you will let us know what helped, what inspired and even what you thought could be done better. No author grows without an honest look at their work.

Writing is Easy became a monumental work for us. The book has been three years in the making. Three years is deceiving, however. Rebekah published her own book (*Motherhood is Easy*) as has Tracy and I (*Loves Lost and Found*). Jeff's book, *Flight from Fear*, is due out summer of 2010. We all blog regularly and are involved in other writers groups as well as other writing projects.

The bottom line is – writers MUST make things happen. Network. Learn. Network. Write. Network. Have I mentioned networking? Writers should surround themselves with other writers. They should also find a place of solitude to work.

Get out there. Submit your work. Take on the challenge to do something you've always dreamed of accomplishing in your life. A truer statement has never been made – if we, the Rogues Gallery Writers can write and produce a book, anyone can. You just have to want it bad enough and stay focused. After all, we all know that writing is easy. This is what we live for. It's the publishing that's the bitch.

The first step is to get it written. Then the real work begins…

The Rogues Gallery Writers

Rebekah Hunter Scott

Originally from New Jersey, Rebekah got her B.A. in creative writing from Florida State University. Her first book, *Motherhood is Easy* (ClearView Press, Inc.) debuted in May 2010, and excerpted in *American Baby* magazine (July 2010). She is a member of the Florida Writers Association, has been published in *The Flagler Review* and won first place for short fiction in *The Storyteller's* People's Choice Awards, Spring 2008. Her fiction is featured in the anthology *From Our Family To Yours* (Peppertree Press). Her work is also scheduled to appear in *American Baby* and *Parents* magazines. She lives in St. Augustine with her husband and two kids. Visit her at www.motherhoodiseasy.com.

Jeff Swesky

Author and ghostwriter Jeff Swesky has had his fiction featured in the FWA Collection, *From Our Family to Yours* (Peppertree Press), and has ghostwritten Rabbi Samuel Cywiak's award-winning Holocaust memoir, *Flight from Fear*, which has recently been published by Bayou Printing. Jeff is finishing his literary coming-of-age novel, *Such a Dreamer*. He is also beginning work on *Before the Crush*, the biography of David Schave, a miracle survivor of severe head and spinal cord injuries. Jeff resides in Palm Coast, FL. Website: www.jeffswesky.com

Michael Ray King

Michael Ray King's books include *Fatherhood 101, Loves Lost and Found* and coming summer of 2010, *The Writing Life*. Michael has written for trade magazines and won RPLA Awards for his *Fatherhood 101* book as well as for his poem *Rendezvous*. In 2006, Michael founded ClearView Press, Inc. as a vehicle to assist writers in their quest for publication. Michael lives in Palm Coast, FL with his wife Bobbie and children Ivy, Nick, Allie and Veronica. Website: www.michaelrayking.com

Tracy McDurmon

Tracy McDurmon aka "Tracy Panthera" is a Florida girl. She is a divorced mother of two awesome boys, Kasey and Dalton, who are the reasons she rolls out of bed and stays strong each day. Tracy lives life like it is the only one she has and from time to time gets off track like anyone else. She has great friends who have helped her on her journey and cherishes each and every one of them. Tracy loves the beach, the arts and the metaphysical. With her open heart and mind she explores all the wonderful experiences that cross her path. Tracy can be found on the web at: www.tracymcdurmon.com

Other Books by Rogues Gallery Writers

Flight from Fear – Jeff Swesky

Motherhood is Easy – Rebekah Hunter Scott

Fatherhood 101 – Michael Ray King

Loves Lost and Found – Michael Ray King/Tracy McDurmon

Rogues Gallery Writers Author Sites

www.michaelrayking.com – Michael Ray King

www.jeffswesky.com – Jeff Swesky

www.rebekahhunterscott.com – Rebekah Hunter Scott

Blogs by Rogues Gallery Writers

motherhoodiseasy.blogspot.com – Rebekah Hunter Scott

jeffswesky.wordpress.com – Jeff Swesky

traceypanthera.blogspot.com – Tracy McDurmon

michaelrayking.blogspot.com – Michael Ray King